THE KILLER...

As Darci drove back to Albuquerque, with the baby in her arms, she knew that Ray would be wondering where she was, and she had to have an explanation. She described herself as frenzied at that point, but her actions were methodical and controlled, anything but "hysterical." In fact, every indication is that she had a plan in mind.

...HER VICTIM

And all this time Cindy lay in the grass behind the little grove of trees. The light rain pattered down upon her. The blood had flowed freely from the gaping tear in her body. She couldn't have lived more than a few minutes after the delivery.

And while Sam searched for her and tried to think where she could be, and while little Luke asked, "Where's my Mommy?" Cindy was already dead, sacrificed to Darci's fanatical needs.

Lullaby and Goodnight

Most Pocket Books are available at special quantity discounts for bulk purchases for sales promotions, premiums or fund raising. Special books or book excerpts can also be created to fit specific needs.

For details write the office of the Vice President of Special Markets, Pocket Books, 1230 Avenue of the Americas, New York, New York 10020.

Lullaby and Goodnight

D.T. HUGHES

POCKET BOOKS
New York   London   Toronto   Sydney   Tokyo   Singapore

An *Original* Publication of POCKET BOOKS

POCKET BOOKS, a division of Simon & Schuster Inc.
1230 Avenue of the Americas, New York, NY 10020

Copyright © 1992 by Dean Hughes

All rights reserved, including the right to reproduce
this book or portions thereof in any form whatsoever.
For information address Pocket Books, 1230 Avenue
of the Americas, New York, NY 10020

ISBN: 0-671-72405-3

First Pocket Books printing March 1992

10 9 8 7 6 5 4 3 2 1

POCKET and colophon are registered trademarks of
Simon & Schuster Inc.

Cover photo of Darci Pierce by Aaron Wilson
Cover photo of baby by the University of New Mexico
Medical School

Printed in the U.S.A.

For Luke, Millie and Bradyn

CHAPTER 1

Murder is not big news in the United States. In Albuquerque, which is not exactly New York or Los Angeles, most local murders don't make the front page. But Cindy Ray's murder did. And it stayed there. Much of the interest centered on the killer, Darci Pierce. People wanted to see what she looked like and know what sort of person she was. The crime was, after all, brutal and grotesque—many said unthinkable. It shocked hard-nosed murder investigators who thought they had seen it all. And yet, the face that appeared in the *Albuquerque Journal* was lovely. This was no tough-looking street kid, but a pretty girl of nineteen—a wholesome, well-groomed "girl next door."

On July 23, 1987, Darci Pierce strangled a pregnant woman into unconsciousness, used a car key to rip open her body, and stole the fetus from her womb. She then left the victim, Cindy Lynn Giles Ray, by the side of a mountain road to bleed to death.

The crime *is* stunning. In America we may not treat pregnant women with quite the same reverence that we once did, but we have hung on to a fair share of our motherhood and apple-pie values. Something deep within us instinctively knows that a woman in that condition represents our origins—life itself. She is not only a mother, but she is *the* mother we hold in a symbolic place of honor. We know there are bad mothers—child abusers, drug addicts, women who sell their babies. We see those stories on the news every night. And because we see such stories, we're not so maudlin in our praise of motherhood as we once were. And yet, there remains in us some resonance we all respond to: The giving of life is sacred, one of the few human acts that deserves automatic reverence.

For the people in Albuquerque—and across the country—who were to read the newspaper accounts of Cindy's murder, the crime was deeply disturbing. The easy reaction was to write Darci off as an aberration. That was a convenient assessment because it made her either a disgusting throwaway, deserving of the death penalty, or a psycho who should be locked away from the rest of society. But either way, the conclusion was much the same: She was not human, not within the range of what we would call normal.

And yet, those who knew Darci considered her likable, intelligent, responsible, and caring. She had never committed a crime, had never injured anyone, and she had never shown any obvious signs that she ever would. She lived and acted much the way most of us do. She was pretty and athletic. She went to church, was a nice neighbor, a good friend, and her young husband considered her a wonderful wife. Everyone who knew her was certain that she was pregnant and about to become an excellent mother. After all, she had read everything she could about infant care, had talked about little else, and she had prepared a beautiful nursery. Only after the crime did her family and friends learn that Darci had been lying about her pregnancy, faking the symptoms—or perhaps even experiencing a pseudo pregnancy in response to her obsession with the idea of being a mother.

Psychologists would eventually decide that powerful forces were at work inside Darci. These same psychologists would not agree, however, on whether she was responsible for her crime. *Insanity* is a legal term. The prosecution would argue that Darci knew what she was doing, planned her "theft," and in spite of some psychological problems, was sane at the time of the murder. The defense lawyers would contend that she was a disturbed teenager whose mind had shattered into multiple personalities.

For both the defense and the prosecution, proof of their case was Darci's life. And so, when March 1988 came, and the trial began, witness after witness talked about Darci's background. Friends, family, husband, coworkers, and a whole parade of mental health specialists presented their views. What gradually came together, in a disjointed chronology, was the astoundingly complex picture of Darci Kayleen Ricker Pierce.

The trial would proceed carefully and correctly. It would all be very civilized. But on trial was the heart of darkness. The woman sitting across the room—the woman with the beautiful eyes and pretty, long dark hair—had done something unspeakable. She had violated a delicate human body, taken a life, and endangered another. She had stolen a young couple's child and claimed it as her own. She had told every kind of lie to cover herself—both before and after the murder. She had crossed some barrier into behavior too dark to comprehend.

And yet, there she was. She looked entirely normal, even lovely.

The jury had to piece together the testimony presented to them and try to see Darci's life for what it was. And ultimately, they had to decide how Darci would lead the rest of her life. The death penalty was not at issue; life in prison was.

Life in prison.

We say it easily enough. We think we understand what it means. But how many of us have had to look at another person and make the judgment? The jurors didn't have the luxury to speculate and philosophize; they had to decide.

They had to attempt to put their shocked emotions aside and try to understand Darci. They had to judge whether Darci was, in fact, a victim herself. Was she an abused child, and if not, how could she have known enough to seduce her seven-year-old cousin—when she was only six? Were her wild tantrums as a child and teenager evidence of developing psychological problems, or was she merely spoiled? And as the layers of lies were stripped away, the jury had to decide what to make of Darci's strange life of deception and fantasy.

This lovely girl, it would turn out, was a remarkably talented liar and manipulator. Underneath that pretty image was a baffling history of absolutely bizarre behaviors. From sex to Sunday school, nothing in her life would turn out to fit the image she had managed to carry off. But was she mentally ill? Her defense lawyers would enlist four experts who would testify for hours that she was.

She strangled a woman about to give birth. She cut that woman open with a car key and took out the living fetus. She left the mother to die. Well, then, we say, the only explanation is that she was sick. That's the safe way to look at the case. But Harry Zimmerman, prosecutor, would say that she was no more mentally ill than any other common crook who uses a

LULLABY AND GOODNIGHT

gun to rob money from a victim's pockets. She wanted a baby—desperately needed a baby to cover her own lies—and so she took one.

That's what Harry Zimmerman believes to this day, and that's what he told the jury. The twelve jurors had to decide. And they had to try to be objective and fair—no matter what this woman had done.

All while the trial progressed, Darci sat with her head down, usually wearing a pretty white blouse, with her dark hair falling down her back, her quiet eyes focused on the table in front of her. Nothing about her hinted that she was capable of the crime that she had committed. Who could help but feel some pity for her?

But the jury also had a responsibility to a tall, soft-spoken young man named Sam Ray, to his blond-haired, two-year-old little boy, Luke, and to a bright-eyed little survivor named Amelia. And they had a responsibility to another pretty, dark-haired young woman. That, of course, was Cindy Ray, who at twenty-three still had so much to look forward to, who had wanted to raise these children with the young husband she had met in high school.

Darci Pierce wanted a baby. Cindy Ray had lived through eight-and-a-half months of pregnancy and was anxious to deliver her second child. When Darci's and Cindy's pictures appeared together in newspapers and magazines, readers were struck by the similarity of their appearances. They were similar in another way: Both had looked forward, more than anything, to being mothers. They believed in the traditional middle-class American dream: meeting the right guy, settling down, buying a house, having a family, living happily ever after. The lives of the two young women crossed by coincidence, but their dreams, as it turned out, were on a kind of collision course.

Yet Darci and Cindy did not see their "happily ever after" dreams come true. Darci's dark act destroyed more than a life; it left a crowd of victims. Cindy's and Darci's families were devastated, and two husbands had their lives changed forever. All who heard the story were left to wonder whether any barrier to human behavior remained in place.

And yet, just as little sprouts of life begin to appear through the ashes on Mount Saint Helens, so does a new life provide a glimpse of loveliness in this story. This book is about Cindy and Darci, but it is also about Sam and Luke and Amelia—known as Millie. It is a wonder that Millie is alive at all. Her life seems to represent the human power to survive and continue. And in her survival—her vitality—is also the survival of at least one part of Cindy's dream.

CHAPTER 2

Sam awoke in a panic. He sat straight up and looked around. For a few seconds nothing was making sense. It had all seemed too real to be a dream, and yet he was struggling now to remember the details.

He sat in bed, still breathing hard, sweating. He had never experienced a nightmare like that, and something in him even now kept telling him that it hadn't been a dream at all.

"Cindy?" he called, but there was no answer.

Sam got up and grabbed his robe. He walked out to the living room. It was a hot July day in Albuquerque, almost one o'clock in the afternoon, and the heat was building inside the mobile home. Sam had worked the night shift, and he usually didn't get up for another couple of hours. Cindy often took Luke and went somewhere during those last two or three hours of his sleeping time, just to be sure he got enough rest.

So nothing was wrong.

And yet, everything seemed wrong. Maybe it had really happened, and the dream had been some sort of warning. Maybe she was dead.

"Cindy?" he called again, and he walked into Luke's bedroom. But he knew they were not there. He checked the time again. It might be three or so before she would come back. How could he stand to wait that long?

But he couldn't do this. It was irrational, silly. Sam was not one who let his emotions get in the way of clear thinking. So what if he had had a dream? Why should that mean anything?

He sat down on the couch and took some long breaths. He knew he ought to go back to bed and sleep some more, but there was no way he would be able to do that.

He kept trying to remember what had happened in the dream. But all he knew was that she was dead, and Sam was left with Luke and the new baby. One clear, intensely real picture remained in his mind. He was holding the baby, looking at it, and Cindy was gone. But how could that happen? A car wreck? Sometimes in an accident, the fetus is saved even though the mother dies. It was possible, but . . .

Sam chided himself. This was stupid. It was only a dream.

Sam thought he heard a car pull into the trailer park. He jumped to his feet and hurried to the window. But it wasn't Cindy. He paced back across the living room, and then back to the window. He was letting himself get entirely too agitated.

He went back to the bedroom and dressed. As he did so he tried to think of something to do to occupy his time until Cindy returned. But nothing interested him. Not food. Not reading. He just kept pacing and watching the window.

And then Sam did something he rarely did. He began to cry. How could he live without Cindy? How could he raise Luke and the baby he had seen in the dream? Cindy was Mom; Cindy was the center of

LULLABY AND GOODNIGHT

everything for Luke. How could Sam go on, alone, and be a daddy, and try to keep everything going?

He couldn't do this. He had to get hold of himself. It was only a dream. He had had all kinds of dreams in his life. They didn't have to *mean* anything.

All the same, Sam kept pacing and watching out the window. But the cars kept whizzing by on the busy street outside, and the heat inside the trailer intensified. Two hours passed in segments of three or four minutes between glances at his watch.

When Cindy finally drove in, Sam was waiting at the door. He grabbed up Luke and hugged him, and then he bent and took Cindy in his arms. He tried not to be too obvious, but his grasp was too tight; his welcome too intense. When Cindy looked at him, he had tears in his eyes and his lips were shaking.

"What's wrong, Sam?" she asked. "Why didn't you stay in bed?"

"Where have you been?"

"I took Luke over to the library. Why? What's wrong?"

"I . . . well, I . . . had a dream."

"What kind of dream?"

But now Sam wasn't sure he should tell her. "I dreamed you had been hurt or something."

"Hurt?"

"Well . . . killed."

Tears came to her eyes. She seemed touched. But Sam saw something else too. Maybe she was just picking up on his own emotion, but she looked scared.

"It was just a dream," Sam said. "But it was incredibly real. I've never had a dream that real."

He wasn't sure he wanted to tell her the other fear, the one that had been developing all afternoon. He had told himself everything was all right. She would be home in a little while, and then he could put this thing behind him. But something else kept saying, "What if she's okay now, but what if the dream is some sort of warning? Maybe God is getting me ready for what I'm going to have to deal with."

"How did I die?" Cindy wanted to know.

"I don't know. You were just gone, and I had the kids. Both of them. Luke and the new baby. And I felt like I couldn't make it—like I couldn't go on living without you. I was holding the baby, and I was crying—and it was so real, I . . ." But he didn't know exactly how to explain the panic that had hit him.

"Oh, Sam." Cindy put her arms around him and pressed her face to his chest. "Let's not talk about it, okay? Everything's all right now."

But she was obviously uneasy. And the fear was as tight as ever in Sam's chest. He wanted to forget the whole thing, but the shakiness, the panic he had been feeling all afternoon, was still there, even with Cindy in his arms.

For four years now, Sam and Cindy had been married. But most everyone who knew them said that the honeymoon had never really ended. They had created a little self-contained world for themselves—and for Luke. And the great focus of their lives now was on the new baby who would soon be born.

Sam Ray was only twenty-five, and Cindy twenty-three, but their attachment to each other had already lasted over eight years. They had met in 1979, when Cindy was a high school sophomore and Sam a senior in Payson, Utah. After their marriage they had moved away from Utah, but they were still tied to the values and worldview they had grown up with in their hometown.

Payson is a little town about sixty miles south of Salt Lake City. It rests in the foothills of the Wasatch

LULLABY AND GOODNIGHT

Mountains, beneath massive Mount Nebo. It's a mostly Mormon town where a bottom lip full of Skoal—or even the circle in the back pocket of a boy's Wrangler jeans—could identify him as a backslider. And a girl could get a "reputation" by being a little too quick to kiss a boy.

As in most high schools, the kids at Payson High had names for some of the identifiable groups. The kids with western-style clothes were called *cowboys*. Most of these were Mormon black sheep. They liked to "drag Main" in their pickup trucks, maybe with a six-pack of beer. They got in fights, used hard language, and they slept in on Sunday morning when the *churchy* kids were attending services.

Cindy Lynn Giles was one of the churchy kids. She was committed to her Mormon faith. She had developed a clear image of the sort of person she wanted to be. She disliked the narrowness of some Mormons, but she loved the ideal of service and love that she often saw in actual practice.

And yet, she was only fifteen. She liked those boot-cut Wranglers and cowboy hats that some of the bad boys wore. She knew she shouldn't find those guys attractive—since they weren't doing all the right things—but she still thought they were cute.

And maybe that's not so surprising, given her background. Her parents, Larry and Vickie Giles, liked country music, and her dad was something of a cowboy himself. But even more, Cindy's parents didn't go to church very often, and Dad spent most of his evenings at the Wee Blu Inn, a local tavern. He had a drinking problem, and he and his wife struggled with their marriage. They had separated a couple of times.

Cindy was a girl with a vision of a perfect family. But she lived with the very real threat of a breakup in her own home. The thought of it terrified her. And so Cindy, at fifteen, was a little mixed-up, but she was really rather simple to understand. She lived in a community—went to a church—that had created for her an ideal, and she longed to possess it. She imagined a tender, loving husband who would never break his vows to her. She pictured a warm, wholesome family in a well-kept home. She imagined the beautiful little babies she would someday raise to be strong, good people, true to the faith.

And then she met Sam.

Sam was no cowboy. He was an active Mormon. He planned to serve for two years as a missionary when he turned the minimum missionary age of nineteen. And yet, he was a little crazy, and he didn't seem very comfortable with the good Mormon boy image. He loved rock music, for one thing, and some of the groups he liked were pretty "hard." But all that was okay. Cindy's vision was of a strong man—a future husband—but not one who was so pious that he couldn't have fun.

She remembered something about Sam from the year before, when he had shown an interest in Tonie, Cindy's older sister. Tonie had asked him to the Sadie Hawkins Day dance. But he had turned her down. And the reason he gave was that his parents wouldn't let him date a girl who wasn't sixteen. That was a guideline that strict Mormons held to. Sam had honored his parents and his church. Cindy liked that. She wasn't sure she liked his haircut—a permed light brown sort of globe he called his Afro. But he was tall, six-foot-two, and he had very nice eyes, soft and gray-blue, a sort of impish smile, and behind the zaniness, a desire to be good.

Of course, Cindy was pretty sure Sam wouldn't ask her out—not until she was sixteen—and that was half

LULLABY AND GOODNIGHT

a year away. To a shy girl who finally had found a handsome guy who liked her, half a year seemed half a lifetime. But Cindy underestimated Sam's ingenuity —and his interest in her. Maybe Sam couldn't ask Cindy out on an actual date, but he found plenty of opportunities to be around her. She had joined the band and was learning to play the cymbals. Sam was the leader of the percussion section. The band provided practice time together, and Sam was kind enough to give the cute little sophomore lots of extra training. After the practice sessions—or after evening band parties—he was sometimes also so generous as to give her a lift home.

It was after one of these little lifts one night that he quickly and rather awkwardly surprised her with a kiss. Cindy had never been kissed—not really—and she wasn't sure she liked his abruptness. But a week or two later, while returning from a band competition on a bus, Sam kissed her again.

And this time she liked it. She kissed him back.

That night Cindy went home to her little basement bedroom she shared with Tonie, and she admitted, shyly, that she really did like Sam.

But the guy was so hard to figure out. In spite of his zany style, he was actually a brain: an A student, member of the honor society, and one of the best math students in the school. She wondered if he was toying with her. After all, she was only five-foot-three, and she wore glasses. She didn't think of herself as attractive. She knew that Sam could have his choice of almost any girl in the band. Why had he chosen her?

But Sam was hooked. Cindy may have been small, but she was athletic and shapely, and under those glasses were very pretty, dark eyes. He also liked the fact that Cindy was bright. She had received almost all A's in junior high, and she had played every sport.

There was a certain tomboy quality that added a little spice to Cindy's prettiness.

For a few weeks Sam and Cindy saw each other as often as they could. And then one night Sam parked a couple of blocks away from Cindy's house, and they began to kiss. Gradually Cindy felt something new: a numbness, a building passion that she had never experienced. Sam was breathing hard, getting excited. Cindy was sure she ought to be scared, but she trusted Sam. She had heard lots of girls talk about making out. As long as she didn't let him do anything really wrong, she was . . . and then she was not sure what was wrong and what wasn't. She just wanted him to keep kissing her, keep holding her. She wanted whatever he wanted.

Cindy had never imagined anything so wildly good, so tangibly necessary. And then Sam backed away. He looked scared. But they hadn't *done* anything—not anything really bad. Her teacher at her Young Women's meeting at church had talked many times about the temptation to let boys go too far, but she hadn't done that.

Sam was still taking deep breaths. "Wow," he said. And then in a moment, "I better take you home." But he didn't say, "We shouldn't have done that," and Cindy wasn't sure.

That night she lay awake wondering. She found herself imagining how nice it would have been to let go. But the idea frightened her and she turned it into thoughts of marriage. Someday it would be Sam. She was sure of that now. She could admit she was in love. Fifteen was young, and Sam still had his mission ahead. But she could wait. She wrote in her journal the next day, "Sam and Cindy," and drew a heart around the names.

On Monday, something had changed. Sam didn't

LULLABY AND GOODNIGHT

say much to Cindy. As the week continued, he seemed to withdraw. And then one night he gave her and another girl a ride home from a school activity. Sam took the other girl home first, and she lived in Elk Ridge, near the mouth of Payson Canyon. As Sam drove back toward town, along the foothills of the mountains, the lights of Payson were spread out in the valley just below them. But Cindy was hardly noticing any of that. What she was hearing was Sam's soft voice, explaining that he didn't think they ought to go with each other anymore.

He didn't say why, and she was not sure she understood. He said some things about their being too young, and he hoped they would date again—after his mission. But he didn't say what was wrong now.

Cindy said very little. She hurt too badly. But she didn't dare tell him what she was feeling, how much she loved him. She had never known how to open up and discuss things, and she was especially afraid of her emotions now.

What followed for Cindy was the hardest time of her young life. Sam had represented more to her than just a good-looking boy to go out with. She longed for something permanent in her life. She could see that her own family was on the edge of breaking up.

Cindy prayed every day that somehow her parents would work things out and stay together. She feared for Kipper, her little brother. He needed a dad. And she wondered how their family could be together in the next life if they broke their bonds now.

That was, after all, one of the most basic Mormon beliefs: The family can exist throughout eternity, *sealed* together in the temple. A *forever family*—that was the term Mormons liked to use. They embroidered it on wall hangings and sang children's songs about it. And most Mormon kids grew up secure that their eternal family was as available as tap water. For Cindy, the thirst for that permanence was constant.

Sam was symbolic of the things Cindy wanted. He planned to go to college next year at Brigham Young University, and he told Cindy that she could get a scholarship and go there too. He wanted a temple marriage—a forever family. Cindy knew she was young to think so far ahead, but just when she dared to look into the future and see Sam there, he walked away.

And so, Cindy and Sam stayed in touch with each other, but they didn't date. Gradually they became good friends. Sam became the big brother Cindy talked to when she had troubles. Sam was not sure he wanted that. He liked to think that after his mission, something might come of the relationship again. But Cindy was not going to be hurt again. Whenever Sam showed interest in rebuilding their relationship, she resisted.

After Sam graduated he worked for a summer and then moved twenty-five miles to the other end of Utah Valley. He enrolled at BYU and moved into an apartment nearby in Provo. But he often came home on weekends, and he sometimes went to high school games and band competitions where he would see Cindy.

Cindy usually used those chances to unburden her problems, and her worries usually involved boys. That was not easy for Sam, especially since he didn't like the cowboys she chose to date.

Soon after Sam's first semester at BYU, he turned nineteen. He was called by his church to serve a mission in England. Cindy told him she would be happy to write to him, but she was still cautious—because of the pain he had caused her. Sam wrote soon after he left, and then again in another couple of

LULLABY AND GOODNIGHT

months. Cindy didn't answer for a time. But she wrote occasionally, and she used the chance, as usual, to express her worries to her "older" friend.

Cindy's life was, in one sense, going very well. She continued to get mostly A's, and she performed well on the gymnastics and track teams. She learned the snare drum and still had a good time with Payson's prize-winning band. All through her junior year of school she kept her personal goals high, and she managed to excel at everything she did.

But her journal expressed her constant unhappiness with her life. And the center of that unhappiness was her inability to find someone—the right person—to love and care about her. Tonie graduated from high school that year, and she got married shortly after. Cindy knew she didn't want to marry that young, but she envied Tonie her attachment to her high school sweetheart, Mark.

Her other great worry continued to be her parents' problems. Finally, the breakup did come. In the summer of 1981, just before Cindy was to start her senior year, her parents announced they were getting a divorce.

And then came the impossible task. The judge considered Cindy and Kipper old enough to make their own decisions. They could live with either parent, but they had to choose for themselves.

One afternoon, after school, Cindy took Kipper in her mother's truck, and they drove into Payson Canyon in the mountains nearby. It was a drive Cindy often took when she had to think. The fall colors were fading now and the canyon was not so breathtaking as it had been a week or two before. Rain was falling. To Cindy it seemed that everything was dying.

Kipper was fourteen. He was scared. He had grown very quiet lately, and Cindy wasn't sure what he was thinking. She pulled off the road at a spot where a stream meandered down the canyon. She left the engine running, so the heater would operate, but she set the brake and turned to Kipper. "What are we going to do?" she asked. "We've got to decide."

They talked for some time, but neither answer seemed right. They would hurt one of their parents no matter what they did.

"Kip," Cindy finally said, "I just keep thinking that Mom can maybe make it on her own, but I don't think Dad will. And it seems like a boy ought to have a father. I'll be gone before long, but you'll be home for quite a few years."

Kip didn't like the answer, but he had no other, and he trusted Cindy. She was someone to rely on when his parents let him down.

Cindy suggested that they pray about their decision. So she and Kipper got out of the truck, and they walked into the woods. The ground was damp, but they knelt down in some fallen leaves. Cindy poured out her feelings, asking that sooner or later their parents would come back together, but that in the meantime she and Kipper could do the right thing. She also asked for help in breaking the news to their mother.

And so she and Kipper stayed with their father, and Vickie moved out. The judge had decided that the one who got the kids also got the house.

Cindy did not handle the breakup well and filled her journal with the pain she felt. But in that pain, she also turned to Sam. He was someone she could write to and express her feelings, and she knew he would understand.

Cindy's senior year of high school had its good moments, but it was a time filled with pain. Nothing felt right with her parents separated. At home she

LULLABY AND GOODNIGHT

found little consolation. Her dad had promised not to drink if the kids stayed with him, but his promise didn't last long.

Cindy dated some, but as spring came on she became extremely busy. She had enough high school credits that she only attended in the morning and then drove to Orem in the afternoons to attend a college class at Utah Technical College (now called Utah Valley Community College). She took a chemistry class that she found very difficult. She finished her gymnastics season with a first place in her region in the compulsory vault exercise and third in the uneven bars.

Cindy graduated with high honors. She was bright, and a very good student. What one finds in her journal, however, is simplicity, not brilliance. She was a nice person, concerned to do right. And though she cared about college and career, she also talked about the children she hoped to raise. She even picked names for them. She liked the name Luke for a boy. And one girl's name she liked was Amelia.

One night, not long after graduation, she wrote in her journal:

> I can't figure out why I am so sad and depressed all the time. I know it isn't right to feel this way. I have this kind of suspended feeling like I keep waiting for something to happen but it never does. I just can't understand it.

But something was in the works. She had a letter from Sam that she had saved, a letter she thought about from time to time. Sam had told her:

> *I don't know what it is, but ever since I got to know you, you've always been in a certain place in*

my heart. I've tried to kid myself. I've gone out with all different kinds of girls, you know, but in my heart and mind there has always been something there. That is why I always keep coming back.

*With love,
Sam XOXOX*

Cindy was not sure she wanted Sam to make a rush for her when he got home. But when she got the letter, his return was another year away, so it wasn't something to concern herself about for now.

And then events took a surprising turn. The Mormon Church announced that the term of missionary service would be reduced from two years to eighteen months (missions were later returned to the full two years). That meant Sam was coming home in August instead of the following February. Cindy had received a half-tuition scholarship, and she was about to move to Lindon, closer to Provo, where she would live with her grandparents and go to BYU. She was sort of frightened that Sam might come home with ideas of marriage.

When Sam returned on August 27, he only waited until the next morning before he called. He asked her to go to a movie that night. When he showed up at her house, she was surprised that he had grown even taller. He was six-foot-four, more than a foot taller than she was, and he looked good—older and more handsome than ever.

They ended up searching for a movie they wanted to see, and finally going to a drive-in theater in Provo. When the film ended, Sam took Cindy in his arms and kissed her. Later that night she wrote in her journal:

LULLABY AND GOODNIGHT

It was our first date in about three years and I shouldn't have let him kiss me. If he doesn't talk to me for a while I guess I will know that he got the wrong impression.

But Sam didn't seem to mind. He didn't stop calling. Not even for a day.

A couple of weeks later Cindy moved to her grandparents' home and started college. She was excited and scared. Her classes, which included chemistry and zoology, were challenging, and the university was bigger than all of Payson. But she studied hard and found that she could compete well, and she liked the quiet peace of her Grandma and Grandpa Giles's house.

On weekends Cindy returned to Payson, and Sam asked her out every week. When he asked her to spend a Saturday in Payson Canyon, she wondered whether they would have enough to talk about all day. But the day turned out well, and Cindy discovered something about Sam. As they sat high atop the mountain and looked out over the vast ranges of valleys below, they were not only at ease as they talked, but he told her how much he loved the out-of-doors: four-wheeling, hiking, fishing—the things she had grown up doing. And even more, he could talk about his feelings: his hopes for the future, the things he cared about. This was a man she could build something with.

But she hesitated. Sam definitely fit the description of that special someone she had longed for. But she had told herself she wouldn't get seriously involved with anyone until she had some years of college behind her.

Then something happened that deepened Cindy's feelings for Sam. One Saturday the two of them drove to Salt Lake City, where they walked around the Mormon temple grounds and spent some time in the visitors' center near the temple. This was the temple where her grandparents had been married, the temple that had taken Mormon pioneers forty years to build. For a long time it had been a powerful symbol for Cindy.

Because Sam had served as a missionary, he had entered the temple and had taken the vows known as the *endowment*. He had committed himself to his church through a series of promises to and from God, in a way that she had not yet done. Cindy felt that Sam's spirit was more refined, that he was further along in his *eternal progress* than she was. The two of them talked about the meaning of eternity, of commitment that went much beyond "to death do we part." She felt vibrations of goodness, sincerity, and trust that she hadn't felt with anyone else.

Later that night Sam told Cindy he was sorry for the way he had treated her in high school. He explained the complicated feelings that had frightened him away from her—and apologized for his immaturity in not explaining to her at the time. But Sam seemed very serious, and he wanted more of a commitment to a relationship than Cindy was ready for.

But Sam and Cindy kept dating every weekend. During the week Cindy studied hard and Sam worked hard. For the present, he was working with his dad in the roofing business. But times had been hard for his dad, and he was in no position to help much if Sam was to return to college. Sam couldn't see how he could support himself while he went to school full-time, and so he began to think about the air force. If he joined, he could get some education while he was in, and GI Bill money for study once he was out.

LULLABY AND GOODNIGHT

Gradually Cindy told Sam more about the difficult time she had faced while he was in England, and she told him about some of the guys with whom she had gone out. When she told him how some of them had treated her, Sam was outraged and even though he was a recently returned missionary, his instinct was to go after them. But Cindy told him that would accomplish nothing. She had forgiven them, and he should too. Sam was a little embarrassed, but he saw something in her he would notice many times in future years. Cindy's Christian spirit ran deeper than his own; she was always more able, and more willing, to forgive than he was.

Meanwhile, Cindy was very busy, but her mind was not entirely on school. By late October, when Sam had been home two months, she wrote in her journal:

> I am beginning to love Sam more and more. One day, when the time is right, I will probably marry him. . . . I still want to go with other guys, but not so much as I used to want to.

And then she didn't get back to her journal for a long time. In the middle of December with classes about to end and finals about to begin, she tried to catch up on what was happening in her life. She felt good about school, but she had decided she couldn't continue the next semester. Even with a scholarship, college was expensive, and her dad was struggling financially. He would never tell her she had to stop, but she knew it would take a lot of pressure off him.

Then she wrote:

> Sam . . . understands me, which is almost next to impossible because sometimes I don't even understand myself. I am going to marry him so I

can be with him forever. I know it will be hard at times but we can make it.

They were not yet engaged, and they hadn't picked a date for the marriage, but they were now committed. And the plan was developing. Sam would join the air force, and he and Cindy would marry that spring before he began his basic training.

On January 17, 1983, on a cold Monday afternoon, Sam picked Cindy up and drove her to Provo. While Cindy waited in the car, he ran into one of the jewelry stores they had previously visited. The mystery about his purpose couldn't have been too great, but Cindy wasn't exactly sure what Sam intended at the moment.

Sam drove to the Provo foothills, where the Provo temple sits in the mouth of Rock Canyon not far from the BYU campus. This was not the majestic old pioneer temple in Salt Lake City, but the same sealing ordinances were performed inside.

It was hardly the day for romance. No birds were singing. No trees were budding out. It was deep winter, cold, and threatening to storm. But Sam led her by the hand around to the east side of the temple into a little garden area where very few people ever walked. With the temple closed on Monday evenings, and with the weather so cold, it was certainly private that day.

Sam sat down on a little bench that faced the east side of the building. He pulled Cindy onto his lap and looked into her eyes. She was so much shorter than he that their eyes were even. He wrapped his arms around her, in her bundled coat, and he said, "Cindy, will you marry me *in the temple . . . forever?*"

He might have only said, "Will you marry me?" But he knew the exact words that meant so much to

LULLABY AND GOODNIGHT

Cindy. All through those painful years when she had longed to see her parents settle their differences and be sealed, and all through those years of longing for that person who could make that kind of commitment to her, she had wondered whether things would ever work out.

But now she had it. Everything she wanted.

"Yes," she cried. "Oh, yes!" She put her arms around him and kissed him. They clung to each other for quite some time, and Cindy cried. And then they got the ring from Sam's pocket.

He put it on her finger and they sat in the cold and talked about the happy future that lay ahead for them. About then, rain began to fall, but it didn't bother them. At that moment, no force—no malignancy—in the world seemed powerful enough to interrupt their joy.

During her engagement, Cindy did not write in her journal very often. She was too busy, too happy. But her joy was so intense that one has to think of young Juliet, so happy and so childlike in her enthusiasm—and so unaware of the future.

When Cindy did write, she discussed her wedding plans, her family, and her delight in finding someone so wonderful to spend eternity with. The wedding date was set for April 15. Just before the wedding, Cindy tried to describe her feelings for Sam: "He is so—I just can't think of a word that describes him. Take all the words that describe good, wonderful things and it still isn't even close to what Sam is. He is everything."

No crowds attend a Mormon temple wedding. Only the immediate family and a few close personal friends and relatives are invited. When the marriage is performed, the couple enters a *sealing room*. These are handsome but relatively unadorned rooms with a glass chandelier hanging above a pretty, upholstered altar. On opposite sides of the room are mirrors that reflect the chandelier. As one stands in the middle of the room and looks into the mirrors, the image of the chandelier—and the couple—bounces back and forth from mirror to mirror in endless, diminishing succession. It is the symbol of eternity.

The person performing the marriage always has the bride and groom look into those mirrors and think about the meaning of their eternal commitment. The marriage ceremony itself is very brief. The man and woman, dressed in white, face each other and kneel on opposite sides of the altar, and they join hands. They promise to love each other throughout eternity—the eternity they see in those ever-reflecting mirrors.

Sam and Cindy decided on the Salt Lake City temple for their marriage. It was the one that meant so much to Cindy. When they came out of the temple, they posed for pictures at the east doors, Sam in his white tuxedo, with tails, and Cindy in her white dress. Then they changed clothes and drove away together. The festive part of a Mormon wedding is the big reception, with lots of guests, usually held that same evening. Sam and Cindy had a number of things to do to be ready for that, so they stopped at a little hamburger stand and got themselves something quick to eat, and then they drove back to Payson.

They had trouble imagining that all this had really happened. They were really married at last. Cindy kept trying her new name on for size, and they laughed about not feeling very grown-up. And rightly so. Sam was twenty-one by then, but Cindy was not quite nineteen.

That night the church cultural hall—a fancy name for the gymnasium—was draped in blue and white. In front of the draping stood the wedding line. Tonie was

LULLABY AND GOODNIGHT

the matron of honor, and some of Sam's sisters were bridesmaids, all dressed in blue print dresses with white ruffles. Sam's older brother, Willie, was the best man. He and Mark and Kipper, along with the fathers of the bride and groom, were dressed in light blue tuxedos with dark blue trim—with a hint of "western" in the cut. The mothers wore dark blue.

Cindy's parents, though divorced, stood side by side in the wedding line. They had always been willing to be friends, and they were less uncomfortable being around each other by now. But only Cindy could have talked them into appearing in public together this way.

Cindy looked beautiful and simple in white. She didn't wear shoes (having slipped them off), even though that accented the difference in height between her and Sam. She didn't want to look taller than Tonie, and when Tonie wore heels, and Cindy didn't, they were about the same height. She had also worn Tonie's dress, partly to save money, and partly because it created another bond between them.

When the reception was finally over and a few details had been taken care of, Sam and Cindy changed in the church rest rooms, and then they went outside to showers of rice. Sam's pickup had not only been decorated but Sam's brother had changed the wiring so that the overhead light went on every time he stepped on the brake.

The newlyweds didn't worry about that. They drove to Provo for a one-night honeymoon. Along the way, on the radio, an Alabama tune came on: "Take Me Down." It was about making love all night, and the two laughed at the appropriateness, but they were still rather shy and a little nervous about sleeping together for the very first time.

Sam scored so high on his air force entrance examinations that he had plenty of choices as to what he could do. But he settled on police work. It was something he had long thought he might like. But his larger goal was to take as many college classes as he could find time for.

As the day approached for Sam to enter the air force, both he and Cindy dreaded the separation. They expected Sam's training to last ten to twelve weeks. At the Salt Lake airport, less than two months into their marriage, they clung to each other until the very last second, and then Sam walked away. Three months sounded like three years to the newlyweds, but Cindy kept telling herself it wasn't very long and she shouldn't be such a baby about it. Sam would be back.

During Sam's absence Cindy went back to live with her dad and Kipper. When she got home she was stunned to see how dirty they had let things become in such a short time. She got after them, however, and she tore into the house. Her dad was actually pleased, of course, but he was also amazed at how much confidence she had gained and how mature she seemed.

On June 17, 1983, Cindy had her nineteenth birthday while Sam was at Lackland Air Force Base in San Antonio, Texas. She counted every day until she would see him again. Finally the wait became just too long and she and Sam agreed that she should join him in Texas as soon as the initial stage of his training was completed.

On August 18 Cindy flew to San Antonio. She was scared to leave her family and the little town where she had always lived—and she was a little frightened of flying, since she never had—but she didn't struggle with her choice.

LULLABY AND GOODNIGHT

San Antonio seemed huge to Sam and Cindy, and they lived in a poor neighborhood. Sam was sometimes away for as many as four days on training programs. Such times were lonely for Cindy, but in certain ways, expanding.

Cindy had had little contact with people of other races and backgrounds. She had not even known all that many people of different religions. She was also shy. Still, she had always been open, and once she got past the initial step of getting acquainted with someone, she was very friendly. But mostly, when evening came, Sam and Cindy were together. They depended on each other entirely for their mutual joy.

During this time her journal was full of Sam, and full of her love. Best of all for Cindy were the weekends, when she and Sam could spend lots of time with each other:

> This weekend has been a really good one. Sam and I have lain around for hours and just talked. It was great. He's such a special man. I'm so glad I saved myself for him. It makes being with him and making love so much more special. It wasn't easy to wait . . . but by waiting, it has made us stronger. And the waiting was worth it.

All the same, Cindy was often homesick. She wondered in her journal about Payson and her family. When she learned from letters that quaking aspen were ablaze in Payson Canyon, she longed to escape the south-Texas humidity and spend time in "her mountains." When deer hunting season opened, she thought of being with her family. She wished she could be in Payson long enough to see some of the marching-band competitions and to see Kipper play football. She had, after all, given up all the things she had ever known for a little apartment in a big city, where she spent most of her time alone.

Cindy was simple in her needs and aspirations. She believed her "happily ever after" ending had begun with a marriage, just as it does in fairy tales. She and Sam sometimes got upset with each other. They both had stubborn streaks in them. But they seemed to live in an age gone by, when "I" wasn't nearly so important as "we." They could always work things out, Cindy trusted, and they did.

By October Sam and Cindy knew they would be going to Germany for three years. They were able to spend a week at home and then flew to Europe in December, arriving just a few days before Christmas. On Christmas day they were living in temporary housing on base in Bitburg, not far from the border of Luxembourg. Sam took a paper bath mat off the floor and drew a Christmas tree on it—complete with ornaments. They leaned it against the wall on top of a writing desk, and around it they placed the presents that they had brought in their luggage with them.

As she adjusted to a foreign culture, the early days in Germany were rather frightening to Cindy, but the compensations were great. She and Sam found an apartment on the edge of a little village named Prumzerlay. The building was really a guest house, used mostly by summer tourists, and so it was attractive, with vaulted ceilings and picture windows that looked out on a picturesque valley and green hills. As spring came on, Sam and Cindy wandered the nearby trails or jogged through the town.

The village was something out of a storybook, and the two never stopped marveling at the idea that they were in Europe, eight thousand miles from home, living among scenery that seemed too beautiful to be

LULLABY AND GOODNIGHT

real. They bought an Alfa Romeo Alfetta GT sports car, and they took long weekend drives into Luxembourg and Belgium, or to the surrounding cities in Germany.

But not all was perfect. Sam went through a serious illness that winter, and the lovely apartment—with the vaulted ceiling and spacious glass—proved to be extremely costly to heat. By spring Sam and Cindy were getting by without heat to avoid buying additional heating oil, and sometimes they got up in the morning to freezing temperatures. The Alfa Romeo proved to be a great headache too. It broke down constantly.

By summer, two things had changed: Cindy was pregnant, and she had begun to work part-time on base at a youth club. The work gave her a way of being around people—young people she enjoyed—and the money eased financial pressures. But most of the money went toward setting up a nursery for the baby. And above all, this baby gave Cindy a new sense of purpose.

Part of the reason money was tight for Sam and Cindy was that they wanted very much to travel to Holland and England that summer. It was important to Sam to show Cindy the places where he had lived and worked as a missionary in England. In addition, a close friend of his—a fellow missionary named Hans—was getting married that summer. The civil wedding would take place in Holland, where Hans lived, and the Mormon temple marriage would take place in London.

When Sam and Cindy returned from the trip, Cindy wrote a long account of all their travels. She was excited about all she had seen in Belgium, Holland, France, and England. She had seen the famous landmarks of London, stayed in bed-and-breakfast rooms, crossed the English Channel on a ferry. She had come a long way from Payson, Utah, and she loved the bigger view of the world she was getting.

Cindy's baby was a boy, born on a stormy winter day, February 9, 1985. Partly because of ice and snow on the roads and the snow still falling, Sam took Cindy to the hospital somewhat sooner than he might have. But at the base hospital the nurse told Cindy she was barely dilated. The doctor told her that she might as well go home for a while.

Sam made the tedious drive home, but within a very short time, Cindy's contractions were coming hard and fast. They headed back to the hospital. Cindy's water broke in the car and the contractions set on very hard.

Cindy screamed with the intense pain. "Oh, Sam. Oh, Sam. I'm going to have the baby. It's coming. I can feel it."

"Just relax and breathe," Sam told her. "Don't push."

"I can't help it. I . . . oh . . . oh." And she kept screaming.

Sam couldn't reach out to her, couldn't even glance away from the treacherous road. He was going as fast as he dared, but their progress was slow. "Hang on. Hang on," he kept telling her. "We'll be there in another few minutes."

When he finally pulled into the maternity entrance to the hospital, Cindy jumped out of the car and ran. Sam pulled the car out of the way and then ran after her. But she had already sprinted down a long hallway and turned the corner.

The nurses prepped Cindy as fast as they could. After only one contraction, they moved her into the delivery room. The doctor kept telling her not to push

LULLABY AND GOODNIGHT

yet, and Cindy felt that she was going to burst. There was no time for any medication.

But it was all over quickly. Once the doctor let Cindy push, the first contraction produced the baby's head, and on the second one, the baby was born. Cindy would not soon forget the pain of the delivery, but she was suddenly transported by the results of it all. A little boy was born: Luke Jesse Ray. She had chosen the names long ago, at age fifteen. If the baby had been a girl, she was to be Amelia Monik.

Cindy was convinced from early on that Luke was not only beautiful but very intelligent. She wondered whether she was worthy to raise such a special person. But he didn't eat very well at first, nor sleep, and he was amazingly alert and active. He also liked to spit up. Sam teased Cindy that the baby's name should have been "Puke" instead of Luke.

But Sam was as proud as Cindy of his little boy. People who saw the three together—at the base exchange, or in town—would stop and smile because they all seemed so wrapped up in each other, and they were such an attractive threesome. And in many ways they soon became a world unto themselves. Before they had been lovers, a couple, but now they had created another life and every act, every decision, focused on their new reality. Luke was their purpose, and their family was the center of life.

Sam continued to take college classes in his off-hours, and Cindy no longer worked. This meant that Sam was gone many hours every day, and Cindy was home most of the time. She walked sometimes, with Luke strapped on her back, and by now she did have lots of friends, especially among the Mormons in her air force ward (congregation).

In June Cindy turned twenty-one. Most of her

journal entries, aside from some doubts about herself, expressed more satisfaction about her life than ever before. Money was still tight, but not as bad as before. Part of the reason was that she and Sam saved carefully and used their money well.

Sam and Cindy traveled again to Holland, and once to Switzerland to the Mormon temple. Later they took a tour of southern Germany. Toward the end of their time in Germany, they took a train trip to northern Germany and Denmark.

Cindy got back into terrific shape after Luke was born. She worked out and became thinner than she had ever been in her life. Sam thought she was more beautiful than ever. Sometimes, however, he worried about her. He had been advanced to the Office of Special Investigations, assigned to the Joint Drug Enforcement Team. He had arrested men who lived on base or around the little town of Bitburg. He would run into them at the BX or commissary. He wondered whether someone would take revenge on him by attacking his wife, and so he instructed her on what to do if that were ever to happen. He told her that if she was ever abducted, to cooperate at first until the attacker relaxed. She might then be able to escape. On the other hand, if her life was threatened, and she had to fight, he told her to be unmerciful. He told her to ram her finger into the assailant's eye—to push it through—or to grab at his groin and rip with all her power.

But he wondered whether she would really do it. And he always assumed that if such a thing ever happened, the assailant would be a man, perhaps even a rapist.

Sam had advanced as quickly as was possible in the air force. He had saved enough money to make a down payment on a new Blazer 4X4, which he would pick up on the East Coast and drive to his new assignment in New Mexico. And another excitement had come into their lives. Cindy was expecting again. Their forever family was going to grow.

Sam and Cindy arranged to pick up their Blazer in South Carolina. They had a reason for that because another one of Cindy's dreams had come true. Kipper had made the choice she always hoped he would make—to be a missionary. Her brother was serving a mission in Virginia and Cindy wanted to visit him.

Sam and Cindy and Luke visited Kipper and then set off across the country for Albuquerque. They stayed long enough to find an apartment, and then they headed north to Utah.

The homecoming—after three years—was wonderful. Both sides of the family were thrilled with little blond-haired Luke, and they were very impressed with Cindy's firm but loving manner with him. He was an active little boy, a real handful, but Cindy had a soothing way of talking to him, and she was very patient.

In Albuquerque, Sam and Cindy continued to dream of their future. The family would be expanding again that summer, and that was the main focus of their lives—along with Sam's continued education. Cindy also looked for a way to expand her experiences and earn some money without leaving home. She decided to sell Tupperware. She could do Tupperware parties in the evenings, when Sam could be home with Luke, and she could take Luke with her on deliveries. But Cindy was still shy, and making contacts with strangers was not easy for her. She did it, however, and Sam watched her confidence take another leap as she found that she could succeed.

Those first months in Albuquerque were busy as

Sam took another class and Cindy raised Luke and pursued the Tupperware business. Before long Sam was made a dispatcher in the Security Police headquarters. This meant intense pressure. He was the one to take all the calls, to dispatch police, and to log every action. Sometimes the phones would light up and multiple responses had to be quick and accurate. He would come home from a shift, tired to the bone, with his head still spinning. And then he had to dive into his home-study class work.

There were times when schedules and needs conflicted, and Cindy felt that Sam was paying too little attention to her and to Luke. There were also times when the pressure was hard for Sam to handle. To ease the pressure, he and Cindy decided to buy a mobile home and move closer to base so that he could ride a bicycle to work and leave the car with Cindy.

The move did help in some ways, but it added new pressure. Every penny in their budget was committed. With payments on the car and trailer, and with all the usual bills, Cindy sometimes wondered how they could manage if anything at all went wrong. The Tupperware sales were minimal at first, but she had high hopes of using what she earned to buy what was needed for the new baby and to buy a computer she badly wanted to get for Sam. She felt he needed one to help him with his schoolwork.

As summer came on, Cindy, moving into the last trimester of her pregnancy, was very uncomfortable in the Albuquerque heat. The trailer was equipped with an air conditioner, but Sam and Cindy decided not to use it. They felt the electricity bills would be too high. But they did what they could to make the trailer feel like a home. The trailer park was a rather poor looking place, without a blade of grass anywhere. Most of the trailers looked shabby at best. But Sam

LULLABY AND GOODNIGHT

and Cindy planted grass, even raised a fairly decent little patch of lawn outside, and they tried to kill the ants. Sam fenced off a little area where Luke could play outside.

Cindy played baseball with two-year-old Luke out on that lawn during the many hours Sam was gone. Sam had built a little T-ball stand so that Luke could take his whacks at a Whiffle ball with a little baseball bat. Sam and Cindy were incredibly proud of their little athlete—who was active enough to drive them crazy sometimes—and they felt good about the tiny yard they had created next to their trailer.

When they had moved to this new area, they had entered a new Mormon ward (congregation), and the people were quick to welcome them and make them feel part of the group.

Life was coming together nicely. Sam and Cindy had so very far to go, but the plan was working. Sam was getting his education—if slowly—and the family was growing. They had learned to believe in themselves and to trust each other. Life seemed so certain to get better and better.

Then Sam had his nightmare.

No matter how hard Sam tried he couldn't get it out of his mind. He told himself a thousand times that it didn't matter, that it was only a dream. But he didn't believe it. Something kept telling him that the dream had been a warning, a chance for him to prepare himself. Cindy was going to die.

CHAPTER 3

During the next few days Sam kept trying to forget the dream. But it wouldn't go away. A feeling kept returning to him, and the feeling always turned into the same thought: The dream had been too real to be ignored. He was a religious person, but very practical. He had never been one to take much stock in mysticism. But now his rational mind battled with his feelings. He kept telling himself that dreams were random and purposeless; he had no reason to pay any more attention to this one than to any other. But he couldn't convince himself, and the thought that plagued him was that he had been warned and should start preparing.

After a few days, when these feelings wouldn't go away, he finally brought up the subject with Cindy again. He started carefully: "Cindy, I just keep wondering why I had that dream the other day. It might not mean a thing, but maybe we should decide what I would do if something like that really happened."

Cindy wouldn't hear of it. She pushed the subject away quickly, and Sam saw in her a discomfort that seemed unusually intense. Because of that he had all the more reason to let the subject drop, but her reaction also made him wonder whether she was thinking the same things that he was—and fearing the thoughts.

Over the next few days he tried to bring up the subject again, and finally he even asked whether, if one of them were to die young, the other should remarry. But Cindy refused to give an opinion. "I don't want to talk about it," she told Sam emphatically. "I *won't* talk about it."

There was something she did want to talk about, however. Some of the people in their new Mormon ward were going to take a trip to Mesa, Arizona, to visit the Mormon temple there—the closest one to Albuquerque. Cindy had been saying for some time that she would like to get to a temple again, before the baby was born. Once she had the new baby and would be breast-feeding, such a trip wouldn't be possible for quite some time. Sam agreed, but he also knew that a trip like that would not be easy for her. The baby was due in less than a month, and the heat had been hard on Cindy. She hadn't slept well lately.

But Cindy wanted to go, and a Mormon sister had agreed to take Luke for the two or three days they would be gone. Sam wanted to go, too, now maybe more than before. In spite of the heat and the discomfort of the long drive they made the trip. They traveled with three other friends, two men and a woman. Cindy found the ride uncomfortable and rather scary, what with the driver pushing hard, but they arrived safely on a Friday afternoon in time to attend one endowment session at the temple that evening.

When Mormons who have already received their endowments return to the temple, they repeat their vows and listen again to the theological instructions. They receive the endowment in proxy for persons who have died without the chance to take such vows, and at the same time they renew their own commitments.

The Rays spent that Friday evening recalling their own promises to each other and their marriage, and envisioning, once again, their purposes on the earth. Afterward, they slept that night in an inexpensive motel—or tried to sleep. Cindy actually slept very little, but she returned the next morning to repeat the ceremony twice more.

The other three friends went back for a third session, but Cindy was exhausted by then. For a time Sam and Cindy walked around the temple grounds and then they sat talking in the cool waiting room inside the entrance to the temple.

Cindy seemed to relax. When they met a high school friend who now lived in the Phoenix area, they chatted with her for a few minutes, but once she was gone, the chance meeting set off memories, and they found themselves reminiscing. Cindy was amazed to think how far she had come. She could hardly remember the little girl she had been a few years before. She was not one to express much confidence in herself, but she had to admit that she had grown. She felt that her faith had grown, that she was making some progress toward being a better person.

They also talked about the future. Sam had made up his mind to leave the air force once he had completed these last two years of his six-year commitment. He was glad he had joined, but his progress toward a college degree was too slow, and he was frustrated with the life of an enlisted man. He didn't feel that he was using his abilities fully, and he was sure that better possibilities existed once he finished his degree.

But as the two of them sat there, quietly talking, they had to admit that things had gone very well. They

LULLABY AND GOODNIGHT

had seen some of the world; they had built a solid relationship with each other; they had a lovely son and another child coming soon; they had both grown and learned a great deal and even managed to make some progress on their formal education; they had been prudent with their money and begun to build up a little equity on the mobile home; and they were proud of the shiny new red Blazer and the other possessions they had acquired. Best of all, they had returned to the temple, taken stock of themselves, and committed once again to live the best lives they could.

Cindy had known what she had wanted for so very long. She wanted someone who believed in the eternities as much as she did, and she wanted children who would stay a part of her life forever. The forever family was actually taking shape, and here in the temple she had time to relax for a little while and see that life, no matter how challenging at times, really was very good. Maybe "happy every second" wasn't possible, but "happily ever after" didn't have to be a fairy tale. She still got depressed at times, and she knew that life in a trailer with two children was not everyone's idea of perfection. But the way she felt now, it was mostly good and getting better.

She held Sam's hand, sitting next to him. "I love you," she whispered.

"I love you too," Sam said.

For a few minutes they simply clung to each other and wished time could hold still. Sam didn't want the other thoughts to come back: the dream, the warning. But even there, in the temple, seemingly cut off from the world and all its complications, the thought kept coming back: I'm not going to have her much longer.

The ride home from the temple was an ordeal. Cindy was nervous the whole way—and that was not like her. They did get home safely, if worn-out, but

Cindy was not feeling well. She couldn't get enough sleep to recover from the trip, and the baby seemed quiet within her, rarely moving at all. Her appointment at the Ob/Gyn clinic on base would be on Thursday. Sam tried to talk her into going in early, but she decided she would wait. Still, she worried all day on Monday.

That evening Sam and Cindy went to bed early. As they lay side by side, Sam asked Cindy what was bothering her. She said that she was worried about the baby, but she admitted that her fears ran deeper, that she was scared about the birth. She remembered how very painful the first delivery had been. But more than that, she was afraid that something might happen to her this time.

Sam didn't know whether he had scared her with his account of the dream, or whether she had been afraid before that. Even before the temple trip she had done some things he couldn't explain. A month or so before, she had called Tonie and both her parents. Sam had listened to the conversations and wondered what she was thinking. She had told Tonie that she wouldn't be able to call her anymore. He knew that she was being careful with money, but she didn't give that as her reason, and Sam had certainly never told her that she ought to stop calling. She had told her mother how much she loved her and missed her, that she was sorry for the strain that had come into their relationship during the time of the divorce. Sam sensed that she was trying to set everything right.

At the end of the conversation with her father, Cindy had said, "Dad, I love you." When he apparently said, "I love you, too" she had said, "Daddy, I really mean it. I want you to know that I really, really love you. Do you understand that?"

It had crossed Sam's mind not only that she was

LULLABY AND GOODNIGHT

trying to get things in proper order, but there was something final in the conversations, as though she were saying good-bye, although at the time, he didn't know why she would feel she needed to do that.

But that was before the dream. And now he wondered whether she too had been given some sort of warning. He tried to get Cindy to talk about the whole thing again—the dream and his worries, and the fears she seemed to be having. Once again, however, she resisted, and so Sam forced her to react by taking a direct, almost cruel approach. "Cindy," he said, "I'm scared. I'm afraid you're going to die and I'm going to be alone. And I don't know what you want me to do. I don't want it to happen without our talking about it. If we don't, I'll never know what you want from me. If it happens, should I get married again? Or would you rather I stay alone with the kids?"

But Cindy got upset. "You just want me to leave so you can get someone better than me!" she told Sam.

He held her and consoled her, and he promised it wasn't true. "Cindy, I'm just scared I'm not going to have you much longer," he told her. But he didn't back off. He asked again. Did she want him to remarry if it did happen?

Cindy was still crying, but she mumbled softly, "Yes."

"How would you handle that?"

For many that would be a strange question, but Cindy knew what he meant. They were committed to each other forever, and they believed that the one to go first would wait for the other.

Cindy whispered very softly, "I don't know. But I will."

Sam turned and reached his arms around her. She turned toward him and he arched around her big stomach. She was crying now, and in a way Sam was sorry that he had done this. It wasn't something he was happy to know; it was survival information.

He wanted to say, "Cindy, let's forget all this. It was a silly dream and I've been acting stupid about it. We're going to be here together for a long, long time." The words were all there, running over and over through his mind, but he couldn't get himself to say them. He just didn't believe it.

And so he held her and they both cried.

That was Monday. Early in the morning on Thursday, July 23, Sam hesitated on the step of his mobile home. He was standing one step down from Cindy, which made them closer to the same height. But they didn't want to say good-bye that morning. He leaned over her bulging front and held her in his arms and kissed her, and then they chatted a bit longer before he kissed her again.

Sam had not forgotten about the dream, but now that they had talked about it, he was relieved. He kept telling himself that it may not be anything to worry about. And mostly, now, he was trying not to dwell on it.

Cindy was still wearing a robe, and she looked tired. She smiled and wished Sam a good day. She had cooked breakfast while he was in the shower, but she had eaten very little herself. She wasn't feeling well, and she hadn't slept well all week.

The morning was warm and the day was going to be blistering. But Cindy had things to do. She had to pick up Tupperware from her distributor, and she would be going in for a checkup at the Ob/Gyn clinic that afternoon. Sam went with her to these visits whenever he could, but now that he was working day shifts, she would have to go without him. She had arranged to leave Luke with Jackie Bloomfield, her Mormon *visit-*

ing teacher—one of two women assigned to visit once a month and be of help where they could.

Sam rode his bicycle to work so Cindy would have a car. And he had a busy morning. The dispatcher's office was the nerve center of the law enforcement unit on base, and it could be hectic. The activity was intense, as usual, and the morning passed quickly, but around noon Cindy called. "Hi, Cin, how're you doing?" Sam asked.

"Hi, Sergeant Ray," she said, joking, but she sounded just a little upset. "I've been looking through my Tupperware order, and they didn't get it right. I've got to run back out there."

"I'm sorry," Sam told her.

"Oh, it's not that big of a deal. I'm just tired."

"What time is your appointment at the clinic?"

"Two. I'll pick you up from work when I'm finished."

"Okay. I'm not exactly sure when I'll get out of here."

"That's okay."

"Why did you call? It wasn't just about the Tupperware, was it?"

"No. I just wanted to tell you I love you."

"I love you too, Cindy."

A long pause followed, and Sam felt a little awkward. He was pretty sure their conversation about the dream was still on her mind. He wanted to tell her to forget it.

"Are you still worried about the baby?" Sam finally asked.

"Yeah, I guess I am. It's moved some today, but not much. Not like it should."

"Don't you think when it's so hot, and you're tired and everything, that the baby feels some of that?"

"I guess. I just hope it's okay."

"I'm sure it is." And Sam *was* sure of that. It was not the baby he was worried about.

"Well," Cindy said, "I better let you go."

"I'm glad you called," Sam said. "I love you."

"I love you too, Sam."

Sam said good-bye, but his feelings were hard to understand. He felt a strange nostalgia. He wanted to hang on, to push aside his fears, but he also felt a kind of sadness—a sense that he would soon lose her and he could do nothing about it.

He went back to work and he stayed very busy. Later, he would cherish the kiss at the doorstep that morning, and this brief conversation. He would remember her words: "I just wanted to tell you I love you." But now he had no time to think about that.

As quitting time approached, Sam received a phone call from the nearby Ob/Gyn clinic. Sister Rosemary Homrich, a nun and midwife, called to tell Sam that Cindy was going to be longer than usual. Because of Cindy's anxieties about the baby's inactivity, Sister Rosemary had hooked her up to a monitor to check the baby. This had taken more time than Cindy had expected and she was worried about Jackie Bloomfield, who hadn't planned to have Luke so long. She asked Sister Rosemary to call Sam and have him pick up Luke if he got finished at work before she was finished at the clinic.

Within half an hour of Sister Rosemary's call, Sam left work and walked around the corner and across the street to the clinic. He saw the Blazer in the parking lot, with the Tupperware on the seat. So he put his holster and a few of his other things inside and then walked into the clinic. The receptionist told him that Cindy was around the corner in the first room, still being monitored. Sam walked into the room, only to

LULLABY AND GOODNIGHT

discover another woman and her husband there. He was embarrassed. He apologized, and then went back to the receptionist. He finally learned, from a nurse, that Cindy had left just a few minutes before.

That didn't make sense. The car was still outside. But Sam assumed she had to be close by. He walked to the pharmacy, checked outside again, and then, beginning to worry a little, made a systematic check of the clinic area. He was trained to make such searches, and the policeman in him took over immediately. But Cindy was simply not there.

Luke had been at the baby-sitter's much longer than Cindy had promised, and this concerned Sam. But he spent about forty-five minutes searching before he decided he better go get his son. Along the way, as he drove, his eyes searched the base. He kept trying to think of some explanation for where she might have gone.

Sam picked up Luke, who had had an "accident" in his clothes. Jackie Bloomfield had found a pair of oversize, worn-out training pants, left over from her own older children. Sam laughed about that and apologized for leaving Luke with her so long. He and Luke then drove back to the base.

But Sam was getting very worried by now. Nothing made sense. The temperature was near one hundred degrees and Cindy was in frail condition. She wasn't likely to walk anywhere. She had been concerned about Luke and was not likely to leave him any longer than necessary. Sam's mind raced to every possibility, but he kept hoping that he would return to the base and find some simple explanation.

When he reached the clinic, which was closing for the day, an office employee told him that an insurance briefing was being held in a nearby building. Expectant parents were supposed to attend at some point in the pregnancy. Cindy had said nothing about the meeting, but Sam was grasping for some logical explanation. Maybe she had walked over and expected him to go get Luke. Maybe she had left a message that somehow hadn't gotten to him. It was worth checking. But shortly after Sam arrived, the meeting broke up and everyone came out. Cindy was not there.

Sam asked Sergeant Null, a fellow policeman, whether Cindy had been in the meeting, but she hadn't been. He even had Null's wife check the rest room.

Sam was trained to deal with emergencies. He didn't panic, but inside, as he fought to suppress his escalating emotions, he could feel a frantic sense that something was definitely wrong. He tried to be calm, for Luke, for Cindy. He tried to think what else to do.

For the next couple of hours he pursued every possibility he could think of. He checked at his workplace to see whether she had come by or left a message. He returned to the clinic and checked every corner, including the rest rooms. He drove about the base, checking everywhere he could think she might be. He went home and looked there. Had she gotten sick? Had she passed out somewhere? Had she gone into labor?

It was not usual to file a missing person's report until an individual had been gone for twenty-four hours, but Sam returned to the police headquarters and filed a report anyway. His fellow security policemen knew that Cindy was near her delivery date and that she wasn't the sort of person to wander off. So a missing person's bulletin was released less than three hours after she had disappeared.

The desk sergeant who had relieved Sam earlier told Sam to go home and to stay put so that if someone

LULLABY AND GOODNIGHT

located Cindy, Sam would be where they could get hold of him. Sam knew there was nothing else he could do, so he took Luke and went home.

While filing the missing person's report, Sam had realized that he didn't know what Cindy was wearing. And so he called Jackie Bloomfield to find out. He also told her that Cindy had still not been located. Before Sam left the police headquarters he received a call from his *home teacher*—a Mormon brother assigned to look after his family. By the time Sam reached his mobile home, his phone was ringing. Even though he had only been in his present ward a couple of months, word was spreading through the membership, and they were calling to see what they could do.

The Mormon bishop, Ted Prettyman, was one of the first to call. Sam told him there was nothing he could do for now, but the bishop told him to sit tight, he would be right over.

And then the wait began.

The phone rang from time to time, but it was never the call Sam was hoping for. Slowly the truth of the situation was becoming undeniable. No simple misunderstanding could explain Cindy's disappearance. Something was seriously wrong. Foul play had to be involved. But why would anyone abduct a woman who was about to have a baby? Who could possibly want to hurt her?

As the evening wore on, Luke was quiet. He sensed the trouble. When bedtime came, Sam helped him get his pajamas on, and then he knelt with him while little Luke, only two-and-a-half, said his own prayers. "Daddy," he said, when he was finished, "where's my mommy?"

Sam held him in his arms and said, "I don't know, Luke. She's lost. We can't find her. But everything's okay. You've got your daddy."

He wanted to say, "Don't worry. We'll find her." But he was starting to think that might not happen.

Luke went to bed and went to sleep, but over the next few days—actually, months—he would ask over and over, "Daddy, where's my mommy?"

The vigil at Sam's mobile home continued. Several of the Mormon men began searching the desolate area between the base and the Bloomfields' home. As darkness came on, they used searchlights, and they checked every abandoned car, every weed patch.

Sam sat at home—or paced—and tried to think what could have happened. Friends called all the hospitals. Sam and Bishop Prettyman tried to consider every possibility.

Sam told himself that either Cindy couldn't come home, or she didn't want to. He tried to think whether anything was wrong between them, whether she would try to leave for some reason. He remembered the kiss that morning, the telephone call. "I just wanted to tell you I love you." Had that been some sort of good-bye?

But no. Definitely not. She had been too sweet to him on the phone. It wasn't that.

Sam called Cindy's parents, and that wasn't easy. He was the young man who had taken their daughter away from Payson, and he felt responsible for her. Now he was calling to tell them that she had vanished, and he hadn't protected her.

But the Gileses hadn't heard from Cindy either. No one had. The wait continued. Sam had been up very early that morning, and the stress of the long day left him exhausted. The bishop finally suggested, around midnight, that they try to get some sleep.

"Sure, but why don't you go home?" Sam suggested. "There's nothing you can do here now."

"That's all right," Bishop Prettyman said. "I'll just

LULLABY AND GOODNIGHT

sleep here on your couch. If you get a call during the night, and you have to go somewhere, someone's going to have to stay with Luke."

"We'll manage all right," Sam told him. "I really think you ought to go home and get a good night's sleep."

Sam knew that the bishop had to go to work in the morning. He was a lay clergyman and worked as a superintendent for a construction company. Besides, Sam knew he also had other responsibilities to deal with.

But Bishop Prettyman was not an easy man to tell what to do. He was a strong man who had gotten through college on a wrestling scholarship. "Listen, Sam," he said, "if you think you can throw me out of here, go ahead; otherwise, I'm staying for the night."

Sam felt the support; knew he needed it. He was grateful for the strength of the young bishop.

And so the two agreed they would try to sleep. But first they knelt together and prayed. "Heavenly Father," Sam said, "please help us to find out where Cindy is, *soon*. And bless her that she's not suffering."

His premonitions over the past two weeks and the logic of the situation were telling him that he was not likely to get good news. He was not ready to admit that the worst had happened, but something told him that he had to be prepared for that possibility.

He had stayed tough all evening. He hadn't cried, hadn't gone to pieces. But now, alone in his own bedroom—their bedroom—he couldn't hold back any longer. He lay down on the bed and sobbed. He wondered whether he would ever see Cindy again. He finally let himself think of all the terrible things that might have happened. He had seen so much in his police career, and he knew what destructive forces were out there in the world. But what kind of person would hurt or rape a woman who was so obviously pregnant?

Sam was bone tired and he eventually dozed off, but the phone rang soon after. It was about two o'clock. He was startled for a second, but he jumped up and ran from his bedroom, through his living room, and into the kitchen. He grabbed the phone. It had only rung a couple of times. He hoped that somehow it would be good news, but he didn't really expect it, and so his heart was pounding. It was Sister Rosemary calling from the hospital. She said she had a "few questions," but Sam sensed something strange in her voice. She also put a doctor on the phone, who had some further questions. They wanted to know more about Cindy, her disappearance, even her blood type. Sam was not clear what was going on. He understood, however, that the hospital staff couldn't reveal anything until they were sure about their own facts.

Sam hung up the phone and went back to bed. But he lay there wondering. He was sure that Sister Rosemary knew more than she was saying. Had they found Cindy? Or did they have some lead? He was too dazed to think what it all might mean.

Sam was accustomed to odd hours and sleeping whenever he could. He willed himself to stop speculating and to get the sleep he was going to need. But he slept fitfully, waking up many times.

During the night, his Security Police friends were busy searching every inch of the base. One of their own was in need, and they felt a personal stake in doing what they could. Sgt. Vickie Mitchell—a friend of Sam's, an experienced dispatcher, and a mother—was on duty. She kept in constant touch with the Albuquerque police. Toward morning she picked up some information about a woman showing up at the University of New Mexico Hospital with a baby that

LULLABY AND GOODNIGHT

was not her own. Her instincts told her this could be significant, and so she contacted the Air Force Office of Special Investigators (AFOSI), and agent Steve Coppinger was quick to check out the situation.

In the morning Luke came in and hugged his daddy. He again wanted to know where his mommy was. Sam struggled to know what to tell him. But he tried to make Luke feel secure.

Soon after Sam got up, a friend of his from Security Police knocked at the door. He had worked all night searching the base for Cindy. He wanted to see how things were going for Sam. Once again, Sam had the feeling that the man knew more than he was telling.

"Sam," he said after a time, "Captain Hall [Squadron Vice-Commander] thought it would be a good idea if I picked up any weapons you have in your house. You know about the policy on that."

Sam had seen this before. When people in the military go through some kind of serious stress, they are required to give up their weapons. Revenge or even suicide can be dangers at such times. Sam didn't mind turning over his little .22-calibre rifle and a hunting knife, but he wondered whether this was a precaution for his current situation or preparation for other news to come.

Gnawing inside was the fear that Cindy was suffering or dead, or worst of all, that she would never be found and he wouldn't know what had happened to her. And he wondered about his baby, whether it too would be lost forever. At the same time, he was quite sure that something was going on at the hospital—something no one wanted to tell him about. He was a controlled person, trained to be careful and logical in the heat of stress, but the wait was almost unbearable. How much longer would it last? What if it were to drag on for days, weeks? He had to take long, slow breaths at times, and tell himself that he could not fly apart. For one thing, Luke needed him.

The bishop took the chance, while others were there, to leave long enough to check in at work. He said he wouldn't put in a full day, that he would get things started and be back. Sam was left trying to think what else he could do. He called Cindy's Tupperware supervisor. Had Cindy said anything to her? Who were some of the other Tupperware people? Some of them had seen her the day before. Did anyone know anything?

Sam also called his parents. In Utah, the Pioneer Day celebration had begun. On July 24, 1847, Brigham Young had arrived in the Salt Lake valley. It was now a day of celebration, a state holiday. His parents were about to leave for the parade in the town of Spanish Fork. They were stunned to hear that Cindy was missing.

Around eight o'clock Captain Hall and Sam's first sergeant, Ed Dickson, came to Sam's home and asked him to come to the base with them. The commander of AFOSI, Colonel Young, wanted to meet with Sam. Sam took Luke along and rode to the base with Hall and Dickson. Colonel Young assured Sam that everything possible was being done. He wanted to know every detail about Cindy's plans for the day, her clothing, etc., and Sam tried to help as best he could. But once again, Sam sensed that Colonel Young knew something, that the OSI was merely getting its facts together before they broke the bad news to him. This was not typical at all for a colonel to be so personally involved with Sam.

But Sam went back to his mobile home, and the terrible wait continued.

Again and again Sam came back to the reality that

LULLABY AND GOODNIGHT

Cindy could not be safe and unharmed. As he looked at Luke, he wondered what the future would hold for the two of them. He thought of the dream. In the dream he also had the baby. How could that happen now?

The phone rang again. Every time it rang, Sam's pulse would take off, and he would pick up the phone hoping for something positive or at least some resolution. This time it was the Tupperware supervisor. She had checked with some of the other salespeople and had learned nothing that Sam didn't already know, but then she said, "I'm not sure whether this could have any connection, but one of our ladies told me that a woman was brought into the University Hospital last night. She had a newborn baby and claimed it was hers. But when they checked her they found that she hadn't given birth." The woman also told Sam that a Detective Tom Craig, of the Albuquerque police, had been assigned to the case.

When Sam put the phone down, he knew. The whole thing finally made sense. Whoever had abducted Cindy had wanted the baby. Maybe it was a black-market operation. Surely someone else besides this woman must have been involved. But what had these people done to Cindy to get the baby? The pictures that came to mind were too awful to deal with. Sam tried to turn the emotion into action. He called Colonel Young. If the air force investigators didn't know about this, they needed to. If they did, maybe the colonel would tell him something.

But Colonel Young was out. Sam left a message about the information he had received.

By now the bishop had returned. Others of his Mormon friends were showing up, with food, with offers of help with Luke, with the hope they might do something to ease his pain.

After about fifteen minutes, Sam called the colonel again. He was desperate to bring the whole thing to some sort of conclusion. What he thought he now knew was devastating, but he would rather know it for sure than simply live with the likelihood.

This time the colonel came to the phone. He told Sam that his commander, Major Webb, was on her way to Sam's house. "Just stay there. She'll be there in a few minutes." He wouldn't say anything else.

Sam knew how these things were done. He knew exactly what this all meant. No one would give him such terrible news over the telephone. The squadron commander was coming because she now had the information and would only give it to him in person.

Cindy was dead. The baby at the hospital was his.

Sam waited but he knew.

He tried to tell himself that some other possibility existed. But he knew.

A growing numbness was engulfing him. He tried to think what he would do. How could he go on living without her? He and Cindy had been each other's universe. He kept clinging to Luke, trying to hold on to what was left of his life. But how could he ever make little Luke understand? How could he raise him alone?

The minutes crawled by.

He was surrounded by friends, but no one was saying much now. They knew better than to tell Sam that everything was all right.

Sam was watching out the window when the commander arrived. The pretty blond major was wearing her dress blues. Those weren't working clothes. She was there to perform a special function. Again, Sam knew what that meant.

And she was not alone. Msgt. Ed Dickson was there

LULLABY AND GOODNIGHT

and so was a Mormon chaplain. And a nurse—although Sam didn't know that's who it was until she came inside and was introduced.

But Sam knew the whole procedure. He had seen it before. He wanted to let go, wanted to cry, but he held on. Something told him that he could do this with some dignity, and something even deeper said that if he ever let go, he might be swallowed—might fall into some black hole that he could not climb back out of—and he couldn't do that. And so Sam let the professional in him take over; something automatic in him told him how to behave.

Major Webb introduced everyone and then she asked Sam whether he could say, under oath, that he had turned over all his weapons.

Sam gave his word.

Everyone sat down.

"We have bad news," Major Webb began. "We normally wouldn't have come yet—until everything is verified—but you found out some things on your own. So we thought it was only fair that we not make you wait any longer."

Sam nodded, waited. But he knew.

"A woman was admitted to the University Hospital last night, as you know. She had a baby that she had not given birth to. She now admits that she took the baby out of another woman's body. We are pretty certain that it's your wife. She left the woman in the mountains yesterday afternoon."

Sam nodded. He tried to breathe.

"A team is heading into the mountains right now—to verify the story. We're not sure it's your wife, but she matches the description."

Sam sat quietly. He was looking at the floor. He wanted to think, but mostly the numbness had taken over. People were around him—the bishop and the chaplain—but he heard little of what anyone said. He picked up Luke and held him.

Tears welled up in Sam's eyes, but he didn't let go. He was still holding on. And he knew immediately what he wanted. He wanted to see his baby.

Major Webb's beeper went off several times in the next few minutes, and she was on the phone most of the time. Every time she put the phone down she had a little more information. But it was only detail. And it all didn't matter. Cindy was gone.

"I want to see my baby," he told the major. "I've lost a member of my family, but I have a new one. I want to see her."

Major Webb said she would see if she could arrange that. She called the hospital and at first was told that until the investigators had located the body and verified Darci's story, they could not let Sam see the baby. But in a short time word came that the body had been located and Sam could come to the hospital.

Bishop Prettyman drove Sam, while the major and her group drove in their own car. The administrator of the hospital was waiting when the entourage arrived. Sam was given special treatment as he was directed to a private room in the nursery area. The head pediatrician entered after a few minutes. He placed the baby girl in Sam's arms.

Sam tried to escape all that he was facing at the moment. He focused on the lovely little child, much smaller than Luke had been but seemingly perfect. He loved her instantly, as he had loved Luke. But this experience carried a new poignancy. This was, after all, what was left of Cindy.

"Is she all right?" he asked.

"Mr. Ray, it's something of a miracle considering

LULLABY AND GOODNIGHT

the conditions under which she was born. We've run a lot of tests, but we can't find a single thing wrong."

A miracle.

As Sam held the delicate little newborn in his arms, it occurred to him that Cindy had prayed for her. That would have been the last thing she would have thought to do. And Cindy's prayers always got through. He had seen the power of her faith many times.

And so he held his little miracle and tried to think what his life would be like now. He felt comfort in the miracle; he felt love for what was left of Cindy, what she had given him in her final moment on earth. But what would he do without her?

The room was filled with people—the air force team that had come to his home, Bishop Prettyman, hospital staff, the doctor. They were all watching. Sam held the baby while little Luke leaned against Sam's side. This was Sam's world now, and he focused on that.

But he didn't let go. He sat and held the baby. His emotions were too overwhelming, too complicated, to deal with. Instead he focused on the lovely child in his arms and his son by his side. He knew that he now had to be both a father *and* a mother. He was in control. He had to go on. He couldn't let his children down. And he couldn't let Cindy down. He knew what kind of mother she would have been; knew what her dreams were; knew how much she loved this little baby. She had given her life for it, and now he had to give his.

Sam spent the rest of the day surrounded by people, but he felt alone, wrapped in numbness. He didn't know who had done this to Cindy. He assumed that someone was working with the woman, that maybe black marketeers were at work. But he couldn't concentrate on the killer; he had to think about the survival of his family. He kept his mind on the tasks before him. He knew that anger and hatred would only eat him up.

Sam also asked himself what Cindy would do. She had always been able to forgive. Somehow he had to do the same. Someone had harmed her—and him—but he knew the hatred could be worse than the injury. And so he put it aside, immediately. He told himself not even to think about the killer.

But Sam was the only one who reacted that way. As the story broke in Albuquerque, and then around the nation, the same question was on everyone's mind. What kind of person—or monster—could do such a thing?

CHAPTER 4

Darci lay in the street, flat on her back, her arms to her sides, and her legs stretched out. She couldn't help smiling.

"Okay. One's coming," Rachel McCrainey said. She sounded excited.

"Good. Let it come."

But the car was still a block away. Darci didn't turn her head. She listened until she could hear the sound of the tires on the pavement and see the headlights out of the corner of her eye, but she didn't move.

"Darci, it's coming!" Rachel said, and now there was anxiousness in her voice.

"I know. I'm going to let it run over me. I'm not scared." Darci's voice was calm and serious.

Rachel waited, waited, but the car was getting close. "Darci, get up now!" Rachel shouted. "Darci.

"Darci!

"Darci!"

Rachel couldn't stand it any longer. She rushed into the dark street, waving her arms. The car slowed, suddenly, and rolled to a stop. Only then did Darci get up and walk off the street.

"You ruin the whole game if *you* stop the cars,"

Darci told Rachel. "Why even play if you're going to do that?"

"I don't *want* to play. It was your idea." And now Rachel was struggling not to cry.

Darci laughed. "Don't be such a baby," she said. "So what if a car runs over me? It's not your problem."

Darci obviously liked playing chicken, found it exciting. When Rachel tried it, she would jump and run when the cars were still far away. Not Darci. She really didn't know how long she dared wait; Rachel always intervened before she could push her courage to the limit.

That was in 1979, the year Sam Ray and Cindy Giles first became interested in each other. Darci Kayleen Ricker turned twelve and began seventh grade that year. In many ways, her life was different from Cindy's or Sam's. She lived in Portland, Oregon, a large city (especially compared to Payson, Utah). And she lived in a tough part of town. There was little sense of a tight-knit community around her, and certainly no homogeneous culture pressuring her toward any one way of life. And yet, the similarities of Darci's life to Cindy's are more striking than the differences. Darci's parents, like Cindy's, were working people. Darci's father worked at a lumber mill, put in long hours, came home tired, and often had to work nights and sleep in the day. Cindy's dad worked in a steel mill when he wasn't on strike or laid off, working long shifts or night shifts. Often he came home beat. Cindy's mother worked as a nurse's aide, and later at the steel mill with her husband. As a part-time source of income, Darci's mother decorated cakes or she took in children to tend.

Both the Gileses and the Rickers struggled with each other, and often fought in front of their kids.

LULLABY AND GOODNIGHT

Each couple had three children and lived in homes that were anything but fancy. Darci and Cindy both grew up going to church, but Darci's parents were more active in their church than Cindy's were. Both families enjoyed hunting, fishing, picnicking, and camping as their main sources of recreation.

Cindy never had a lot of friends her own age when she was growing up. Neither did Darci. But Darci's best friend was Rachel McCrainey. Rachel always thought Darci was a little strange, but it never even occurred to her that Darci might hurt anyone, at least not seriously. Later, however, she remembered curious qualities about Darci that she had never understood.

It was not that Darci tortured animals or lived in psychotic delusions. For the most part, Rachel remembered an ordinary girl. Darci always did well in school, and she was a chatty, outgoing person. If she didn't have a lot of friends, she didn't seem concerned about it. She liked to spend time alone.

But Darci's moods could change suddenly and unexplainably, and her fantasies were unusually real to her. Darci told Rachel on one occasion that her mother had ordered her a new party dress from Paris. She described the gown in vivid detail. Rachel had learned to doubt such stories, but she was always amazed at Darci's complete certainty of her own facts. When Darci appeared at the party in an ordinary dress, Rachel asked her what happened to the beautiful white dress her mother had ordered from Paris. Darci seemed surprised at the question. She laughed and said, "What are you talking about?"

Rachel reminded her about their conversation and even told her some of the details about the dress. Darci didn't say, "I was just joking," or, "Didn't you know I was making that up?" Not even, "Okay, I lied." She seemed genuinely confused by what she heard. She could look Rachel right in the eye, her own eyes steady and confident. She told Rachel again that she had never heard of such a thing and she didn't know where Rachel had gotten the idea. Strangely enough, Rachel believed her friend. Darci really didn't seem to be acting or lying.

One of Darci's continual fantasies had to do with her "real" mother. Darci had been adopted. Her parents had met a pots-and-pans salesman at a sales party. Quite by accident, as they conversed with the man, they learned that he had an unmarried teenaged daughter who was expecting a baby. He said that he was looking for a family to adopt the child. The Rickers already had two sons, but Mrs. Ricker had suffered a very difficult and dangerous delivery with her second child. She was afraid to give birth again; still, she wanted more children. When she and her husband learned that the child would be available at birth, they arranged through a lawyer to adopt. They received the baby girl when she was eleven days old, and they named her Darci Kayleen Ricker.

Adoption had been very common in the Rickers' families. They saw no special problem with it, and they believed it was important to be open about the adopted child's birth. So Darci learned at a young age that she was not the Rickers' biological child. Darci would later say that her brothers, one of whom was mentally handicapped, teased her about her origins. When they became angry with her, they would tell her that she wasn't their real sister, that she didn't belong to their family. She would become enraged, but her usual reaction was to withdraw to her room and refuse to speak to them.

Virtually everyone who knew Darci in more than a passing way, knew how she felt about her adoption:

She resented her biological mother for giving her away, and she often said she disliked—or hated—her adoptive mother. She was especially bothered by Mrs. Ricker's obesity. Rachel could not remember that Darci ever said anything positive about Sandra Ricker.

Darci often fantasized about her natural mother. She told Rachel one day that her real mother had approached her while she was playing outside and told her that she wanted her back. This mother was young and pretty and thin. Darci was animated and happy, and she told Rachel all about the talk she and her mother had had. Her mother had told Darci how much she loved her and how sorry she was that she had ever given her up. Rachel saw the happiness and certainty in Darci's face, and she bought the story completely in spite of her usual skepticism for Darci's tales. How could she have a doubt? Darci could repeat every word of the conversation.

But that was on Friday, and on Monday, when Rachel asked Darci whether she had heard from her mother again, Darci's confused look returned. "What are you talking about?" Darci asked. "I've never met my mother. She gave me away when I was eleven days old."

Rachel was upset. "Darci," she said, "you talked about it all day on Friday. You told me all that stuff your mother said to you."

Darci laughed and shook her head. "I don't know who tells you stuff like that. I never said any such thing."

Rachel gave up and vowed not to believe Darci ever again, but she still wasn't sure whether the girl was lying, or whether she really didn't remember.

Rachel, like most everyone who knew Darci in her growing-up years, knew that Darci made things up.

The fantasies about the dress or about her mother were only two of the more convincing stories she told Rachel. Often the line between fact and fiction was more obvious. Darci pictured herself in glamorous Cinderella stories of every kind. Sometimes she didn't pretend the stories were true, but presented them as wishes. Other times she would report rich uncles who were going to take her away, or exciting trips she was about to take.

Rachel, at the time, perceived all this as relatively harmless. So did most people. Everyone recognized the more extreme fictions. They laughed about Darci's imagination, and saw no sign of anything terribly dangerous in it.

Rachel felt that Darci always had to be better than other people. Once Rachel got a higher grade than Darci on a test, and that normally didn't happen. Darci was not willing to accept the grade, and she placed the blame on the teacher. She grabbed hold of her desk, lifted it in the air and screamed, "I'm going to throw this at you!" She looked wild, angry enough to carry out her threat.

The teacher, needless to say, was shocked—and frightened. "Now, Darci," she said soothingly, "please put the chair down and we can talk about this."

Darci stood with the desk still suspended for a few more seconds, and then the rage seemed to pass. She set the desk down and her teacher asked her whether she would like to take the test over again.

She agreed to that. And when Darci did better the second time—and better than Rachel—she was satisfied.

Such extreme reactions were nothing new for Darci. Even though she was usually quite placid, once, when she quarreled with another student, she picked up a

LULLABY AND GOODNIGHT

chair and struck the girl with it. Part of the reason for the fight was that the other girl was black, and Darci, according to Rachel, was very prejudiced. In fact, Darci didn't think she should have to go to school with blacks.

Darci's sixth-grade teacher, Sharon Gray, had also seen these kinds of outbursts. Darci, she said, was a favorite student: bright, sensitive, and very attached to her teacher. But on several occasions she lost her temper and suddenly tossed her desk over or became loud and abusive.

And yet, Darci had become completely enamored with her teacher. Mrs. Gray was a pretty, tall, slender woman, and she was educated and refined. She was the antithesis of Mrs. Ricker. Darci imitated her in every way she could. She took to drinking tea because Mrs. Gray drank tea, and she lingered at school as long as she could each day, just to be near her. She talked about her teacher at home all the time, and she tried to imitate the way she spoke and walked.

Mrs. Gray saw Darci as a complex and perplexing child. On the one hand, she was her best student, articulate and very motivated to do well—one of the "most brilliant" kids she ever taught. And yet, Mrs. Gray had to make Darci sit right next to her desk so that she could keep an eye on her. Darci could change suddenly and shockingly into a different person. On a number of occasions she suddenly became enraged over what seemed trivial matters to Mrs. Gray. She would scream, throw books, or rip up papers.

One day, while Mrs. Gray was out of the room, after school, she heard glass shatter and she hurried back to the room. She found the little window in the classroom door broken, and she found Darci inside, sitting at a desk. "What happened? What went on here?" Mrs. Gray demanded. "Did you break this?"

Darci's head was down, and she seemed repentant. She nodded to admit that she had broken the window, but she continued to look at her hand that was scraped from the glass. Mrs. Gray found out that Darci and another girl had gotten into an argument and that Darci had broken the window, but the information came from the other girl. When Mrs. Gray asked Darci why she had broken the window, Darci wouldn't answer. She seemed distant and confused. Mrs. Gray had seen the look before. Darci sometimes stared off into space and seemed to lose contact with the reality around her: "She would be sitting at the desk doing her work and, you know, maybe once in a while making eye contact with me, or I would walk by and she would look up and smile and then maybe the next minute or within the next five or ten minutes I might catch her staring out the window, which is not abnormal for kids, you know, to daydream once in a while, but then all of a sudden I might see a frown or all of a sudden, you know, I would walk by her and she would just smile, and I would be in the back of the room with some other kids and then the desk would be over and she would be very upset."

What was most perplexing to Mrs. Gray was that she couldn't understand why these things were happening. With some kids, she could see that their outbursts resulted from a specific frustration, or the need for attention, but Darci seemed to act in patterns that had no rhyme nor reason.

Mrs. Gray had to discipline Darci because of her sudden outbursts. When Mrs. Gray made her stand in a corner, Darci would become outraged, but she would often turn her anger on herself. She would begin to scratch her arms, actually digging into her skin. At such times, Mrs. Gray found a way to calm Darci: "There are some students that when they're

LULLABY AND GOODNIGHT

upset you just don't touch them, you give them their space, you let them come down on their own. With Darci I found it very effective to be close to her. I could reach out and, you know, touch her arms and those couple of times when she did scare me, you know, trying to scratch herself, I could put my arms around her and even though she was very strong—in fact, she was much stronger than me, but I had no problem just putting my arms around her and just kind of calming her and never, ever had any—I've been injured by some other students, but I never ever had any physical injury from her at all."

Mrs. Gray was very concerned about the signs she saw in Darci, and she tried to involve the Rickers in finding answers. But she had little success with that approach. She eventually decided that the Rickers were not effective parents whom she could work with: "I just felt that they were ineffectual in helping me trying to deal with behaviors with her. . . . I just didn't feel like they had much control with her."

Darci told Mrs. Gray, as she had Rachel, that she wanted to have her own mansion. She wanted servants and classy cars, and she wanted to travel. Sometimes Mrs. Gray had the impression that she confused her dreams with reality. Once, after school, she stood by Mrs. Gray's desk and told all about a trip she had taken during the Christmas holiday. She had flown to Alaska on a free ticket that had been given to her by a relative who owned an airline. She had skied and had a wonderful time. "Oh, yeah, I'm a great skier now," she claimed. "You should have seen me. I was really hotdogging. I can do jumps and everything."

Mrs. Gray knew that not a word of this was true. She wondered why Darci needed to make up such stories. But the whole vision was so real to Darci. Her face was aglow with the excitement of it all, her pretty eyes intense, and her account was fluid and detailed. Had Mrs. Gray not known Darci better, she might have believed the story herself.

One day Darci told Rachel McCrainey that her boyfriend, Eric Church, had gotten her pregnant and she had had an abortion. Darci was in seventh grade at the time. "But he loves me, Rachel," she said. "My parents don't want us to get married, but we're going to. We're going to run away together. We're leaving this weekend."

Rachel was doubtful. She asked Darci about this boyfriend she had never met but had heard about before. Darci told her he was an older boy, and then she described him in great detail—what he looked like, what he liked to do, the things he said to her. And she explained her plan to sneak away with him. "I won't be back to school on Monday. We'll have to say good-bye today. You'll never see me again."

Rachel still wasn't sure, but the story sounded too real to be invented. Darci expressed her feelings for Eric with such passion, and now, there she stood, seemingly heartbroken to say good-bye.

Then on Monday Darci showed up at school.

"What happened? Why didn't you elope?" Rachel asked her.

"What?"

"I thought you were going to run away with Eric?"

Darci looked at her strangely and shook her head. "What are you talking about?" she asked.

"You know what you told me last week. You said that you and Eric were going to run away and get married."

Darci shook her head again, still seeming confused. "Rachel, I never told you anything like that. Where are you getting that stuff? Is someone telling you stories about me?"

Rachel was angry by this time. "Is this just another one of your lies?"

"Rachel, you're nuts. I don't even know anyone named Eric."

Rachel was stunned. She had listened to Darci go on and on about this boy. How could Darci do that if he didn't even exist? But he didn't exist, and what Rachel discovered was that Darci had no boyfriend at all.

Yet Darci wasn't all talk. Once she actually did run away from home—although not with a boy. She didn't just hide out at a friend's or hitchhike out of town. She and another girl got on an airplane and flew to Salt Lake City. No one seemed to know where she got the money to do that. And her motives were never exactly clear. She had left with a friend who was having trouble at home, but that hardly explained why Darci was willing to go along.

When the two reached Utah, just sixty miles from the town where Cindy and Sam lived, they found a shelter for runaways, and then, almost immediately, they lost their nerve and called home. Laura Davenport, Mrs. Ricker's sister, was at the house when Darci called. According to her, the Rickers were very upset. They talked to Darci and begged her to please come home. Darci's father wired money to Salt Lake, and the two girls flew back to Portland.

Sandra Ricker was so upset that she became hysterical and ill, and she went to bed. Aunt Laura drove with Mr. Ricker to the airport, where they picked up Darci and her friend. In the car, on the way back, and then again in her mother's bedroom, Darci apologized profusely—with tears running down her cheeks. She said she would never do such a thing again. She was sweet and sincerely sorry for the turmoil she had caused.

But Mrs. Davenport saw more to this than a mere whim on Darci's part. Things were not all they ought to have been in the Ricker home. She felt that Darci had been allowed to grow up too fast. She wore nylons and makeup much earlier than most girls, and her parents seemed to have little control. Part of the problem seemed to be that Mr. Ricker, because of his odd working hours, was almost an absentee father. Darci's brother Rick was mentally handicapped and required a lot of special attention. Darci spent an unusual amount of time alone. Mrs. Davenport saw her as a loner who spent too much time inside her own fantasies.

Mrs. Davenport didn't view the Rickers as a close family, although they liked to think they were. They shared a few outdoor activities but they were not nearly as close-knit as her own family. Darci often came to talk to her aunt, and most of the time she seemed to show more love for her mother's sister than she did for her own mother. She seemed to envy the closeness of the Davenports over the tension in her own home.

Part of the problem was the Rickers' marital problems. At one point Ken and Sandra agreed to stay together only until their kids were raised. Yet much of the problem in the Rickers' relationship was Darci herself. The Rickers could never agree on how they should deal with her. Sandra Ricker felt that Darci needed more discipline, needed to be told no more often, and when younger, had needed a spanking from time to time. Ken Ricker was not only not home a great deal, but he was not one to get tough with Darci. She was something of a "Daddy's girl," and could always seem to get away with what she wanted with him.

LULLABY AND GOODNIGHT

Occasionally Mrs. Davenport had gotten glimpses of Darci that were disturbing. Once, when Darci and the Davenport's son Kurt were playing together, Kurt had run upstairs to his parents and yelled for them to come quick because something was wrong with Darci. The Davenports rushed downstairs and found Darci on the concrete floor, seemingly passed out. But Mr. Davenport didn't go for it. He knew Darci too well. He said, "Come on, Darci. Get up. Quit fooling around."

He walked away and Darci got up. Kurt had been completely convinced that something was wrong, and he was troubled by what he had seen. He said that he found Darci in the garage sniffing gasoline fumes. He told her, "That's not good for you, that could kill you." She looked up at him calmly and said, "Well, that's the idea." Kurt didn't know what to think. Was she joking or what? He walked on into the house. And then Darci ran in behind him and screamed, "Kurt, I saw Grandma King," and she collapsed on the floor. Grandma King was their great-grandmother, who was dead.

When Darci got up, she seemed a little odd, unusually distant, but then, within a short time, she returned to normal.

In spite of Darci's eccentricities, Aunt Laura was convinced that her niece was destined for big things. She worried that Darci always wanted to be "bigger and better" than everyone else, but on the other hand, Darci was smart and she was highly motivated. She dreamed of being a stewardess, and she talked about it the way she had fantasized about being a princess or a movie star when she was younger. She thought of stewardesses as beautiful and glamorous—flying about the world, seeing exciting places, living well.

That's the kind of life she longed for. And Aunt Laura thought she had the ability and drive to get what she wanted.

Most of Darci's problems, as far as Mrs. Davenport could tell, were fairly typical of teenagers. Darci argued with her mother, and her parents had some troubles, but that could be said of many, if not most, families. It hardly seemed reason for any really serious concern.

But Darci was always so intense, and so absorbed with certain preoccupations. At about age nine she first tried to find out from Mrs. Ricker who her "real" mother was. Mrs. Ricker knew the mother's name, knew that she was only fifteen when Darci was born, but she refused to tell Darci anything about the woman. "Darci, honey, you're lucky," she told her. "You have two mothers who love you. Your first mother wanted what was best for you. That's why she gave you to me. You know how much I love you."

But Darci wasn't satisfied. Her interest in her biological mother became a kind of obsession. All through her teenage years, she tried to discover her identity. She would eventually go on her own to the city courthouse and try to find records, but she would learn that such information was not open to public research in Oregon. All the same, the issue didn't go away for Darci. She continued to feel abandoned, never forgetting that her mother had not wanted her. And she resented Mrs. Ricker. Sandra Ricker was a very large woman, with a chin lost in deep rolls of fat, and huge, fleshy arms. Darci hated all that fat. She was embarrassed by it, and she found the woman hideous to look at. She believed that her real mother was beautiful.

Darci showed her hatred toward her adoptive mother with her rebelliousness. She seemed to disagree with everything Mrs. Ricker said. Darci was a tomboy —one who never liked frilly things. Mrs. Ricker had wanted to decorate Darci's room in pink, with "bows or something feminine," but Darci chose a dramatic dark blue with red and white stripes across the ceiling and one wall. She loved the room that way, and she spent much of her time there. But she was not happy with her house. It was a moderate two-story house, not ramshackle, but not fancy either, and it was not in a nice neighborhood.

That's not what Darci told people. She lied about her house, told friends she lived in a mansion. "My parents will give me anything I ask for," she liked to tell people. But she didn't invite her school friends to her home because she was ashamed to have them see it. She was also ashamed to have friends see her obese mother. In her later teens, Darci would write a letter to her mother, telling her, as Mrs. Ricker put it, "that I was a terrible person because I was fat and she could not tolerate that. There was no room for fat people in her society. . . ."

Mrs. Ricker had known about Darci's embarrassment long before Darci wrote the letter. By seventh grade, she and Darci were often doing battle, and Darci had expressed disgust with her mother's heaviness many times before. That was not by any means the only problem. "[Darci] was a teenager that was absolutely her own boss," Mrs. Ricker explained.

The Rickers may not have been the most effective parents around, but they tried their best. They put Darci in a private Christian school when she was in second and third grades. This was a family with limited resources, but they paid for the private school because they thought it would give her the challenge she needed. After two years, however, she was expelled.

For lying.

Mrs. Ricker didn't remember that Darci had a big problem with lying. True, Darci often told her parents that she was going to get higher grades than she actually received. But she was sure that all children told lies at times—her sons had told lies too. She perceived Darci's lying as a fairly minor part of her overall personality. In spite of Darci's hatefulness toward her, Sandra Ricker also remembered how loving and kind Darci could be, not only to her but to others.

All in all, Darci seemed quite normal to her mother. She had a few childhood problems, had told a few lies, had been belligerent as a teenager (as many are), and had become more distant as she grew older. But Mrs. Ricker remembered hunting and fishing trips, family birthday parties, lots of normal, happy times.

What hurt Mrs. Ricker the most was that she knew that Darci found her so intolerable. On a couple of occasions Darci told people that her mother beat her. It was not true. Mrs. Ricker denied it, and eventually Darci denied it. But she had lied, and the lie seemed to come from her disgust with her mother. Why would she want to lie and claim to be abused if she wasn't? Mrs. Ricker said it was "to make people feel sorry for her, I think, because she had, again, a fat, ugly mother. I think she was really ashamed."

Mr. Ricker saw Darci somewhat differently. He was an unassuming man with plenty of rough edges, but he had tender feelings for Darci. He noticed the fantasies—even the lies—but he didn't see them as all that dangerous. He got along with Darci much better than his wife did. Mr. Ricker found Darci, for the most part, a charming girl. She could be difficult, but she was also fun to be with, pleasant much of the time, and not very different from most teenagers. He admit-

LULLABY AND GOODNIGHT

ted that at school she seemed to argue a great deal with other kids. She liked "to be a leader," and she had trouble with those who didn't like her bossy manner. Darci was at odds with her mother, but her dad saw her mainly as a fun, active kid, someone he enjoyed spending time with.

One of the things Darci and Mr. Ricker enjoyed most was going deer hunting together. It was an annual event, and Darci loved it. She was a strong, rugged girl even though her appearance was so pretty and delicate. She liked the out-of-doors. She took a hunter-safety course but she actually never carried a rifle on hunts. Mostly, she liked the time with her dad, who was gone from the home so much.

Darci never killed a deer, but she helped her dad clean the ones he shot. He taught her how to gut the animals and to skin them. She wasn't squeamish about that. The blood didn't seem to bother her.

Those who knew the family well could see why Darci got along well with her dad. He was a person she could manipulate, and she never failed to do so. Darci admitted that she got most of what she wanted from her dad, and she knew she was treated better than her two brothers. But then, lots of girls know how to exploit "Daddy." If Mr. Ricker was not a strict disciplinarian, he was certainly not alone in modern America.

Mr. Ricker did notice one thing about Darci that worried him. She slept with a knife under her pillow —and sometimes with a gun under her bed. Mr. Ricker would take them away from her, tell her that it wasn't necessary, but Darci would go back and get a butcher knife from the kitchen and put it under her pillow again. She was also afraid to go to the store by herself. And she was afraid to take a shower.

Her father thought that her fears were extreme, and

it worried him a little, but then, maybe her behavior was understandable. The Rickers lived in "one of the roughest neighborhoods" in Portland, and the house had been broken into three times. When Mr. Ricker asked her why she was afraid, she told him, "I'm afraid someone will break in the house and come after me." When she walked to the store, she was afraid of being approached by some of the tough guys in the neighborhood.

Mr. Ricker also became aware of Darci's natural ability to play roles or act out parts. She appeared in one high school play, but more than that, she assumed her own roles constantly. She learned to convince people of almost anything she wanted them to believe. Virtually everyone she knew was sometimes deceived by her amazing ability to act, to invent—to lie.

Or did she, in fact, invent realities and live in them so completely that they were not lies at all to her? No one who knew her as a teenager thought that was the case. But then, they were not psychologists.

There were other things going on in Darci's life— things most of the people closest to her knew nothing about. Darci was not very good at keeping secrets. But she did keep one: She had begun an active sexual life when she was in the *first* grade. She and her cousin, Kurt Davenport, had begun having sex when she was six and he was seven.

Sexual play at that age may not be surprising. But this was more than that. Darci knew exactly what to do. She had young Kurt undress and she took her clothes off, but she was interested in more than the usual sort of childhood looking and exploring. She showed Kurt how to enter her, and from this very young age, they engaged in actual sexual intercourse. This continued for many years after.

While they kept this secret to themselves, their

families knew them to be very close all during their growing-up years. And Darci *was* a great friend to Kurt. She was domineering, but she could be caring too. She helped Kurt, for instance, get through a hard time when his grandfather died. She walked with him on the beach, and she told him, "God has a reason for what he does." Her voice could be soothing and gentle at such times. She listened and empathized and was there for Kurt at a time when he needed her.

As a teenager, Kurt felt confused emotions about the secret past he and Darci shared. Their sexual involvement had begun when he was so young that he hadn't been sure whether it was right or wrong. But as they began to grow up, at age twelve or thirteen, they both seemed to know that it wasn't the right thing for cousins to do, and so they discontinued without ever agreeing to do so, or without ever talking about it again.

What Kurt never knew was how Darci had learned about sex. Had someone told her or showed her? Perhaps some other child? Or most troubling, was she sexually abused by some adult? Darci would later admit to psychologists that her attitudes about sex were confused. Her life had been one long series of promiscuous sexual encounters, and yet she reported discomfort and absence of pleasure with most of her sexual experiences. All this could indicate a history of childhood sexual abuse, but Darci could not remember that happening.

If no clear-cut proof exists for early sexual abuse, Darci's sexual history is nonetheless bizarre. Along with the very early sexual activity with her cousin, she reported that when she was in third grade an adolescent girl, a neighbor, forced Darci to engage in oral sex and urinated in her face. She also claimed that during the summer between fifth and sixth grade an uncle climbed in bed with her. When she demanded he leave, he did, but she remained frightened of him afterward. And then, as a teen, she was baby-sitting when the father came home drunk and made sexual advances toward her. In fact, Darci later reported that he raped her, but no corroboration exists, since she did not report the incident at the time.

What *is* known is that Darci entered puberty extraordinarily early. At nine years old she developed breasts and began to menstruate. She looked much older than her actual age. And she liked looking older. She began wearing hose and using makeup. As she came into her teens, she claimed to have slept with many men, adults as well as teenagers, most of whom were nothing more than casual acquaintances.

After Kurt and Darci stopped having sex, their friendship continued. While Kurt remembered Darci as caring and kind at times, he also admitted that she was a difficult person to be close to. She was ambitious and driven toward success, and she was highly unpredictable. But she was really not impulsive. She calculated and planned, and she found ways to get the things she wanted. She controlled people more than she let them control her. She also had very clear ideas about what she wanted. Yet, at the same time, she was always something of a mystery. He never saw in her the potential to hurt anyone, but he also didn't really feel that he knew who she was.

The fact is, Darci had a secret life that even Kurt didn't know about. Some things she told no one. She would eventually admit to a psychiatrist that she had learned at an early age to seduce men, and she had begun to have sex with adults before she was even a teenager.

Yet Darci's memories of these experiences were

peculiar and vague. She said that once, when traveling with her family—at age eleven—she went to a motel sauna. There she met a man who was staying in the motel. She made eyes at the man and let him know that she was willing. He took her to his room, and they made love. But she remembered no words being spoken. She made eyes; he took her away; they had sex. Or at least that's the way she remembered it.

But relying on Darci's memory is hazardous. However much her family and friends were willing to ignore certain oddities in her behavior, one picture becomes clear: Darci lived in a world where the lines between reality and imagination had become blurred. Sometimes her fantasies may have been relatively harmless—mere wish fulfillment to a girl who longed for something more than what she had in life. But her stories sometimes showed a wily sort of calculation. She used them to get what she wanted, whether it was prestige, attention, or self-gratification.

But no one noticed.

All while Darci was growing up, not one person worried enough about her strangeness to seek special help for her. Was it because she was so pretty and confident and articulate? Or was it simple denial by those who didn't want to see serious problems?

Of course, once an atrocity has been committed, everyone wants to probe the perpetrator's childhood. But how many of us would have noticed enough in Darci's behavior to do anything about it? After all, she was such a lovely kid in so many ways.

There is also another possibility, and it's frightening. Maybe Darci was a normal child—with an active fantasy life. Many bright kids are imaginative. Maybe Darci *was* the girl next door. Given her crime, most of us would rather believe that she was insane and that her childhood and adolescence are proof of it. And that may well be the case. But those who knew her best thought she was a self-willed but basically normal child. Up until the very day of the crime, no one—not her friends, her parents, nor her husband—considered her dangerous in any way.

CHAPTER 5

By the time Darci entered high school she had become a beautiful young woman, in some ways very mature for her age. She looked older than she was, and she could converse with confidence and fluency. Most adults saw her as competent, intelligent, and destined for big things.

She got good grades, although not as good as she sometimes claimed, and her teachers thought well of her. She was involved in a fair number of school activities, but she never had many friends, and no really close ones. Her relationships with boys were usually brief, and according to her own account, almost always sexual.

It was while Darci was in high school that she first met Ray Pierce. Darci went to a Catholic high school (one of very few non-Catholics attending), and Ray went to a public high school, but the two met at a Rotary function. Darci had been chosen to be sponsored by the Rotary Club to go to South Africa for a year as an exchange student. So Ray and Darci only dated a short time before Darci left.

Ray was a nice-looking young man, boyish in appearance, neat, his brown hair brushed and parted nicely. If Darci looked like the girl next door, Ray looked like an Eagle Scout eager to do a good turn. He was an innocent compared to Darci, and he was as easily manipulated as was Darci's father. Perhaps that's why Darci liked him.

Darci spent her junior year of high school in South Africa. She lived very well. She stayed with wealthy families, and her sense of independence expanded. Ray noticed the difference when she returned: "She seemed to be aloof, if you will. She had lived in a country where you've got two classes, an upper and lower class, and when she came back to a middle-class family it seemed like we weren't good enough for a time."

While Darci was gone she wrote home about her wonderful lifestyle. Her mother later said, "Oh, she had the grandest experience in the whole world. She lived with people that were very rich, that had chauffeurs and maids and swimming pools, airplanes, took trips, that type of thing."

Darci may well have been exaggerating, but she did live with several families, and these were, undoubtedly, well-off white families. She became very close to one of the couples, called them Ma and Pa, and she also lived for a time in the home of a medical doctor. Darci even claimed at the time that she assisted in some orthopedic surgical procedures.

The tension in the Ricker home had reached a very bad point before Darci left, but she returned to a home that was placid by comparison. During Darci's absence, the Rickers found that they could actually get along pretty well. Many of their problems with each other had to do with their philosophy of dealing with the headstrong Darci. While she was gone they talked and agreed on how they would deal with her when she returned.

Not only had the Rickers settled some of their

problems and grown closer, but they had remodeled the house. They had finished the basement and paneled the living room. They had not dared touch Darci's bedroom, but they had converted an upstairs bedroom as a sitting area for Darci, outside her own bedroom. They expected Darci to be thrilled.

But Darci came home earlier than expected and the remodeling was not yet complete. And Darci's reaction was painful to Mrs. Ricker: "Well, it hurt our feelings because she was not impressed. We were really impressed with what we were doing and to us—she was so beyond our home that it hurt our feelings lots." All Darci could talk about was the splendor she had lived with during the past year—and the "parents" she had come to love.

Darci had come home with an Afrikaner/English accent, but one that she sometimes used and sometimes dropped, as though she forgot about it at times. She also claimed to be able to speak the Afrikaner language, which she sometimes began to speak, as though by accident. Others saw this as affectation—but the sort of thing they had always come to expect from Darci.

Mrs. Ricker saw a great change in her daughter. "Everything Darci did was different when she came home because she learned proper manners... a proper way to eat, a proper way to do everything. And so we weren't—we weren't proper, and that hurt me."

Darci's time in South Africa may have been the happiest of her life. She had left a troubled home—a house and neighborhood she was ashamed of—and she had lived a kind of dream in beautiful houses with proper people. However inflated Darci's stories about the experience may have been, she did not adjust well to the return. Her troubles with her parents escalated badly during her final year of high school. She was dating Ray Pierce again, and she wanted to stay out as late as she chose, come and go as she pleased, and live her own life without parental interference. Mr. Ricker was trying to tighten the reins a little, according to his wife's wishes, and this did not go down well with Darci. The arguments were almost constant.

Finally, in the middle of the school year, she moved out. For Sandra Ricker, Darci had become impossible to control. "She had matured beyond me, you know, she—she was her own boss." But she was not happy that friends of the family, David and Karen Head, took Darci in: "Well, I was really angry because I felt that they just gave her an out. . . . If they hadn't said, 'Well, you can move in with us,' maybe we could have gotten some help and counseling or something and straightened our problems out. I felt like they were butting in."

But Karen Head saw the matter from a different perspective. She had known Darci since she was a child. Mrs. Ricker had taken in children to baby-sit at one point in her life, and she had looked after the Heads' children. Darci had become close to the Heads' boys, and Karen had thought well of Darci: "I always saw Darci as a very bright child, full of activity, very loving toward my family. [She had] a very loving relationship with my oldest son." And she saw the trouble in Darci's home as more the Rickers' fault: "As the years progressed that I have known the family, I discovered that there really was a dysfunctional family unit going on. Her father, which became a joke to my husband and I, was always asleep because he worked nights. When he was awake he was, you know, he wasn't much company. I never saw him take the kids anywhere. Her mother always wanted Darci to be in the limelight. When Darci had troubles and she would tell her mom, her mom really didn't believe her. I asked several times for them to get counseling throughout the years. That fell on deaf ears. They didn't want to hear it. I was usually told that I was getting the lies and it was my problem with Darci."

It is entirely possible that the Heads did get a distorted picture from Darci, but they were in a position to see the continuing animosity in the home, and they decided to step in and help. Darci had turned to them before. At fourteen, she had come to Karen and asked for help in locating her natural mother. Karen knew how troubled she was about her "abandonment" and adoption. Karen and David had also seen an oddly changed Darci return from South Africa: "When she came back, she had several more prejudices toward people who were overweight, people who were black. And her mother, who was—it came out very, very strong when she came back—she didn't like her mother because of her obesity. She would talk at times with a different accent in front of me and then would slip out of that and talk in her natural voice. [She] seemed not to have the friends that she did before. I didn't see her with that many friends or hear her talk about so many friends from school." She also noticed that Darci spent more time alone than she ever had before.

At Christmastime, 1984, after Darci had been back from South Africa about half a year, she went to Karen Head and told her that she was planning to leave home. She wanted to live with her boyfriend, Ray Pierce, who was living with two other young men. Karen did not like the idea at all. She told Darci to go home and try to patch things up, and to seek counseling. When this didn't work and Darci determined to move out—and the Rickers told her to go ahead— Karen asked Darci to move in with her and her family. Karen didn't want to interfere, but she also didn't want Darci to move in with three young men.

The Heads had Darci sit down with them while they set out some very strict rules, and they told Darci she could only stay with them if she abided by them. Both Darci and Ray agreed to the rules, but it wasn't long before the independent Darci found the rules too stern to live with. Karen had a conference with her, and told her that if she couldn't live by the rules she would have to leave. Darci was angry and complained about the strictness, but she agreed, again, to live by the Heads' standards, and she stayed.

During Darci's time with the Heads, she became concerned that she was getting overweight, and perhaps she was a little heavier than ideal. She started to live on a pot of coffee in the morning and almost nothing else, and she was fanatical about the idea that she could not become fat. When Karen saw her taking a drug, Darci admitted that she was taking diet pills. A conference followed, and Darci agreed that abuse of the pills was another infraction of the rules, and she would give them up.

But Darci was struggling. She wanted to be away from all this control. She still talked of a career as a stewardess, or of going to college. But more than anything, she wanted to be with Ray.

During that spring of 1985, Darci experienced serious abdominal pains. At first her obstetrician, Dr. Sargent, thought she was experiencing a tubal pregnancy, but he discovered an ovarian cyst, which he removed. After the surgery, she was given prescription pain pills. But here again, Karen observed Darci overindulging in the pills, using them to the point of abuse. Karen took them away and flushed them down the toilet. Darci became irate and belligerent, but then

LULLABY AND GOODNIGHT

once again accepted Karen's authority. The contrition may have been feigned, since Darci knew she didn't have many alternatives, but she had a sweet way of admitting her mistakes, looking at Karen with those beautiful eyes, full of repentance, and asking for forgiveness.

But Darci may have used other drugs during this time, and earlier. She would later claim that as a teenager she had abused several illicit drugs: marijuana, LSD, cocaine, and amphetamines. However, her family and friends were not aware of any of that. It seems possible that she invented this history.

Darci did seek counseling at Catholic Family Services while she was living with the Heads. She was not involved for more than a session or two, however, and the forms she filled out when she began counseling indicated no particular concern about her own mental state. She reported no delusions or any other unusual mental phenomena.

During the time Darci lived with the Heads, Karen saw a tender, caring side of her. Darci had known the Heads' oldest child since he had been two. Darci loved him very much. She attended his basketball, baseball, and soccer games. She bought him and the other children presents. She had a good relationship with all the kids.

Karen felt that Darci really did want to patch things up with her mother. She cried at times, expressed her regrets about the relationship, but said she didn't know what to do to set things right. When Darci's cousin, Kurt's sister, Michelle, got married, Darci was not invited to the wedding. The Davenports feared that Darci and Sandra Ricker's poor relationship would cause tension or even create a scene. But Darci was very hurt that she wasn't invited, and she decided to show up anyway. Nothing bad came of her being there, and Darci and her mother did begin to make some headway in dealing with each other.

The other powerful feeling Darci often expressed to Karen was that she wanted to have a child of her own. And she wanted to be a perfect mother.

In June Darci graduated from high school, and she immediately moved out of the Heads' home and moved into an apartment with Ray. Ray was working at a hobby shop in Beaverton, Oregon, near Portland, and he was going to college part-time. Darci also found work. She got a job at a department store called G. I. Joe's, where she worked in the sporting goods section.

Darci had always struck people as peculiar in some ways, but it was during the time that Darci was living with Ray that her behavior began to take on a new level of strangeness. The change was subtle, not noticed by most, but Darci's fantasies began to focus. There was no bloodlust in Darci. She was not fighting against violent impulses to kill. She did nothing criminal. She simply felt one of the most basic female impulses. She wanted to give birth; she wanted her own little baby to care for and nurture. She wanted to be a wonderful mother.

While Darci worked at G. I. Joe's, she met a young woman named Tina Otis. The two shared a locker and soon became friends. Darci often told Tina about her pain at knowing she had been given up at birth and about her desire to have a child of her own. Darci had begun to express these concerns to almost everyone, even people she had known only briefly.

That summer Darci visited Dr. Sargent again. She said that she had been taking birth control pills but had missed a period. He tested her for pregnancy, but the test was negative. He noticed nothing unusual in

Darci's response. But later that summer, Darci finally got what she wanted, or at least she thought she did. She tested positive on a home pregnancy test. This for her was the fulfillment of a purpose, and she talked of being the perfect mother, of being a better mother than the teenager who had given her away at her birth, and better than the obese mother who never lived up to Darci's idea of what a mother should be.

But the pregnancy was doomed. By September, Dr. Sargent informed her that she actually had a *molar pregnancy*. Ray said, later, that he and Darci both felt bad about the loss. "Yes, it was obviously difficult for both of us, losing a child." And yet, "It appeared to pass relatively normally, as near as I could tell."

Actually, Ray must have listened primarily to his wife's interpretation of events. A molar pregnancy produces a tumorlike growth, not a fetus. The uterus overgrows itself. But to Darci, she had miscarried, and she saw that as a failure on her part. The placenta was aborted with a D and C procedure and Darci recovered quickly. Dr. Sargent observed no out-of-the-ordinary responses other than some mild expressions of concern or regret.

Ray, the man who knew Darci best, saw nothing terribly out of the ordinary in Darci's momentary depression. From his point of view, she handled it well. She soon took a second job and was working at the Hard Luck Cafe as well as at G. I. Joe's. And Ray saw no serious problems ahead for them. They talked about marriage, but Ray was not eager to make that commitment quite yet. He said that Darci had a way of "pushing your buttons," and getting a person to do what she wanted. This tendency caused him to hesitate about making their relationship permanent.

During the fall Dr. Sargent also saw Darci a number of times, and he saw nothing out of the ordinary in her behavior or attitudes. After the molar pregnancy, he did think follow-up was very important, since such a tumor has cancerlike qualities, and therefore he wanted to monitor her with serum HCG tests. These are used to measure hormone output and therefore serve as pregnancy tests. Dr. Sargent used them to watch hormone levels and be certain they fell to normal quickly. Over the next few months, in the fall of 1985, Darci came in often for these tests. As Dr. Sargent saw Darci from time to time, he continued to see her as a normal, functioning, pleasant person. And she certainly wasn't pregnant.

That same fall, however, others saw peculiar signs in some of her behaviors. Darci's brother, Craig, was married and his wife, Mary Ann, was expecting a baby. The couple moved into the apartment that adjoined the one that Ray and Darci lived in. They were gradually getting to be on better terms. Earlier, at the time of the marriage, Mary Ann had not invited Darci to her wedding because she and Darci had been at odds for a long time.

Two years before, Mary Ann had become pregnant and was not married. She had decided to give the baby up. This act was intolerable to Darci. She could not imagine how any woman could give away her own flesh and blood and she told Mary Ann this, bluntly.

But now Mary Ann was having a baby she planned to keep. Darci became rather excited about having the little baby next door. On November 19, little Joshua was born. November 21 was Craig's birthday. Darci threw a little dinner party for Craig and Mary Ann, who came home from the hospital that day. But that's when Darci did something that Craig considered very strange: "We had just gotten done eating and Darci made a statement and said, 'Gee, Mary Ann, wouldn't it be neat if you and I both could breast-feed Joshua.'"

Craig was shocked. He didn't know what to say. Neither did Mary Ann, but afterward, she told Craig, "You'd better do something about it." Darci actually wanted Mary Ann to leave the baby with her a couple of nights each week so that she could take care of it and breast-feed it.

For Craig and Mary Ann the idea was more than illogical. It was out of line. They wondered what was wrong with Darci that she could think of suggesting such a thing. And yet, after that, Darci did baby-sit their baby and was very loving and caring toward him.

All that winter, as Darci worked two jobs, she continued to focus on the idea that she wanted to be a mother. Dr. Sargent had told her that it would be wise to wait a year before she became pregnant so that she could be certain that no lingering problem remained from the molar pregnancy. By spring of 1986 Darci was having trouble with increased pain during her periods. When she visited Dr. Sargent, she told him that she had gone off birth control pills. He advised her to begin using them again.

At that time, Darci did raise the issue of possible infertility, but the doctor saw no reason to suspect that. She would later claim that Dr. Sargent had suspected endometriosis, which could cause infertility, but Dr. Sargent remembered only speculating that something of that sort might be possible. Darci didn't seem overly concerned, and Dr. Sargent suggested they wait and see what happened the next time she went off birth control pills.

Darci, however, was not expressing all her thoughts to Dr. Sargent. The idea of having a baby—and the fear that she was infertile—was constantly on her mind. She fantasized about becoming a mother, and she may have begun to believe in her own fantasies. By the early summer of 1986, Darci told Tina Otis that she was pregnant. It was their little secret. The baby was due in December, at Christmastime, she told Tina, and she was very excited. At work, the two talked about the baby often. Darci told Tina that if she ever lost the baby she didn't know what she would do.

By now Darci was claiming that she had already lost babies before. She began to tell people that she had had a tubal pregnancy the year before, when in fact she knew that the problem had been an ovarian cyst. She also told a counselor at the Catholic Family Services that she had lost a baby in the molar pregnancy, when in fact, even though a "pregnancy" had occurred, no fetus had formed.

Darci told Tina that she wanted to get married. Ray had continued to hesitate about a lasting commitment, but Darci wanted to marry as soon as possible. She even asked Tina whether she would be willing to be maid of honor when the time came.

Darci was gaining weight by then, and she would eventually gain over fifty pounds. During that summer, she saw Dr. Sargent again, and she told him she was not taking birth control pills. She wanted to get pregnant. She took a pregnancy test, which was negative, and so she knew clearly that she was not pregnant. She and Dr. Sargent talked in August and considered the possibility that she was having irregularities in her ovulation. He suggested some possible treatments, but he was not overly concerned. He thought they should give it some more time. And Darci made no move to pursue the treatments.

All the same, Darci filed for maternity leave with

LULLABY AND GOODNIGHT

G. I. Joe's. Ray knew that she wasn't pregnant and Darci did not claim to him that she was. But she took the leave, admitting that it was a deception. Eventually she called Tina Otis and told her that she had delivered a baby stillborn and was brokenhearted. She and Tina cried together on the phone, and Tina was completely convinced that Darci had lost a baby and was going through a terrible time of grieving. Unfortunately, Tina then reported the information to her boss at G. I. Joe's. The man was nice enough to send flowers, but Darci was very upset that Tina had destroyed her ruse. She was never friends with Tina again. She eventually returned to work, but she snubbed her former friend whenever they met. One has to wonder what she intended to tell the boss herself, given the fact that she knew that he believed she would soon have a baby.

During all this time, Darci's relationship with her mother was rebuilding. At the time of the molar pregnancy, she called her mother. Mrs. Ricker hurried to the hospital with a Care Bear to take home, as something to hold, since she had lost her baby. Darci's way of describing the situation made it sound as though it were a miscarriage or a necessary abortion, and Mrs. Ricker felt very sorry for her. She remembered her own difficulty with the deliveries of her boys.

Mrs. Ricker was growing proud of the way Darci was living, even though she would have preferred that Darci and Ray marry. Darci kept the house beautifully, cooked well—even though she had rarely helped with household duties in her own home—and she seemed to be happy with Ray.

Darci had also been very thoughtful when her father had an appendectomy. She had come to the hospital, sat with him for three days, and had shown a great deal of tenderness. All this had begun to rebuild some bridges between Darci and her family. Darci even agreed when a minister suggested that she attend counseling with her parents and work out their problems before Ray and Darci go forward with their marriage.

The first session ended in an explosion. But when Ray pressed the issue and said that he wouldn't marry Darci unless she could work things out, Darci was very sweet during the next session. From that point on the discussions seemed to help, and Darci's parents felt better about their daughter than they had in a long time. What is not clear is whether Darci's attitude toward them actually changed, or whether she was motivated only by her desire to get a commitment from Ray. She would continue to make very negative statements about both of her parents long after the counseling sessions ended.

But then something happened that upset the Rickers. The neighbor from across the street told Mrs. Ricker that Darci had taken maternity leave from G. I. Joe's. When Mrs. Ricker asked her daughter what this was about, Darci came to the house and told her mom what had happened. She admitted that she had lied about being pregnant and about the stillbirth.

Mrs. Ricker cried with Darci, but she was astounded that Darci would think to do such a thing. "Why would anybody—why would anybody say they're pregnant when they're not?"

And then she told Darci what she thought of her lie: "I mainly told her, I said, 'Darci, you and Ray will never be blessed. You're telling a lie on a baby, you know, you're—I was really upset. This, you know, this—you don't lie like that. . . . None of it made sense, and she promised and promised and promised

LULLABY AND GOODNIGHT

that she would never, never, never do it again, never lie again."

But Darci had only just begun. However one views Darci's actions during the time she was living with Ray—as a series of lies or as a gradual descent into madness—clearly her focus was narrowing and her obsession with having a baby was growing.

During the time when all this was happening, Darci went to visit her favorite teacher from elementary school, Mrs. Gray. They chatted and Mrs. Gray pressed Darci a little, asked her whether she was learning to control her temper and whether she had gotten her life into focus. Darci had a ready answer, according to Mrs. Gray: ". . . she told me that she had come to a focus and that the only thing she wanted to be was a domestic engineer, and I had never heard that term before, so I asked her what she meant by that, and it was to be a mother; that she had just decided that she wanted to have children and wanted to stay home with the children and wanted to help them as much as possible."

For many young women, for many generations, this has been the American dream. It hardly seems crazy to want what so many others have wanted. But something was happening inside Darci. What Mrs. Gray saw as a focus was in fact becoming an all-consuming obsession. She had to be a mother—a better one than her natural mother and her adoptive mother had been. She had to get pregnant and she desperately feared that she couldn't, that she was sterile. Too many dangerous forces in Darci's psyche were becoming focused at the same time. Part of that focus was a tremendous need to get a commitment from Ray. They had been together a long time, but she wanted more than that. She wanted him to marry her.

Ray Pierce later admitted that his and Darci's relationship had become rocky at that point. He claimed that they never actually discussed breaking up, but he had thought about it. It seems likely that Darci recognized the possibility, and one of her motivations to become pregnant may have been to keep Ray. She knew that when she tested positive during the molar pregnancy, Ray had temporarily agreed to get married. She had come to view pregnancy as a means to force Ray to commit to her in marriage.

So that fall, not long after the feigned stillbirth, Darci told Ray that she was now really pregnant. And Ray saw the signs: she was gaining weight, her bust was enlarging, and she claimed aversions to certain foods. Perhaps she actually experienced these aversions. Darci's line between fantasy and reality—always hazy at best—was becoming deeply confused.

Darci began to wear maternity clothes almost immediately. She claimed to be seeing Dr. Sargent for treatment, and bills were coming in from his office. Ray had every reason to believe Darci. She would not take any sort of drug, and she wouldn't drink alcohol because she wouldn't endanger the baby. She also began to take prenatal vitamins. Once, when she and Ray traveled to the Oregon coast to visit Ray's parents, Darci forgot her vitamins. She made Ray go buy more, since she didn't want to miss any days of taking them. Eventually, she would have difficulty sleeping because she couldn't lie on her stomach, and she experienced pain when she tried to sleep on her back. She was also constipated, which was a new problem for her. When Ray suggested certain medications, she said she couldn't take them because they might harm the baby.

What Darci didn't tell Ray was that the doctor bills

were really for a visit in August when Darci reported bleeding problems and expressed her continued fear that she couldn't get pregnant. Another visit in September was a follow-up to the August appointment. On both occasions Dr. Sargent administered pregnancy tests, and both were negative. So Darci *knew,* without a doubt, that she was *not* pregnant.

In December Darci went back to Dr. Sargent with a sore throat and the belief, once again, that she might be pregnant. No test was taken because Darci wasn't feeling well, but a couple of days later, she started her period. In February she went to Dr. Sargent, again thinking she might be pregnant, but her pregnancy test came back negative. Or in other words, throughout the crucial period in the fall and winter of 1986 and 1987, when Darci told Ray that she was pregnant, and they planned their wedding, got married, and during the early months of their marriage, Darci may have suspected she was pregnant at times, but evidence was conclusive that she was *not,* and she *knew* that.

Interestingly, however, when Darci visited Dr. Sargent for the last time, in February, she reported having had no menstrual period since December 17. This, along with the observation of her husband and many others about her physical changes, could indicate that Darci actually was going through a pseudo pregnancy. Absolutely everyone who knew Darci believed that she was pregnant when she and Ray got married in December and during the following winter and spring.

Mrs. Ricker reported that she felt Darci's stomach and was certain that she was pregnant. This was a woman who had borne two children herself, and she knew the difference between fat and the round hardness of a swelling uterus. Many others reported the same experience when they touched Darci's abdomen. Kathy Landrum, who became Darci's close friend that winter, said, "I've taken care of fat people in hospitals, and I've been pregnant myself and I feel that I would be in a position to tell the difference." She never had any doubt that Darci was pregnant.

Laura Davenport reported a similar experience. Ray and Darci came to dinner, and afterward, when Darci and Mrs. Davenport were cleaning up, Darci said, "Aunt Laura, look, I'm getting so big." She pulled up her blouse to show her aunt. Mrs. Davenport would later say, "I've been pregnant, so I know the difference between just being fat or pregnant. Her stomach was round, it wasn't just flat here and there and like a waist in between. It was a round shape like you would be when you're pregnant."

Dorothy Spain, who had worked with Darci at G. I. Joe's, saw Darci during this "pregnancy." The two had become good friends during the time Dorothy was expecting her own baby. Darci had shared with Dorothy, as with Tina Otis, her secret that she was pregnant, and then the two had cried together when Darci's supposed stillbirth had occurred. Dorothy had also listened to Darci's elaborate wedding plans and her stories about the elegant house her parents had. Darci claimed she would have no trouble with furniture once she and Ray were married because her parents redecorated often, and they would pass their fashionable furniture on to Darci and Ray. Dorothy wondered why Darci's parents would live in such a lavish house in a neighborhood that was anything but elegant, but she believed Darci, as people so often did. When Dorothy saw Darci during her "pregnancy," Darci took Dorothy's daughter, Whitney, in her arms and held her. And she seemed to go off into another world. "As a matter of fact," Dorothy would later say, "she was so much in her world she didn't really seem to respond to people for a moment or two while they were talking to her."

When Darci visited Dr. Sargent in February, however, and she once again proved not to be pregnant, he reported that her abdomen was not hard, but that she had gained a great deal of weight. Then why did so many people report that her abdomen was round and hard? One wonders how that could be possible unless Darci taught herself to fake the hardness by straining her muscles in some way.

In any case, Darci not only looked pregnant, but she seemed the perfect future mother—absolutely dedicated to the idea of having her own child, and enraptured with the love of babies.

One might wonder how Ray Pierce could have lived with Darci and never have realized that she wasn't pregnant. But doctors and nurses who observed Darci immediately after the crime said that she did indeed look pregnant. One doctor reported a slight change in the pigmentation of her nipples, a typical sign of pregnancy, although the change was not quite as great as one would expect. Darci probably could have put on weight on purpose, but she may have gone through the actual symptoms of carrying a child. Her periods may have ceased, although no conclusive proof exists that they did so. Her body did seem to change in some ways, and she went about planning for the baby in every way. Perhaps Ray was young, at twenty, and inexperienced, but one suspects that any husband would have believed in Darci's pregnancy, just as her mother and friends did.

What becomes very apparent in following Darci through the winter and spring of 1986–87 is that she entered her own myth completely. In the fall the Rickers, believing that Darci was pregnant, began to pressure the young couple to get married. Ray was talking about joining the air force, and the Rickers wanted him and Darci to get things settled before then and before the baby was born. Ray did agree and Darci seemed to enter fully into the excitement of the domestic haven she had long desired and would now create.

Since Ray would be leaving in January for his basic training in the air force, the wedding was set for December. The marriage might have occurred earlier, but Mr. Ricker suffered a minor heart attack that fall and was in the hospital for six weeks. Darci was very attentive to her father during that time, and then, in mid-December, Darci and Ray finally married.

Darci's mother and Aunt Laura helped Darci plan the wedding. Mrs. Ricker made a beautiful cake and decorated for a nice, but fairly small reception. Aunt Laura ordered the flowers and made other arrangements. Ray and Darci were married in a church and a nice reception followed afterward. For her wedding gown, Darci wore a pretty maternity dress. She was "too far along" to fit into a regular dress. Or at least that's what everyone thought. Darci was the only one there who knew that she wasn't actually pregnant.

In mid-January Ray left for basic training at Lackland Air Force Base near San Antonio. He also received further technical training and did not return to Portland until the middle of April. During the four months that he was gone, Darci returned home to live with her parents. The baby, according to Darci, was due in April, so Ray expected to return about the time of the birth.

During the time that Darci lived at home, troubles inevitably occurred between Darci and her mother. Nonetheless, Mrs. Ricker worked hard to make the time as agreeable as possible. She held a baby shower

LULLABY AND GOODNIGHT

for Darci, and she tried to make everything as special as she could: "We just decorated the whole house beautifully and put little banners up and all these things, and I baked a cake. I put pink and blue clowns on pillars, then another cake on top of that. I bought a pink ceramic bootie and filled it with icing and put a little bear on top of it because she wanted to do the nursery in bears."

Aunt Donna helped, and she remembered the shower as a nice occasion: "Her parents bought her a cradle and my dad put it together and we put the gifts in the cradle. . . . [Darci] had gotten a new maternity dress and had her hair all fixed. And she came and she looked so nice and we just all had a good time at the baby shower. She was very pleased, opening gifts, just like anybody would be. It was wonderful."

One of the games the women played was to measure around Darci's middle, and then for everyone to guess the number of inches. A prize went to the one who came the closest.

It was all a lot of fun, and very natural, and yet, it was astounding. What must Darci have been thinking? Was she hoping that any day now she really would become pregnant and could somehow explain away the timing of the delivery? Did she consider claiming a miscarriage or another stillbirth? Or did she think at all? Did she *really* believe she *was* pregnant, and was she so immersed in her desire to have a baby that she believed the fantasy her mind had weaved? But if that is so, it's only partly true. She would later admit that she always *knew* that she was not pregnant.

During the time Ray was gone, Darci became close friends with the Landrums, a couple Darci had met earlier, through Ray. The husband was interested in radio controlled cars, which Ray sold at the hobby shop where he worked. The two husbands attended a radio car race together, and afterward Ray and Darci went to the Landrums' home. Kathy Landrum was impressed with this bright and very mature young woman. Kathy knew that Ray would soon be leaving, and she invited Darci to spend some time with her and her husband, so that she would have some company when she was alone.

Two or three weeks later Darci invited Kathy to her baby shower. Kathy couldn't attend, but after that, the two began to get together occasionally. Eventually, Darci would spend a great deal of time in the Landrum home. This was a difficult time for Darci's mother. As usual, Darci was turning to others for her intimate talks and advice, and she was leaving Mrs. Ricker out. But she had no idea how intimate the relationship had become.

One of Darci's strangest acts was to tell her newlywed husband, when he called from Texas, that she had gone to bed with Kathy Landrum and that she had shared a lovely time with her. Kathy would later say that their relationship became sexual at Darci's initiation: "She's a very flirtatious young woman. She was very seductive."

Darci was jealous of any young woman who had anything at all to do with Ray. She continued to believe that Ray had never dropped his interest in a former girlfriend, and she fretted about that quite often. And yet, she could call her husband and admit to an affair with a woman and expect him to have no trouble accepting the idea. Maybe she was right. Ray was apparently willing to forgive this kind of infidelity.

Darci's relationship with Kathy Landrum was not primarily a sexual one, however. The center of the talk—the focus—was upon Darci's pregnancy. Kathy was a mother and she could share with Darci her own birthing experiences. According to Kathy, Darci was consumed with interest: "She was very knowledgeable. I mean, she had the terminology down. It appeared to me that she had educated herself quite well. I could relate to that, as during my first pregnancy I absorbed a lot of reading material and I sought out as much information about the whole process as possible so as to best make decisions about the birth. It seemed to me she was doing the same thing. We could talk on the same level, you know."

Often they talked about Darci's visits to Dr. Sargent. "We'd have lunch together and then she'd inform me she had a doctor's visit that afternoon and we'd talk in the evening and she would recount what happened at the visit or reassure me that everything was fine."

The only problem with all that, of course, is that it wasn't true. Darci only visited Dr. Sargent once during those months, and as mentioned before, on that visit a pregnancy test revealed that Darci was not expecting. Therefore, Darci's entire account had to be invented. Yet her descriptions of the visits and of her conversations with the doctor were all detailed and vivid.

Gradually, the relationship became very close, and Darci clung to Kathy to the point that it concerned Kathy. She foresaw doom in Darci's marriage to Ray. Darci often complained about him, that he didn't care enough about the baby, that he spent too much money on his hobbies. He refused to get started putting a nursery together, which broke Darci's heart.

Darci and Kathy also attended a childbirthing class together. One evening they learned about medications available during childbirth, and then they saw a film about C-sections. The patient in the film was draped so that the audience did not see the actual method of surgery, but the procedure was explained. Darci became adamant, however, and said that she would *never* give birth that way. It was important to her to experience a natural childbirth. Kathy tried to reason with Darci and explain that in an emergency Darci might have to accept a C-section as a viable alternative, but Darci was stubborn and said she could never do that.

As the time for Ray's return approached, Darci often expressed the wish that Kathy could be with her, instead of Ray, at the time of the birth. She and Ray would be moving to Albuquerque for Ray's first assignment in the air force, and Darci was worried about her marriage. Kathy reassured her that the birth would give her life new meaning and excitement. Her time and attention would be centered on the baby. But Kathy confided in her husband that she feared that one day Darci would show up on their doorstep with a baby in her arms. She couldn't imagine that the marriage was going to last.

Ray sensed none of this. He saw Darci as a loving and devoted wife. Was Darci fickle in her relationship, or genuinely confused? Did she play each of her "lovers" for her own advantage? Such answers are always difficult with Darci.

What *is* clear is that Darci had created an enormous problem and one that was becoming more and more intense and stressful with each passing day. She would later admit that when someone touched her stomach, she taught herself how to move her muscles to create the sensation that the baby was moving inside her. She did this for Ray as well as for others. That very act becomes a sort of symbol for her complicated mental state. On the one hand, her body was going through symptoms that were typical of a woman about to give birth and her mind was completely focused on the

LULLABY AND GOODNIGHT

fruition of that fantasy. The birthing classes, the maternity clothes, the self-education, the baby shower, and the purchase of baby clothes, children's books, diapers and a diaper bag, stuffed animals, and nursery items—everything in her life was centered on the baby. She even began to subscribe to *Parents' Magazine*. But the baby did not exist and Darci knew that. One could say that perhaps she was ignoring the doctor's tests and trusting in the symptoms she was feeling. But if that was the case, she wouldn't have rippled her own stomach muscles to create the illusion of the baby's movements. Most importantly, evidence never would come out that she slipped back and forth from one reality to another. Even in the times when she was carrying out her fantasy completely, she would always take steps to cover the truth. This duplicity would only become more intense as the time for the birth approached.

Mrs. Ricker was very upset that Darci would consider traveling with Ray to Albuquerque at a time when her baby was almost due. Ray planned to rent a moving truck, and Darci would drive their car. Darci reassured her mother that she would be all right. But Mrs. Ricker was able to convince Mr. Pierce, Ray's father, to go along with them. Darci was actually not pleased about that, but in April they packed the truck and set off for New Mexico.

One other bizarre episode occurred during this time. Ray was also concerned about whether it was wise for Darci to travel when she might deliver at any time. But one day he received a call from a man who said he was Dr. Sargent. The man told Ray it would be all right for Darci to make the trip. Dr. Sargent, however, would later say that he never made such a call. At Darci's trial, Ray took back the statement. He said it never happened. Either he was confused when he first made the statement, or he decided to cover Darci on another one of her deceptions.

Mrs. Ricker was greatly relieved when Darci safely arrived in Albuquerque and began to get set up in an apartment. But Darci's mother was also confused by some of her daughter's statements, and she wondered exactly when the baby was due. So she called Darci's doctor. A nurse in Dr. Sargent's office informed Mrs. Ricker that Darci's only recent visit had been in February and at that time a pregnancy test had been negative.

Needless to say, Sandra Ricker was stunned. "I mean, I didn't know what to think, and I thought . . . you know, somebody is going crazy here, and it must be me." She called Dr. Sargent's office again, thinking that some mistake had been made, but she received the same answer. Then she called Darci.

Darci's response was to laugh and say, "Well, Mom, you know I'm pregnant." The logic was airtight. Sandra did know that her daughter was pregnant. She had seen her, felt her abdomen, talked with her about her visits to the doctor, shared her own knowledge about having babies. She and Darci had "expected" this baby together for months. The only possible explanation for the response at the doctor's office was that a mistake had been made in the record keeping, or that the nurse was looking at information taken the previous February.

What Mrs. Ricker didn't know was that Darci called Dr. Sargent's office soon after her mother hung up the phone. Darci demanded, in very stern language, that no one in the office ever again give any private information about her to *anyone*. Darci had laughed, and handled her mother casually, but a few minutes later, on the phone with the nurse, she sounded angry and assertive.

Darci, in spite of a possible collapse of the whole deception, remained "pregnant." And Mrs. Ricker talked to her daughter again, soon after she and Ray were getting settled: "Well, they were happy. They had found their house and they were settled. She was making a nursery, fixing a nursery up. She explained it in great length, how beautiful it was, and I think I bought every bear picture Home Interior ever made. Everything was bear, you know. It was really going to be neat."

Ray did tell Mrs. Ricker that Darci wasn't getting much bigger than she had been in Oregon, but that didn't seem to be any reason to suspect anything. Darci was still talking about natural childbirth and learning proper breathing methods and using Ray as her coach. Who would have thought that she wasn't pregnant?

But one matter was very confusing. Darci had begun to say that the original delivery date had apparently been wrong, and that the birth would be a little later. She pushed the due date back again a couple of times later that spring.

Meanwhile, Darci was writing to Kathy and calling her on the telephone fairly often. She told Kathy that she had received an ultrasound and the baby was not as big as she had previously been told in Portland. The doctor had moved the due date back to between late May and the middle of June.

Darci also continued to report details about the pregnancy to Kathy. Once she said she had lost her mucous plug. Another time, she claimed to be dilated a certain number of centimeters, but then the next week reported a different number. Eventually, she reported that she was going to be induced.

Darci had asked for her records from Dr. Sargent to be sent to the base Ob/Gyn clinic, and then called back and had them sent to the University of New Mexico Medical Center. One wonders why she would bother since she was not going in for regular examinations, as she reported to Ray. Every word of her account about doctors, ultrasound, and dilation was her own invention. But when she first appeared at the base clinic to sign up for treatment, Ray was with her. Perhaps he had insisted he go along, and she had been trapped into sending for the records. Or even more likely, she may have invited him along, to make the hoax seem real.

Ray Pierce was inexperienced, and he trusted Darci's many explanations. He reported, later, that he and Darci met people who said that they had experienced ten- or eleven-month pregnancies. Darci had actually been wearing maternity clothes for close to a year, but the molar pregnancy had been part of that, and the young man was perhaps rightly confused by all of Darci's accounts.

But as July approached, and still no baby had been born, certainly Darci's time had run out. And so she told her husband the only logical thing she could say: This baby, who refused to come, would have to be induced. She even gave Ray the date when it would happen, and at that point something had to give. Darci had to have a baby or she had to admit that she had been lying. She would also later say that she considered one more option. She thought about disappearing.

But in the end, she found she couldn't do that. Somehow, she had to get a baby.

CHAPTER 6

Darci sometimes had terrible nightmares. She would suddenly sit up in bed, screaming. Ray would have to console her as she sobbed and told him what she had seen. Usually it was a burglar breaking into the house, chasing her with a knife or a gun. But once she screamed out because she had seen her baby, newly born, and it had no face. Where the face should have been was only a blank place.

Pressure was building on Darci. She later tried to explain what was happening to her: "I feel that I put a lot on myself because I felt, I felt like, you know, any woman can carry a baby to term and have one. Why can't I? You know, what is it that I'm so deficient that I can't do this and so I was trying so hard to do it so that I could prove to myself that I was capable of doing this basic function and also the fact that there was such a void there, such an emptiness, such a longing, because I've always loved children so much."

She described her mental state as the pretended pregnancy kept extending: "I think I was losing touch. I was getting really desperate trying to figure out what I was gonna do, how I was gonna find someone to give me their baby now."

Darci's statement that she wanted to find someone to give her a baby is typical of ideas she seemed to consider perfectly logical. But then, Darci was a person who expected reality to conform to her needs, whether logical or not.

Darci turned the heat up on herself when she announced to her husband, family, and friends that she had set a date to be induced. She later claimed that she almost left Ray on the appointed day. But then she found a way to delay one more time: "So I went into the admissions desk [at the hospital] and the lady that was there. I said to her, I said, 'Can we talk some place?' and she said, 'Sure,' and I went back and I told her that there was a woman who was having my child that was supposed to have delivered . . . uhm . . . today and didn't. My husband thought that I was coming in to be delivered because he thought it was me having the baby, uh, he was supposed to go to a meeting, turned out the meeting was canceled, so he's gonna be here, can you say that the office has been trying to contact us, and it's been moved to next week?"

That's the story that Darci told. But interestingly, even in a confession that seems open and straightforward, her account is quite different from the account given by the woman at the admissions desk, Kelly Jean Lyden. Lyden said that Darci did come in and ask to speak to her, as Darci claimed, and that the two went into an empty patient waiting area. Darci seemed pleasant and normal—not nervous at all—and she began to tell her sad story. She told Lyden some of her background: that she had been adopted, that she was not able to conceive. And then she told the story about the surrogate mother.

To this point, the stories are much the same, except for the number of details Darci was willing to reveal to

LULLABY AND GOODNIGHT

a stranger, which she didn't mention in her later account. But then Darci, according to Lyden, said that she regretted the deception that she had pulled on her husband. "She [said] she was feeling sorry she had lied to him and she wanted to tell him that evening at home. . . . she did not want him to be angry or humiliated there in the hospital."

Kelly Lyden was completely convinced that Darci was telling the truth. Darci was gentle, sweet, and repentant for what she had done. She sat with her hands in her lap, her eyes downcast, her voice soft. How could anyone doubt her sincerity? And so Lyden agreed to help Darci.

But she was not nearly so able an actress. When Darci brought Ray to the office, Lyden did tell Ray that the doctor had been called away and the induction would have to be delayed, but she was nervous and she sounded strained. All the same, Ray bought the story and he and Darci returned home.

Ray was upset. He felt the pregnancy had gone on entirely too long. Darci was reassuring. Everything would be fine. She would call first thing on Monday and schedule a new appointment for the earliest possible time. Darci knew she had bought a few days, but she knew she couldn't keep this up much longer.

Pressure was also coming from other sources. In Portland, Darci's mother was waiting for the call that would announce the birth of her grandchild. She had gathered some friends together for dinner. They prayed for Darci and waited for the call. Darci finally did call, and she told her mother the same story. She sounded disappointed, but upbeat. As with Ray, she reassured her mother that everything would be fine.

But Darci mentioned another detail to her mother that Mrs. Ricker herself found strange. Darci said that she had gone to the hospital very excited, and she had dressed in a color-coordinated outfit for the big occasion. Mrs. Ricker's comment about that was, "When I was ready to have my children, who cares what I wore?"

Most expectant mothers would probably agree with Mrs. Ricker. What Mrs. Ricker did want to know, of course, was when the actual delivery would take place—when would the doctor induce labor? All Darci's other friends, including Kathy Landrum, wanted to know the same thing.

And so the pressure began all over again.

On Monday Darci told her husband that she had called the hospital and the doctor could not do the induction until Thursday. Ray was upset and asked her to call back and try to move the time up, but Darci, after claiming to have made the call, came back and said the change was impossible. But she caressed him and consoled him and told him it wasn't that big of a deal. Maybe she would go into labor on her own by then.

One of the reasons Ray was upset was that his parents were coming. They had expected the induction on the original "scheduled" day, and were coming the next week. If Darci had the baby early in the week, she could be home when his parents came, and they could all do a little sightseeing together. Darci had not liked the fact that Ray's father had driven with them when they had moved to Albuquerque. She had told Ray that she wanted the move to be their own personal "starting out" time together, a time to "cry or laugh" together, and not a time to have someone else in their home. Now she told him much the same thing, that she would rather not have Ray's parents there.

But neither gave way. Darci insisted that the baby

LULLABY AND GOODNIGHT

could not be induced until Thursday, and Ray insisted that his parents were still coming.

Pressure.

Everyone was waiting, and only Darci knew that her womb was really empty. On Wednesday night Mrs. Ricker called to see what was happening and Ray told her that Thursday night would be it.

"I talked—Darci on one line and Ray was on the other," Mrs. Ricker said, "and a lot of joking was going back and forth between all of us on the phone. And he [Ray] said, 'Come hell or high water . . . we are not coming out of the hospital tomorrow without a baby.'"

Pressure.

Or as Darci would later say: "I had to figure out something to do before five o'clock, didn't I, when we were supposed to go to the hospital?"

On Thursday morning—the day Darci had "scheduled" the second induction—one more factor added to Darci's stress. She got mad at her husband that morning. On the previous day they had picked up their new car. They had wrecked one of their cars earlier and had finally settled on a Mustang they purchased at a Ford dealership. There was some delay in getting the car ready and getting a loan approved, but on Wednesday they picked it up. Darci had made a very big thing of buying a car seat for the baby, and when they brought the car home, she immediately took the car seat out to make sure it would fit into the car. But she and Ray struggled to get the seat to work.

On the following morning Ray decided to take the car to work with him, and he didn't want the baby seat in the back. The car would actually be Darci's after that one day because that was the car with the seat belts, but for one day Ray wanted to enjoy his

Mustang: ". . . macho or whatever it was, I just didn't really want to have the baby seat in there. I wanted to drive it as a car for that day, so I took the car seat out."

But Darci got very upset. "What are you so ashamed of?" she demanded. "Don't you want to be a father?"

This was a woman who, within twelve hours, was faced with admitting to everyone she knew that she had been lying for almost a year. Did she never ask herself what Ray might say about the car seat when she finally had to deal with the obvious, larger issue that she had been lying to him for many months?

Or did she already have her plan set as to how she would get herself a baby that day?

Ray left Darci angry, but he came home for lunch, as usual. Ray had to travel almost twenty minutes to get to his home, during a one-hour lunch, which meant he would only have a few minutes to lunch at home, but it was something he did almost every day. The brief visit seemed to mean a lot to Darci—and to Ray—in spite of troubles they sometimes had with their relationship.

All seemed fine at lunch. But Darci wanted to buy a stroller for the baby. Ray sat at the kitchen table in their little duplex apartment. "Darci, we really can't afford it right now," he told her. "Can't we wait a month or two on that?" Darci reluctantly agreed.

Before Ray left, he told Darci that he would try to get off a little early so he could get home in plenty of time to go to the hospital. Nothing Darci did suggested to him that anything was wrong. She seemed normal and not even very upset about the stroller. She didn't even bring up the car seat that had concerned her that morning. Ray returned to work and was allowed to leave at about two o'clock, considerably earlier than he had expected. But when he came

LULLABY AND GOODNIGHT

home, Darci was not there. She had taken their old white Volkswagen bug. Ray was not concerned at first because she had "previously gone out just to get a grip on herself, psych herself up for the baby."

But time kept passing. Where could she be? Ray was not a nervous young man, but as the minutes turned into hours, he began to worry. Darci had a certain unpredictable quality, and her moods could change so dramatically. But where would she be now, with the appointment at five o'clock?

Darci had decided to leave Ray. She had come to the point that she felt trapped by her own lie. She considered trying to steal a baby, but it would have to be a newborn, and she wasn't sure that she could pull that off. Her only alternative, other than admitting the truth about the baby, was to disappear. And that's what she decided to do.

Or at least that's what she claimed. That was the story she would later give investigators. But her actions raise serious questions about the truth of that claim. She took nothing with her—no clothes, little money, not even a toothbrush, and she walked out the door almost as soon as Ray had backed out of their driveway. She later explained that by saying, "This time I was gonna leave, but I didn't take a bag. I was just calling it all quits and, you know, let everybody figure out where I had gone if they could."

But she didn't leave. She drove to a gas station on base and filled the tank, and instead of heading out of town, she drove over to the base hospital. She had no real explanation for that except that she hadn't been there since she first arrived in Albuquerque. As she tells it, she walked through the building, which was newly remodeled. She looked at the new carpets, picked up a brochure, and walked back out. And then,

"I think it was almost one o'clock and I was getting ready to drive off and I realized the Ob/Gyn clinic was around the other side. . . . I went back out to my car and was driving like I was gonna go out the Gibson gate and—uh—a woman caught my eye and she was very pregnant and she had just climbed out of a red Blazer . . . and I decided that I was gonna wait for her to come back out and I was gonna talk to her and try to get her to give me her baby."

What?

Why would this woman want to give Darci her baby? Is this the mind of a person beginning to break from stress, someone who had lost all touch with reality? Darci had to have a baby by five o'clock. Even if the "woman" was very pregnant, how did she hope to "talk to her" about delivering that afternoon? Maybe Darci was slipping into her own fantasies so deeply that her logic needed no grounding in reality.

Or maybe Darci knew exactly what she would have to do. Maybe she had made a decision to take what she wanted by whatever means was necessary. Maybe she had given in to the pressure and told herself that she would make things work out in her own life no matter what it cost someone else—exactly the way a thief decides to steal no matter how much the theft will affect the victim.

Or maybe two "mind states" were functioning in her head at the same time. Maybe one of those states knew exactly what she would have to do to get the baby. Maybe the other one was admitting only to the idea of talking to her.

What is certain is that Darci did wait.

And the pressure was building.

Had she noticed that the woman had similarities to herself? Her dark hair, her height, her athletic figure? She would later describe her in exactly those terms.

Had she decided that the mother was near full-term simply on the basis of her very round front? Or had she seen the mother two weeks before in the base library? Had she even talked to her and learned something about her scheduled visits to the clinic? A librarian later reported that she thought she had seen them in the base library at the same time. But no one was ever able to verify that Darci and Cindy had actually met each other.

People did see Darci out in the parking lot in the terrific heat, waiting all afternoon. And the wait was much longer than either woman could have expected. The delay came because Cindy was worried about the lack of movement she felt inside herself. And the delay was nearly long enough—almost providential. Had Cindy been perhaps five, maybe ten minutes longer, Sam would have met Cindy, and he would have walked from the hospital with her. Cindy's life might have gone on without a thought of the other pregnant woman she might have glimpsed outside. And what would have happened to Darci? Would she have gone home and told Ray the truth? Would she have run away? Or would she have sought another fetus from another woman?

But the razor's edge didn't cut that way. When Cindy walked from the clinic, Darci was parked in her white VW next to Cindy and Sam's cherry-red Blazer.

What we know about Cindy's abduction and eventual murder comes mostly from Darci, and so it is filtered through her own perception. Even when Darci tells her notion of the truth, one has reason to wonder whether it entirely fits with reality. But another factor enters in. Darci claimed, once she finally admitted to the crime, that her memory of most of the events was gone. Mental health specialists hired both by the defense and by the prosecution tended to believe her.

Her story seemed credible, and the patchy memory, the confused mental state, all seemed plausible. Both sides concluded that the amnesia was probably real, not feigned.

In any case, we only have Darci's story, plus a certain amount of objective corroborating evidence to go on. Putting all the information together, however, a fairly detailed account of the murder does come together.

Darci waited for Cindy outside the clinic for about two hours. The day was extremely hot, approaching one-hundred degrees by mid-afternoon, and Darci waited in her VW, or outside, and watched for the pregnant woman to come out. But the wait became too long. She was about to give up and leave when Cindy walked from the clinic. Darci told the story this way: "... I got out of my car, the passenger side, her driver's side 'cause she was getting in and I asked her to get in the car with me, that I needed someone to talk to, that I had some problems right now, I didn't know anybody, that I just needed to talk. And she looked startled and I told her, 'Please, I just need somebody to talk to, I'm not gonna hurt you,' and so she got in the car with me and I said why don't we go back to my place and we can sit over a couple of glasses of iced tea and we can talk, 'cause I think even just to talk with somebody would have been real nice. Well, I drove down San Mateo and turned left on Marquette and saw that Ray's car was in the driveway and recognized the car so I did a 'U' real quick and got back on San Mateo and ... (pause) ... and I ... I think I drove back over to Central and drove down Central and went past UNM.

"... I thought it would be real nice just to drive around and talk to her and I asked her ... uhm ... if

LULLABY AND GOODNIGHT

her husband was in the military and she said yes. I asked her what he did and she said he was an SP . . . uhm . . . I never got around to actually telling her what my problem was. I . . . I don't remember the conversation between us. I do remember that she rolled down the window and just relaxed, sat back, we were just talking."

Some of the essential facts in this account seem accurate. Ray had come home early, so the drive home and the U-turn ring true. And, of course, Cindy must have told Darci that Sam was a policeman. It is unlikely she could have known that any other way.

But almost surely, Cindy did not get in the car voluntarily. She was already upset and concerned that she had been in the clinic twice as long as she expected to be. She had already called Sam and asked him to hurry to the baby-sitter's if he finished before she did. She also knew that at any minute Sam would be walking across the street to meet her. Perhaps she would have taken a minute or two to talk to someone who looked pitiful and had a sad story to tell. But to get into the car and drive away with the idea of going off to the woman's house was simply not possible. Aside from the fact that Cindy didn't drink iced tea (Mormons abstain from coffee and tea), she simply would not have taken that kind of time out of her day when she felt so responsible to get back to her child and relieve the baby-sitter.

Cindy also learned, while at the clinic that day, about an important "Champus" meeting that would occur at 3:30. Champus is the insurance benefit for military dependents that would provide for Cindy's delivery and pediatric care. She told a friend, inside the clinic, that she would probably go to the meeting, and she promised to save a seat if she got there first.

But this was before the long delay. She may have thought that she could pick up Luke and then return to the base once Sam was home to watch the baby. In any case, it was one other reason for her to hurry that afternoon.

What Darci didn't mention at that point was that she had a gun with her. It was actually a replica pistol. The outer portion of the gun was real, but the inner workings were plastic—it was a demonstration pistol. Although it would not shoot, it was not a toy. Anyone would have considered it a lethal weapon from its outer appearance. Darci must have used the pistol to get Cindy into the car.

Darci did admit, when asked, that she had the gun, but she said that she merely pulled it from the pocket on the door and set it on her lap *after* Cindy had gotten in the car: "She [Cindy] saw it, but it didn't involve her. She didn't look at it, uh, I just told her again I wasn't going to hurt her, you know, and she, she trusted me. She was very relaxed." But Darci kept the gun there because "I just didn't want [Cindy] to leave."

Cindy couldn't have been relaxed. But she may well have remembered her husband's advice. Sam had told her a number of times that if she was ever abducted she should pretend to go along with the person, and then wait for an opportunity to get away.

Darci described herself, on the other hand, as hysterical, and she later remembered only snatches of the conversation between the two. One thing she did not remember—or know—was Cindy's name.

Darci headed out of town toward the mountains on Highway I-40. Near the mountains a light afternoon rain began to fall. Lightning flashed and Darci remembered Cindy telling her that she liked thunderstorms, but the noise of thunder always scared her. She also remembered Cindy saying that she and her husband often came to this area to go four-wheeling.

All this rings with authenticity, and in Darci's mixed-up state, Cindy must have seemed chatty and friendly. But Cindy was certainly terrified. The gun was in Darci's lap, and she was driving Cindy away from the city—away from her husband and son—to some unknown destination. Cindy would have been praying and thinking, probably contemplating a chance to get away when she could somehow do so safely. But that would mean safety to the baby inside her as well as safety to herself.

Darci drove on the freeway until she reached an exit near the little town of Tijeras, and there she had an option. She could head into the mountains, as she apparently had decided to do, or she could make a left-hand turn, under the freeway, and another left back onto I-40. This is exactly what Darci contemplated doing: "Okay, and I decided I was gonna turn around and take her back. I . . . I had had enough. I was gonna turn around and take her back and level with my husband on everything, just tell him that, you know, I can't take any more. I feel like everything's falling in on me." But Darci didn't turn back. She started up Highway 14 into the Manzano Mountains: ". . . because [Cindy] was still talking and she was real relaxed. . . ."

Darci continued up the winding road through a pretty canyon, the road lined with piñon pines and junipers. But she "didn't feel like driving anymore." She just wanted to "stop and talk." So she pulled off the paved highway onto a gravel road and continued forward to another turn to the left. She crossed a cattle guard and drove a short distance forward. She was in a little canyon well out of site from the highway. It was normally a dry place, the grass yellow and the junipers faded by the summer heat, but on this day the drizzle of rain was falling and the little dry gulch had a trickle of a stream running through it.

In this remote spot, where Darci might not have expected anyone to be around, she stopped the car. She had an explanation for that: ". . . there was a nice place on the road so I stopped the car 'cause there was a bunch of trees that overhung and we could be outside 'cause it was so humid, 'cause it was so hot in the car."

The two, according to Darci, walked under the trees and then "stood around," and talked. But Cindy must have been wondering every second what was about to happen. She must have sensed that something was wrong with Darci, no matter how softly and gently she might have spoken. The gun was enough to tell Cindy that Darci was a desperate woman.

Cindy may have thought of running. All her life she had been able to outrun even most of the boys she knew. But run with the baby inside her? And run where? So, she must have told herself to stay calm, to reassure Darci. She must have hoped that Darci only needed to talk, and that she wouldn't really become violent, no matter what strange forces had pushed her to abduct Cindy.

And Darci must have told her story, talked on and on. She always did.

Maybe Cindy came to believe that the talk would be enough, and then Darci would take her back. "I won't hurt you," Darci had told her. And Cindy surely wanted to believe that. As Darci talked about herself, one thing is clear. Cindy would have felt compassion for her. Even though she would have looked for every chance to protect her baby, she most certainly found Darci a person she could pity and console. It was simply Cindy's nature to react with compassion toward people who suffered.

All this time, Darci claimed, the gun was in the car. But Darci still didn't ask Cindy for her baby: "I asked her all about her baby, when it was due, how the pregnancy was . . . and I was just coming to the point of asking her to give me her child and I decided, no I wanted to go home, 'cause I just was gonna forget the whole thing and go home . . . and we were getting back in the car and then . . . that's, I don't know from the car until I was driving real fast down the road and I had the baby in my arms and I don't know what happened from the time we were getting in the car. I don't know."

When pushed, however, Darci remembered a few important details. She said that she got back in the car and then she hit Cindy, "not with her hand," but she didn't remember with what, although she thought it might have been the gun. Darci was able to hit Cindy hard on the back of the head, so she must have struck suddenly and without warning. Cindy must have been lulled into thinking that Darci meant no harm.

The two wrestled and fell out of the car on Cindy's side. Darci said that Cindy scratched her and pulled her hair. Both women fell on the gravel road, and Darci said she didn't hit Cindy any more after that. But Darci must have hit Cindy hard enough to subdue her because she offered no resistance from that point on. And Cindy had several bruises on her head.

Darci then strangled Cindy. She used the monitor strap that was in Cindy's purse. At the Ob/Gyn clinic, earlier that day, Cindy had used the strap to hold a monitor on her stomach. The nurses had told her to take it home and wash it and bring it back for her next appointment. She had tucked it in her purse.

There in the gravel road, near the car, Darci pulled the strap very tight and held it until Cindy was unconscious. By this time Cindy was not fighting back, and so the strangling was a calculated choice, not a reaction to a struggle between the two.

Crucially, Darci held on long enough to render Cindy unconscious, but not dead. Blood was still pumping to the baby. Somehow Darci had delivered exactly the right amount of "anesthetic" for the operation she was about to perform. Had she continued to strangle Cindy perhaps a few, ten, fifteen seconds more, Cindy might have died and the baby would not have lived very long. Darci would have had only a couple of minutes.

With Cindy still breathing, Darci dragged her down a steep drop-off by the side of the road and into a little grove of piñon pines, with some low-growing junipers beneath. The natural inclination is to imagine Darci in a wild, hurried frenzy at this point, desperate to get what she wanted and then to get away. But that was not the case. Suddenly, at this crucial moment, an eyewitness appeared, and he saw anything but frenzy in Darci's behavior.

Just as Darci was preparing to begin her surgery, a man in a pickup truck drove up the road and was stopped by the Volkswagen parked in the road with the doors open on both sides. The man was Theron Hartshorn, who was building a house for his family a little farther up the road. He couldn't get by on the narrow road, and so he got out of his truck. Until then, he hadn't seen anyone.

The razor's edge again. Cindy was still alive. And suddenly a man appears in this isolated valley, as if sent to save Cindy. Caught in the act, many a murderer might have panicked and run, or tried to hide—or anything but what Darci did.

As Hartshorn was walking toward the Volkswagen, Darci appeared from behind the trees. She was straightening her dress. "My friend and I need to be left alone," she said.

"Fine," Hartshorn said. "I have to get around. You'll have to shut your door."

His thought was that the woman was planning to have sex with someone in the bushes, beneath the trees. She seemed nervous but not irrational or out of control. He had no sense that she seemed out of touch with reality. When he walked over to shut the car door, she repeated, "We need to be left alone." She said it three or four times. Mr. Hartshorn had no desire to do anything but get on by, so he shut the door and got in his truck. But as he drove by the VW he glanced into the trees and saw "somebody lying on the ground and the woman that I was talking to was crawling up toward her."

The woman on the ground was not moving. Mr. Hartshorn thought it was merely "two women playing around in the bushes." Later, he would regret that he hadn't been more suspicious, that he hadn't done something to stop Darci. But he saw no blood or any evidence that anything criminal was happening.

Earlier, at the clinic, a few minutes might have saved Cindy's life. Here in this little valley, a minute or two might have made the difference. But Darci's self-control, her ability to lie, to manipulate others, worked for her once again. Even at the most traumatic moment of her life, she could control herself enough to handle the threat and take care of the business at hand.

Darci said she did not remember the murder, but she did remember Mr. Hartshorn. And she told the story exactly as he did. "I told him that my friend and I had to be left alone." She was not crazed and wild, even in her own account.

Once Hartshorn was gone, Darci had to get the baby. She had brought no knife with her. She calculated her options, and she made a good decision. Once again, she used Cindy's purse for the source of the instrument she needed. At some point, Darci got hold of Cindy's set of keys that included a fairly new key to Sam and Cindy's Blazer. She had few choices, but as it turned out, the choice of the key was an excellent one.

Darci raised Cindy's maternity top and plunged the key into Cindy's taut abdomen and broke through the skin. Cindy was still unconscious. She did not react, did not twist or fight. She almost certainly felt nothing.

Darci used the sharp, ragged edge of the key to cut and tear her way through the fat tissue and muscle. Either Darci knew where and how to cut, or she was very lucky. She cut across the abdomen, very low, just above the pubic area. This is the area where the muscle wall is thinnest, and where the cut is made by experts. The incision—about five and a half inches across—was also the approximate length typically used in a cesarean operation. When the key broke through the uterine wall, the blunt end was an advantage, since it would not be as likely to cut the baby.

The original incision was not big enough, however, and Darci took hold of the top and bottom of the gap and stretched it, ripping the incision a little longer. Then she reached inside Cindy and pulled the baby through. But all this was done with deftness and precision. The operation couldn't have been performed any better in an operating room.

Or that is to say, the operation couldn't have been

any better for the *baby*. The mother, of course, had no chance to survive.

At that point, some of Darci's memory returned. She later remembered the bitter taste in her mouth when she bit through the umbilical cord, and she remembered holding the cord so that it wouldn't bleed. She was very careful with the new baby. She cleared its mouth, as best she could, and tried to protect it: ". . . I pulled off my dress and wrapped the baby in my dress and put the baby against my chest because my slip was real low to keep the baby warm and I got in the car and I was driving really fast, really fast. . . .

". . . I had the baby clutched against me. I was driving with one hand and I don't remember how I shifted. I think I took my hand off the wheel, I don't remember, but I remember there was a big curve and I knew that I needed to slow down 'cause I was going so fast and I lifted my left foot to go for the brake, but I hit the clutch and the car started sliding and I couldn't stop the car from sliding and I was going backward on the road and then I hit the side of the mountain thing.

". . . I ran over a tree and I was thinking with a Volkswagen and all the weight is over the rear end, so I can get out of here, but I thought what if I'm stuck, and I got out of the car, I got out of the car, I didn't think I got out of the car, I got out of the car and I remember because my seat had fallen back. I'm short; I'm short to drive that car and the seat doesn't work right, so my husband had to put two bricks behind the seat to keep it up to where I can drive it and the bricks fell out of the way and the [seat was] back, so I couldn't reach the pedal."

Darci placed the baby on the seat while she replaced the bricks. But she was very careful. The baby was

". . . wrapped in my dress, all covered up and the seat covers are sheepskin, so I knew it would be warm and it would only be for a second. . . ."

Some cars came by, and a motorcycle, but no one stopped, and Darci was able to drive away from the little accident. She continued back down the winding highway to the freeway. And at that point, she had to plan her next action: ". . . I started thinking, I can't just show up someplace with this baby in my arms around here and not have some kind of a story."

But Darci left something out.

She must have had a "story" in mind long before she reached I-40. After delivering the baby, and before getting in the car, she spattered her slip with blood. She spread the blood along her thighs, obviously to create the illusion that she had given birth to the baby. She then washed her hands very carefully, probably in the trickle of a stream nearby. In her own account of events, her only concern was for the baby, but she had to set the baby aside while she prepared her ruse, and she had to begin calculating her story from the moment she had what she wanted.

Or maybe she had thought all those steps through long ahead of time. Maybe she was carrying out a careful plan that she had rehearsed in her mind many times.

Along the way, Darci had made one mistake, although she wasn't yet aware of it. She always wore a Krugerrand on a necklace. It was a memento of her time in South Africa. But sometime during her struggles with Cindy, the chain broke, and the Krugerrand ended up under Cindy's body.

As Darci drove back to Albuquerque with the baby in her arms, she knew that Ray would be wondering where she was, and she had to have an explanation. She described herself as frenzied at that point, but her

LULLABY AND GOODNIGHT

actions were methodical and controlled, anything but hysterical. In fact, every indication is that she had a plan in mind.

Cindy lay in the grass behind the little grove of trees while Darci constructed her story and prepared to put it into effect. A light rain pattered down upon her body. The blood had flowed freely from the gaping tear made by Darci. Cindy couldn't have lived more than a few minutes after the delivery.

While Sam searched for his wife and tried to think where she could be, and while little Luke asked, "Where's my Mommy?" Cindy Ray was already dead, sacrificed to Darci's fanatical needs for what she had to have most . . . for what she could not be denied . . . for what she would have and take at *any* cost.

CHAPTER 7

A few days before the murder, during the time when Darci and Ray had been looking at cars, they had stopped at the Montano Acura dealership, and they had met some of the salesmen there. One of them had been particularly friendly and interested in the baby Darci seemed to be carrying. As Darci raced back toward Albuquerque with Cindy's baby, she decided to go to that Acura dealership: "So I drove to I-25 and I . . . I knew that if I pulled in at the Acura dealership, because we had known a guy in there, whose wife had had a couple of kids . . . I could tell him that I had been leaving and decided to come back and delivered the baby on the road on my way back and that I needed an ambulance 'cause we needed to get to the hospital. That particular salesman wasn't there, but one of the other guys that we talked to was and he came out and he had our home number and everything . . . uhm . . . I asked him to call an ambulance, for him to call Ray to tell him to meet us at the hospital, 'cause that's where we would be going. Uhm, one of the salesmen, well, quite a few of the salesmen came out and they were leaving and I didn't want to stay by myself, so I asked one of them to stay and he was really nice and he had been saying, you know,

LULLABY AND GOODNIGHT

you're incredible, you know, you did this yourself, you know, my wife and I have had two kids and, wow, you know, you're quite a lady, you did this yourself."

Darci asked, by name, for Rob Mohr, one of the salesmen at Montano Acura. When he got to her car, he saw Darci sitting in the driver's seat, holding the baby, who was wrapped in Darci's dress. Darci was "perspiring profusely." Her hair was matted, and her white slip was soaked through with sweat. He could see the bloodstains on her slip as well. The car was also muddy, and the back taillight and fender were damaged. He didn't doubt Darci's story, for a minute. She seemed "distraught," he said, and she told her story very believably. She mentioned details: fighting with her husband and her deciding to run away, taking only four dollars and no baggage, labor beginning as she changed her mind and returned on I-25, experiencing one pain so severe she swerved from the road and wrecked the Volkswagen, and then, delivering the baby. Mohr even asked her how she cut the umbilical cord, and she said that she bit through it. And she had the baby's name ready: Amanda Michelle.

All this was told in a disjointed, incoherent, flustered manner, and she seemed genuinely upset. But these actions may have been part of a preconceived plan. When Ray and Darci took their new car for a test drive the day before, they had driven on I-40, toward the mountains where Darci had taken Cindy. Then, as they returned to the Ford dealership, Darci suggested that they drive over to the Acura dealership —just to drive the car a little more. Had she wanted to scope that area out again? Had she planned that part of her return trip from the mountains? Had she thought this all through before she ever picked Cindy up?

133

We'll probably never know answers to those questions, but we do know that throughout this "distraught" period, Darci continued to lie very effectively. She wanted to have someone call her husband, and she wanted an ambulance. John Drexler, another salesman, talked with Darci while Mohr called Ray. Drexler knelt by the side of the car with the door open and helped Darci check the baby, but she held "her" daughter close and wouldn't let go.

The ambulance arrived after about twenty or twenty-five minutes. As the paramedics were coming to the car, Darci thought of the gun. She told Drexler there was a toy gun in the car that she wanted him to stick away in the pocket on the door. She explained that she had taken it along for protection, even though it wasn't real. She may have been upset, but she remembered the things she had to take care of—or cover up.

The paramedics wanted to check the baby, but Darci resisted at first. Finally she handed the child over and got out of the car, but she became weak as she walked to the ambulance. She slumped over and the paramedics had to let her down easily and then give her oxygen. She kept pushing it away, however, and asking about Amanda. No one doubted her genuine concern for her new little baby.

The ambulance took Darci and the baby to the University of New Mexico Medical Center, the place that had been arranged for air force families to deliver their babies. John Drexler rode with her because she asked him to do so. She had attached to him quickly, and she seemed to need the assurance that someone she knew was with her.

Darci's explanation for stopping at the Montano Acura dealership is interesting not only for what Darci said, but what she didn't say. As she drove into

Albuquerque, heading west on I-40, she actually passed a turnoff that would have taken her a short distance south to the medical center. She had been there a number of times. She and her husband had even practiced driving there so they would be able to make it quickly on the day that Darci went into labor. In other words, she did not pass the hospital by accident, but purposely passed the turnoff, continued west until she met another freeway, I-25, and there she turned to the north, heading farther away from the hospital. The extra drive would have taken perhaps fifteen minutes. Then the ambulance had to be called, with a further delay.

What was Darci's motivation for doing all this? That becomes clear in the story she would tell at the hospital. She told hospital personnel that that afternoon she had decided to leave her husband. She used the argument over the car seat to justify her account. She claimed to have driven north on Highway I-25, toward Santa Fe, but then had changed her mind and was returning to Albuquerque when she went into labor and delivered the baby on the side of the highway.

That was the story. It was designed to explain her absence and the reason for the baby being born away from home. But the account also placed her on I-25, north of town, instead of on I-40, east of the city. She knew that eventually the body would be found, and she had now placed herself away from the area. It is exactly this kind of calculation that argues that Darci did think very clearly about pulling off the crime. In spite of Darci's claims to be primarily concerned about the baby, the extra travel time seems to indicate that her overriding concern was to create a cover story.

When the ambulance reached the hospital, Ray was

waiting. Darci said that he was pleased: ". . . he was real proud because, you know, here was our baby and everything was okay, you know; I had been leaving him and decided to come back and had the baby on the road and it was okay."

Ray trusted Darci's story, he would later say, because she had talked before about leaving. Finances had been a big problem, and she had told him that he would be better off living in the bachelors' quarters, where he could use all his money on himself.

Darci's own explanation again demonstrates how carefully she thought about covering herself: "I decided that I was going to say that I had been leaving him and was going north, 'cause I have some family in Colorado. . . ."

But Darci had a problem. Naturally, the emergency room personnel would want to examine her. Darci knew she couldn't allow that: ". . . I wouldn't let them examine me for obvious reasons, 'cause it was very obvious that I didn't have the baby. . . . uhm . . . I played it up to how I felt about the other doctors that I had supposedly dealt with on base, 'cause I did go in there right after we moved here to establish my records there. . . ."

And so, she told the doctors at the hospital she would prefer to see her own private doctor, and they need not worry about her; she was fine. She became, in fact, angry and hostile as she continued to refuse treatment. The first reason she gave her husband was that she didn't want a woman to examine her, and the doctor was a woman.

Darci claimed that she had been treated "crappy" at the base clinic. But what is interesting is her admission that she knew she was acting, creating a motivation that would justify her actions to the doc-

LULLABY AND GOODNIGHT

tors. She "played up" her dislike for the doctors she had dealt with in the past.

At the same time that she was calculating her moves, doing what it took to avoid detection, those who observed her reported a woman who was overjoyed with her new baby. In fact, one of the first things Darci and Ray did was begin to notify their families. The baby had finally arrived!

Mrs. Ricker received a call from Ray. He told her that Darci had delivered a baby girl, to be named Amanda Michelle. Sandra Ricker was very happy as she had been hoping for a granddaughter.

Darci called Kathy Landrum herself: "I had the baby," she announced excitedly. Kathy was ecstatic: "She was calling me, however, from the delivery room of the hospital. She stated that she wouldn't let anybody touch her until they would give her a phone and she could call me with the good news." And then she reported "a bizarre story" to Kathy. She told the whole story, including the detail about cutting the umbilical cord with her teeth. She added that she felt very dizzy and weak but that she had driven, covered with blood, until she recognized the Acura dealership. But the baby was fine, a beautiful little girl. "She seemed very excited about the whole thing."

Only one detail was changed from the version she had given others. In this account, Darci said she had started out to leave Ray and was "driving home" to Portland. "I was coming to see you and suddenly I had a very sharp pain and I had to swerve to the side of the road." It's only a slight alteration, and yet, the calculation again seems evident. This version is to please Kathy. She was heading to Portland, not to Colorado, and she was coming to Kathy's house, not her own.

But then Ray got on the phone and told Kathy that Darci was refusing to be examined. He asked Kathy to talk to her and try to convince her to accept treatment. "Darci," Kathy told her, "you have to let the doctors check you. You know, in such a quick delivery you may have ripped. You may be bleeding. You'll need repair. They need to check to make sure you don't have any complications." Darci calmly reassured Kathy. "It's okay. I'll see my doctor tomorrow morning and I'll have him look at me." Then she told Kathy to call her the next day at home.

On the surface, it would seem that Darci had no chance of deceiving the hospital staff. It even seems odd that she would go to the hospital rather than go home and tell her husband she had delivered the baby herself and she and the baby were fine. But there were several reasons why that approach simply could not work for her. In the first place, she must have known that Ray would not sit still for that. They would have to have the baby checked and have the umbilical cord clamped correctly. Perhaps Darci did not show all the concern for the baby that she might have, but she knew enough about infant care that she at least would want the baby examined and cared for.

Even more importantly, throughout the evening Darci continued to bring up her central focus: the desire to have a birth certificate. Darci didn't want the baby ever to have a doubt about its origins. Her own adoption had pained her too much. Darci's other considerations are matters for speculation only, but she must have thought her decision through, and she may have reasoned this way: Women give birth at home, often with the help of a certified midwife. When they do, they sometimes go to the hospital if any trouble develops for the mother or the baby. Wouldn't it be reasonable to take a baby in, whose

LULLABY AND GOODNIGHT

birth had been outside the hospital, to request care for the baby, but ask to be treated outside the hospital? Wasn't that her right to make such a decision? Darci always saw the world from her own unique perspective, and she tended to think that others should give her whatever she wanted.

Actually, her method might have worked. Hospitals are allowed to release a patient "Against Medical Advice," so long as the patient signs a release form. If Darci had seemed well enough—if she had acted a little more the way the staff expected someone in Darci's situation to behave—if certain other clues hadn't made the doctors suspicious, Darci could have been released to her own doctor. She then might have deceived her husband, as she had so often before, and told him that she had seen a doctor.

It was a long shot, but it might have happened. Darci, however, who always believed she could pull off such things, and who often was successful in her deceptions, sometimes had very little sense of expected behaviors. She did a number of things that caused the hospital staff to deny her the release—and the birth certificate—she wanted.

On the one hand, Darci's story seemed reasonable. There she was, disheveled, with blood on her slip and mud on her feet. Certainly women are sometimes forced to deliver under such circumstances. For Ray the matter was simple: His wife had been pregnant, and now she wasn't. And she had the baby in her arms.

But to the doctors, Darci simply didn't "present" the way most new mothers do. Dr. Susan Graham, a resident obstetrician and gynecologist, was the first physician to speak with Darci. She was on duty in labor and delivery when she received a call from the emergency room. What she heard was not unusual. A woman had given birth outside the hospital and had been brought to emergency. According to normal procedure, she was then moved to the labor and delivery area where she could be examined. Shortly after, Dr. Graham received the report that Darci had arrived but was refusing to be examined and was "really quite angry."

Perhaps it was the anger, as much as anything, that first seemed odd to Dr. Graham. She went to the room where Darci had been taken and found her on a delivery table but with her legs flat, not in stirrups, as would normally be the case. She was wearing a blood-covered slip and she had "blood and mud from her midthigh down her legs and on her feet."

Dr. Graham explained to Darci why an examination was necessary, what the possible dangers were. But Darci told Dr. Graham, angrily, that she "wouldn't have anyone put their fingers up there." She told her story once again, but when Dr. Graham reached over and touched her abdomen, Darci rolled over and refused to be touched anywhere. She told Dr. Graham that she wanted a birth certificate for her baby, and then she wanted to go home.

But Dr. Graham had touched her, and what she felt didn't seem right. The abdomen was quite soft, which meant either that the uterus was still "boggy" or that she had not delivered and therefore no firm uterus was present. The first case seemed unlikely to someone with experience in such matters. Dr. Graham saw no blood in the area around the birth canal. All the blood was lower on her legs. And her agitation struck the doctor as being unusual: "Yes, that was extremely odd. We have a lot of agitated patients on labor and delivery, but they're agitated during the time they're giving birth to the babies and almost instantly they become calm. They fall asleep and become happy.

This woman was exceedingly agitated and I had never seen a woman who had given birth that agitated at that point."

Dr. Graham's instincts told her that something was wrong, and she wasn't about to release Darci from the hospital. But she also wasn't going to try to force her into treatment. She merely told Darci, "Fine. When you're ready to be examined, let me know, and in the meantime, we'll move you somewhere else." She left the room.

Dr. Graham spoke with Ray and explained to him, as others had done in the emergency room, why the examination was important. Ray agreed, of course, and said he would try to convince Darci. Darci was left in the examining room for the present, with Ray there to try to talk some sense into her. He was used to her strange moods and quirky preferences, but this all seemed so illogical. He kept trying to talk to Darci, but she was adamant. What didn't cross his mind was that the baby was not theirs. Darci kept rehashing her story, talking, talking, talking, and as she filled the pieces in, everything seemed to make sense.

Normally Dr. Graham would not have contacted her superior at that point, but Dr. John Slocumb, supervisor of Obstetrics and Gynecologic Service at the hospital, was preparing for surgery and came into the labor and delivery area. Before he went to surgery, Dr. Graham spoke with him and told him what was going on with Darci. So Dr. Slocumb and Dr. Graham spoke with Darci again, along with Ray, and explained all the reasons why the examination was necessary. Dr. Slocumb was equally mystified by what he saw: Darci's anger and refusal to be examined, the pattern of the blood and amniotic fluid on Darci's legs rather than near her pelvic area.

Dr. Slocumb had no more success with Darci than

Dr. Graham had had. She lay upon the table, but she didn't seem exhausted and serene, as one might expect. Her eyes were resolute, and she talked with force. "Just give me the birth certificate," she told him. "I want to go home." So Dr. Slocumb took the same approach that Dr. Graham had used. He left Darci and told her that she could not be released. He went to perform surgery, and then, when a patient came in with an emergency, he did another operation, with Dr. Graham's assistance.

When they returned to the labor and delivery section around nine-thirty or ten o'clock that night, the troubles with Darci had gotten more complicated. She was still refusing to be checked, and several indications were suspicious to the doctor. When Dr. Slocumb had first seen Darci lying on the bed, she looked as though she might have had a baby. Her abdomen looked "fairly full," somewhat distended. But when he touched her, he discovered that the abdomen was soft. There were no "masses present," nothing to indicate the shape of a uterus.

Dr. Slocumb also saw Darci attempt to breast-feed the baby, and he noticed what seemed a slight alteration in the pigmentation of her nipples but not as much as one would expect.

Even more conclusive an indication was the baby's head, which was round and well-shaped, as one would expect from a cesarean birth. If the baby had recently passed through the birth canal, as Darci claimed it had, the baby's head would be more cone shaped, with the bone plates overlapping. This was the most startling of Dr. Slocumb's observations, and one that Dr. Graham and the nurses both in emergency and in the labor area had noticed.

Dr. Slocumb also discovered a scratch on the baby's leg. In a normal vaginal birth, one would not expect any scratches. "But if there had been an accident or the baby had somehow had a problem or been slippery or something and the baby had been grabbed, it might be possible, but it was a fairly deep scratch on the leg."

With the eye of a detective, Dr. Slocumb noticed one other little detail that didn't fit with the story Darci was telling. On Darci's dress, which she had used to wrap the baby, were some little twigs and cedar leaves. (Throughout the west, one variety of juniper is usually called cedar, although it is actually a juniper and not a true cedar.) Darci had claimed that she had delivered the baby along highway I-25, which is in the desert. Dr. Slocumb knew that cedars didn't grow there; they grew in the mountains, however. When he asked Darci if she had been in the mountains, she seemed to react, to get a little nervous.

Besides all these clues, something less specific, more abstract, had bothered Dr. Slocumb from the first time he had met Darci: ". . . she was talking about the baby, but was directing a lot of attention and conversation to the husband, and I felt somewhat uncomfortable in that she did not appear to be really concerned as much about the baby as she did about the presence of her husband and what was going on, what her husband could observe her doing with the baby."

He explained that normally a discernible bonding takes place immediately between the mother and child. As the evening wore on, and the lie became ever more apparent, what Dr. Slocumb thought he saw was much more interest in deceiving the husband than in care for the baby. "I felt that her concern was not so much for the baby as it was for what the baby meant to her and her relationship with her husband."

Darci's motivations are not easy to read in this case.

Her passion to have a child—to be a mother—was certainly great, but her deepest need may not have been for the baby but for the symbolic value to herself.

Finally Dr. Slocumb confronted Darci with his suspicions. He and his staff did not believe that Darci had given birth to the baby, and they wanted to know the truth. Darci's reaction was surprising to Dr. Slocumb, but typical of Darci: "She didn't seem particularly upset, didn't seem to deny the fact that we were confronting her with. . . . and [she] immediately switched to what she said had happened, that the baby had been delivered in Santa Fe by another woman and a nurse midwife."

Darci later explained what was going through her head at the time: ". . . I wouldn't let them examine me, but the one doctor asked me . . . he . . . he told Ray to step out of the room that he just wanted to talk to me, because I said no way, I'm not letting him examine me. When [Ray] left, he said I think you need to level with me about what has happened. Uhm . . . he says, we're real sure that you did not deliver this baby . . . uhm . . . I knew they had taken my blood and I figured that they had taken blood from the baby and I hadn't thought about blood types not matching. At that point it hit me that that was a very obvious thing to determine whether a child was yours or not.

"All I could . . . all I could remember was to think of . . . was black market babies."

But Darci knew that it was illegal to buy a baby on the black market, and she didn't want her story to get out. So she offered Dr. Slocumb money if he would sign a birth certificate: "I asked him not to take it wrong, but I asked him how much it would cost for him to sign . . . and he shook his head at me and said no."

Ironically, Darci didn't need to be concerned about

blood type at that point. By coincidence, hers and the baby's blood types did match. What she didn't perceive was that her story simply wouldn't hold up in all kinds of other ways. Nor would the next story about the black market baby. But she tried it anyway. And when she could tell that Dr. Slocumb wasn't buying that one either, she quickly tried another approach. She said that she had received the baby from a surrogate mother who had delivered the baby in Santa Fe. She claimed she had driven to Santa Fe that afternoon and picked the baby up from a midwife, who had dumped blood and amniotic fluid on her to make her appear to have delivered the baby herself. Darci claimed she had paid $10,000 for the baby.

Once Darci had switched stories, she didn't mind being examined. She told Dr. Slocumb that she would be examined so long as her husband was not in the room and that he not be told that the baby was not hers. The two doctors examined Darci, and Dr. Graham reported later that Darci's abdomen appeared to be that of a woman about twenty weeks pregnant, or of someone who had just given birth. It was "nice and rounded." But when she pressed on the bulging area, she felt nothing. "It was very soft and you could push it all the way down." And, of course, doing the pelvic examination, the doctors found no sign that Darci had given birth.

So what should the doctors do? The problem was not gynecological, and Darci was being examined by gynecologists. Both of them felt that the problem was really a matter for psychologists and social workers. In the morning, they decided, they would call in Child Protective Services, but in the meantime, they would have an in-house psychiatrist and social worker speak with her.

Dr. Leiby, the psychiatrist, spoke with Darci briefly,

and he came away baffled. He was very concerned but unclear what was going on. He said that he would have his assistant come by in the morning and begin to work with her. The social worker was even more concerned. She did not wait until morning but called Child Protective Services, and she told Dr. Graham, "You have a pathological liar here. You have got to figure out where the baby came from."

Everything might have stayed on hold for the night, but then a piece of the puzzle came into the hands of Dr. Graham. It was not a piece she could put in place quite yet, but it was a frightening bit of information that sounded all too likely to have something to do with the baby.

After Darci's examination, Dr. Slocumb had gone home for the night, but Dr. Graham was still on duty. After dealing with some other matters for about an hour, she came back to the labor and delivery area. Some of the nurses were standing together, "whispering in a concerned manner." One of the persons in the group was Sister Rosemary Homrich, the midwife who worked at the base clinic but who split her time at the hospital. She had come to the hospital to admit one of her patients. But she was very upset. During the evening she had received two calls from Sam Ray. Sister Rosemary told them that she had examined Sam's wife that afternoon, but she had disappeared shortly afterward and had never come home. That sort of thing was not uncommon with patients served at the hospital, but Sister Rosemary said it was very unusual in this case. Cindy Ray came from a very stable home life, and just wasn't the sort to run off. What worried Sister Rosemary the most was that she was nearly full-term pregnant.

For the first time, the hospital staff had a possible

source of Darci's baby, but the idea was too terrible to contemplate. It became clear to Dr. Graham that the police had to be brought in. She called the police and then notified the nursery to lock its doors. She also asked the hospital security staff to place guards outside Darci's room. If she tried to leave the hospital, she was to be stopped. A pediatrician was called in for another examination of the baby. This time Dr. Graham wanted a specific estimate of when the baby had been born and whether there was any chance that she had been born vaginally.

At eleven o'clock that night, Nurse Elisabeth Koehler came on duty for the night shift in the labor and delivery area. She was informed about Darci. Nurse Koehler was the charge nurse, supervising the night shift. She took Darci as her own assignment and went in to meet her. She checked her vital signs, and found them slightly elevated but not dangerously so. She theorized that the slight fever might have been caused by an infection from a cut on Darci's foot for which she was taking antibiotics.

Darci, in her confession, would later speak of nurses taking her vital signs, and she made one of those strange Darci-like comments that is difficult to interpret: "Yeah, my husband was in the room with me and the nurses kept coming in and taking my blood pressure and stuff and my blood pressure even did what it was supposed to according to a woman who had just delivered a baby. It was low and they got me in the room and got me in the bed and it came back up. Don't ask me how I managed that one."

Elisabeth Koehler found Darci "calm, cool, collected, excited that she had a baby." And she was perfectly willing, at midnight, after a long, emotional day, to chat and get acquainted. She learned that

Elisabeth, as she was soon calling her, had been to Africa, and so the two talked a good deal about Darci's experiences in South Africa.

Ray Pierce had noticed when Darci first came into the emergency room that her gold chain was hanging around her neck, broken, and that the gold Krugerrand that she had brought home from South Africa was missing. Darci asked Elisabeth to check around for it. Could it be in the emergency room, or perhaps in the ambulance?

At about one o'clock in the morning, Darci and Ray, along with Elisabeth, walked over to see the baby in the nursery. Darci now had a gown and bathrobe on, and she had brushed her hair. Darci and Ray talked about how beautiful little Amanda was. Ray thought she looked like Darci, and Darci thought she had Ray's nose. They both seemed excited and happy, really quite typical of new parents. Of course, Darci not only knew that the baby was not hers; she knew that Elisabeth knew. And yet, she didn't mind putting on the act for her husband as Elisabeth listened.

Ray went home to rest and take care of his and Darci's dogs at that point, and the all-night standoff between Darci and the suspicious staff continued. Darci would eventually rest for fairly short naps, but most of the night she talked with Elisabeth. She told the story of the surrogate mother, and she gave much more of her background—the molar pregnancy, the possible infertility, her history with Ray. She also gave more details about the surrogate mother. She gave the woman the name Sherry Martin—the same name she had used the week before when she told a similar story to deceive Kelly Lyden, the hospital receptionist.

Darci told Elisabeth that she paid a midwife $2,000 to deliver the baby and stage Darci's pretended birth. The midwife had even left the umbilical cord

LULLABY AND GOODNIGHT

unclamped so that the birth would appear to have been done by the side of a highway. And she had saved a basin of blood and amniotic fluid to throw on Darci, to carry out the deception. Elisabeth was shocked. She couldn't imagine that any midwife, for any amount, would be willing to do such a thing. Darci quickly adjusted her story. She wasn't at all sure that the woman was really a certified nurse midwife. She may have only been a lay midwife; Darci had never seen any credentials.

Nurse Koehler's impression was that Darci always had an answer. If something didn't fit, she would back up quickly and adjust, but she never lost her confidence in her story, even though Elisabeth found the account beyond her own power to believe. And no matter what accusations came at Darci, her manner remained much the same: "calm, relaxed, and happy that she had this baby." Somehow she continued to believe that she was going to be allowed to keep it.

Dr. Slocumb had failed to see the signs of pregnancy in Darci, even before he had examined her. But Darci told Elisabeth that she had faked the pregnancy and deceived her husband. And she told her she had been adopted and had always suffered with that knowledge. She didn't want the baby, or her husband, to know that she had purchased the child. So she had gained weight, and her body had gone through physical changes. She claimed her breasts had enlarged and the nipples had gotten darker and more erect. And she had developed an aversion for pizza, which she had always loved. She even had morning sickness. She told both Dr. Leiby and Nurse Koehler, "You know how powerful the mind can be. People can fake pregnancies."

But Elisabeth remained skeptical. She certainly didn't believe the story of the surrogate mother. She didn't like Darci's admissions of such cold calculation, and she didn't like the way Darci lied to her husband. Something about Darci's never-ending talkativeness, her absence of regret for her lies, her coldness, all bothered Elisabeth. She found herself not liking the woman.

At one point in the long night, Darci said to Nurse Koehler, "Elisabeth, where did I go wrong? I thought this all out, and I thought it would work without any problem."

During the night Darci also asked about the baby on several occasions. The nursery had reported a slight abnormality in her blood—one that was not dangerous—but Darci wanted to check on this every little while.

Sometime between 1:30 and 3:00, Elisabeth confronted Darci with the information about Cindy. She told her, "Darci, you know things just are getting a little bit confusing here because now there's a missing woman in Albuquerque who is term and we don't know where she is and don't know where the baby is and that's not looking too good as far as the surrogate mother story goes."

Darci looked Elisabeth in the eye, calmly, and said she knew nothing of the woman.

At three o'clock, Dr. Slocumb confronted Darci directly, using Cindy's name for the first time. But Darci said in a confident voice that she didn't know anyone named Cindy Ray. "I'm sorry the woman is missing," she said, "but I don't know anything about it." She did not seem ruffled or worried. Elisabeth couldn't believe the surrogate mother story, but she found herself thinking that Darci was telling the truth about not knowing Cindy.

After this little meeting Darci and Elisabeth contin-

LULLABY AND GOODNIGHT

ued to talk. Some of what she told Elisabeth was part of a familiar pattern of Darci's fantasies—or lies. She said her family was upper middle class and that she got pretty much anything she wanted. She was close to her dad, and she spent a lot of time with him. She told more about her medical history and mentioned her infertility due to endometriosis. And Darci kept coming back to the difficulty she had with having been adopted. Elisabeth had an adopted sister, and so she understood something about the feelings of adoptive children, and the two shared some of their feelings and emotions. Darci seemed to attach to Elisabeth very quickly.

As morning was coming on, and Elisabeth's shift was ending, Darci kept asking whether she would be allowed to leave the hospital. Elisabeth told her that she didn't think so, that the whole matter of the surrogate mother had to be cleared up. But Darci was concerned about her husband's parents arriving that morning. She wondered whether she could be released, and she could use the baby's slightly elevated hematocrit number (a minor blood abnormality) as an excuse to her parents-in-law as to why the baby could not yet be released. She also said she would be happy to talk to anyone about the surrogate mother, but she stuck to that story as her explanation for where she had gotten the baby.

By then, Dr. Graham had called Dr. Slocumb and he had returned to the hospital. And then the two doctors, along with Dr. Leiby, the psychiatrist, and two officers from the Albuquerque Police Department, talked to Ray Pierce. They told him that Darci had not given birth to the baby. Everyone in the room had a hard time understanding how Ray could have lived with Darci all these months and not recognize that she wasn't pregnant. But when they saw his reaction—his devastation—those in the room "hadn't any doubt, whatsoever, that he had completely believed [in the pregnancy] up until that time."

Ray was startled and confused. As investigators asked him about Darci's story, he said he didn't believe that she had access to $10,000. Darci had claimed to have gotten the money from a trust fund, but Ray doubted that any such trust fund existed. He told the police and doctors that Darci had once claimed that if she needed money, she could "get by" as a prostitute, and strangely, he theorized that perhaps she had gotten the money that way. But his overall reaction was sadness and even some guilt. He said that he had been too busy and preoccupied; he should have gone with Darci to her doctor appointments, and then he would have known. Darci, after all, had claimed to be pregnant once before when she wasn't, and maybe he should have suspected something.

At about seven, Darci was told that some police investigators wanted to see her. She got up and combed her hair and put on a housecoat her husband had brought her, and then she sat in a wheelchair that Elisabeth used to take her to a conference room where she could meet the investigators. Dr. Slocumb went along, and they met Detective Tom Craig from the Albuquerque Police Department, who would direct the investigation. With him was his supervisor, Sergeant Lueras, and Special Investigators Coppinger and Thyssen from the air force.

Tom Craig was a no-nonsense kind of man. He was not big, but he was strongly built, and a certain toughness also came through in his voice. He got right to the point: "Darci, before we get started here, I want

LULLABY AND GOODNIGHT

to advise you of your rights, all right? We're investigating a situation here. We know that the baby is not your baby. So we suspect that a crime has been committed. I want you to understand that you have the right to remain silent. . . ." With that he read her all of her rights.

Darci asked, in response, "Am I being arrested for something here?" When Craig told her that he was only there to investigate at this point, Darci asked for the tape recorder to be turned off, and then she asked what the laws in New Mexico were covering surrogate mothers and purchasing babies.

What Darci told the investigators was the same story she had told the hospital staff. The mother of the baby was named Sherry Martin. Darci had met her outside an abortion clinic in Portland, many months before, and she had talked the girl out of having an abortion and had promised her $10,000 for her baby. The young woman had flown to New Mexico and then gone to Santa Fe to have the baby, which was delivered by a midwife. The midwife had put the blood on Darci, and together they had made up the story about having the baby on the highway.

But Darci's story didn't hold up. She couldn't remember the address of the house where she got the baby, and she said she hadn't written it down. She had relied on directions, but now she couldn't remember those, although she made up some vague details about the street being named "Cantrel or Cantran, or something like that." She didn't even know how long the drive was to Santa Fe.

When asked whether she had been on the air force base the day before, Darci lied and said she had never gone there at all that day, nor had she visited any of the medical facilities. And some of her explanations were not even plausible, as when she claimed the mud all over her feet and legs had come from a wet lawn in front of the midwife's house.

In explaining the story that she created with the midwife, perhaps Darci revealed a good deal about the actual lie she was telling at the moment. She said that she and the midwife worked out a complete scenario, and then carried off the deception in a way that would be believable. For instance, why had she taken the baby to a hospital? Darci answered, "To complete the scenario. . . . What kind of concerned parents could deliver their child by themselves and not go to a hospital and have the baby checked to make sure that it's okay? I had to establish with people here that the baby was indeed fine and that it had indeed been born, you know."

Tom Craig became impatient at times. At one point he told Darci, "I'll tell you what. None of this makes sense, okay? As far as we're concerned, none of this makes any sense, as far as this baby is concerned." He then asked Darci whether she knew Cindy Ray.

"No I don't," Darci replied very calmly.

"Is that baby you brought in here really Mrs. Ray's?"

"No, it's not. It's mine. I got it from a surrogate mother, just like I told you."

Finally Craig had had enough: "Yeah, let's get this right, huh? Let's think this out now. We've been sitting here listening to so much crap now for the last thirty minutes and in the meantime, there's a gal out there that's missing that we're worried about and you're not helping us at all. You've lied to us ever since you've sat down there. You've been lying to your husband for years now. When are you going to start telling the truth so we can get this straightened out?"

Darci answered resolutely, "I've not been lying to

my husband for years now and I have *not* been lying to you."

Craig challenged her again. "Everything that you have told us here is the truth? Is that what you are saying?" Darci said it was. "Yeah, and you expect us to believe it?"

At that point Steve Coppinger made a conscious decision to take a different approach with Darci. Coppinger had been putting clues together since he spoke with Dr. Slocumb and with Ray Pierce before he talked to Darci. He had already theorized from the blood and amniotic fluid on Darci—and meconium, a substance found in the amniotic fluid when a baby is under stress—that Darci had performed a C-section, probably on Cindy Ray. He had learned from Ray that Darci had gone hunting and that she had gutted and dressed large game animals, and that she had assisted a surgeon in South Africa. He concluded that Darci might be capable of performing the surgery to take Cindy's baby.

He had also received training on how to detect, in a defendant's behavior, whether an account was true, and he was convinced that Darci was lying: "The defendant in this case was—her eyes were very small pinpoints. She was concentrating very carefully on everything she was saying. There were times when she would get into areas where I felt she was not staying on what necessarily we were asking, she was getting off track. There was a point where we were asking about a midwife area and she started talking about family friends that were in football and stuff which wasn't relevant to what we wanted to stay on.

"I was having problems with what she was telling me. We are trained to pick up when people are creating stories as they go or maybe developing some type of falsehoods and I was getting that feeling as the case was continuing. The information she was giving me was just not very strong. She couldn't back it up with the kind of facts you expect someone to be aware of when they're involved in something that will be this important."

At one point Coppinger had become frustrated with these perceived lies, and he had shown his frustration in much the same language that Tom Craig had used. "I don't believe you one little bit," he told Darci. "We have a pregnant woman that's missing and you're coming up with a story that has all these holes in it and we're concerned." But Coppinger had also been trained in using different methods of interrogation. He was not a slick man by nature, no more than Tom Craig, but he sensed that the confrontational method would not work with Darci. As he would later explain, some people respond better to a "behavioral type of approach, where you show that you're concerned about their needs. . . . I decided to change my technique to the behavioral technique and try to empathize with the subject a little bit, be more friendly, show some concern for her."

The technique apparently worked, although it took a while. After a couple of hours of frustration, the investigators learned that they were going to have to vacate the room they had been using. They moved to another room and continued the questioning, but after a short time, they decided to take a break. During the break, Coppinger went to make a phone call. But he was soon paged and told that Darci wanted to talk to him alone.

What had happened while he was gone was that Elisabeth Koehler had been talking to Darci, and Elisabeth had asked Darci whether she wanted to see the baby. Elisabeth wondered whether holding the baby wouldn't spark some desire in Darci to admit the truth. Darci said yes, that she did want to see the baby and so Elisabeth went to the nursery and brought "Amanda" back. When Elisabeth entered the room, she was struck again by Darci's calm. She sat in the wheelchair with her hands in her lap, dressed in a hospital gown and a robe. She looked tired and pale but not nervous or frightened.

Elisabeth Koehler had seen plenty in her years in the ER and in maternity wards, but nothing like this. She was a young woman herself, and on first appearance she could seem rather frail. But there was a toughness about her, too, an athletic look in her leanness. She could be gentle with patients, but she had learned not to let them use her. She cared about Darci, but she cared more right then about the baby—and the mother, wherever she was. Darci's lying and manipulating really bothered her. She was almost certain by that time that the baby had been stolen from the missing Cindy Ray.

Elisabeth placed the baby in Darci's arms. It was wrapped in a "hospital green" blanket. She sat down across from Darci and watched. Darci was entranced as she looked down at the baby's face. She stroked its hair with one finger then held its little hand. "Amanda Michelle," she whispered.

About then, Dr. Susan Graham came into the room. She said hello to Darci and sat down, but she let Elisabeth do the talking.

Darci was enjoying "her" little baby. She looked up at Elisabeth and said, "I feel like a real person for the first time in my life. This baby is going to live its entire life with me."

Elisabeth didn't want to push things too quickly. She said nothing, and she let Darci enjoy the baby a little longer. "My mother didn't want me," Darci said. "She gave me away. But I won't do that." Darci stroked the baby's hair again, touched her face. And then she said, looking down, speaking as much to the baby as to the nurse, "I never, ever felt like a part of my family."

"Why, Darci?"

"It wasn't my real family. And they didn't love me. No one wanted me."

"But, Darci," Elisabeth said, "isn't this baby going to feel the same way? Don't you think she ought to be with her own family?"

Darci looked at Elisabeth for some time. She didn't answer, but something had changed in her eyes. She seemed to be probing within herself. For the first time all night, she had no quick answer.

"How do you think the baby's mother must feel? Won't you help us so we can find her?"

Still no answer. But Darci was beginning to look troubled.

"You're not going to be allowed to keep the baby, Darci. And we can't keep it here very long. If we can't find the mother, the baby will be put up for adoption —just the way you were. Darci, come on, you *know* this baby isn't really yours."

Darci was looking down now. She seemed ready to cry. "They'll never let me take her home," she mumbled.

Elisabeth spoke softly. "Darci, do you have any idea where this baby's mother might be?"

Something seemed to crack in Darci. Tears finally came. "Maybe something's happened. Maybe something terrible has happened. But I can't bring it up. I can't bring it up."

"Has something happened to the baby's mother?"

LULLABY AND GOODNIGHT

"I can't bring it up, Elisabeth. There may be something, but I can't bring it up."

"But, Darci, we need to help her. Can't you tell us where the baby's mother is?"

"Ray's going to leave me, Elisabeth. If he finds out the baby's not mine, he'll leave. I know he will."

"But, Darci—"

"I don't want to lie to him. If he finds out I've been lying, he'll leave."

"But, Darci, you've been lying all these months. You've been telling him you're pregnant. You told him this was his baby. You can't keep doing that."

Darci didn't respond for a time. She was obviously considering what she would do. But then, rather suddenly, she handed the baby over, and Elisabeth took it back to the nursery.

While Nurse Koehler was gone, Darci turned to Susan Graham. "I'm sorry for the way I acted when I came in last night," she said. "I'm sorry for the way I talked to you."

"That's all right. We just need to get this all straightened out now."

Darci nodded, but then she stared ahead and seemed to think.

As Elisabeth walked back to the nursery she had the distinct impression that Darci had given the baby up far too easily. She had wanted to be complete, a mother, part of a family. But when she saw that possibility begin to slip away, she let the baby go immediately, with very little emotion. Elisabeth also had the feeling that Darci was on the edge of confessing, and that she must convince her to tell them where the mother was, now, before Darci's hard edge returned.

"Darci," she said when she sat down by her again,

"think about the baby's mother. We need to take her baby back to her. Or if she's hurt, we need to help her."

Darci hung her head, and her pretty long hair fell forward. "I've done something horribly wrong," she said. "I'm afraid maybe something is wrong with the woman."

"What did you do, Darci?"

Darci was crying, but she wouldn't answer.

"Maybe you should tell this to someone who can help the mother."

Darci nodded. "I want to talk to that one policeman. The one in the beige pants."

Elisabeth hurried out and asked the policemen outside to get Steve Coppinger. And that's when he was paged. When he arrived in a few minutes, he could see that everything had changed. Darci had been almost upbeat at times, chatting about her baby, but now she had given up the illusion—not just to him, but to herself.

"Darci, is there something you want to tell me?"

"I want everyone to leave the room. I only want to talk to you. I don't want any tape recorders, either, and no notes."

"Okay." It was against regulations to talk to her alone, but he knew he better take what he could get. If Cindy was still alive somewhere, they needed to act fast. He turned to the nurse and doctor. "Could you two wait right outside?"

They said they would, and they left.

Coppinger sat down by Darci, and she began to talk. She was visibly upset, and yet she remained calm and relatively coherent. "I'm afraid I've done something," she told him. "I told you that I didn't go out to the base yesterday, but I did. There was a woman there. I'm afraid I did something. I'm remembering things.

Things are coming back to me now. I'm remembering terrible, terrible things."

"What things, Darci?"

Darci talked of the woman on the base, of taking her in a car, but she was jumping about now, not really admitting anything.

"Darci, what happened? Where is this woman now?"

"I've done terrible things. Terrible things. Oh, God, Steve, I killed her. What's going to happen to me? What will my parents think? What will Ray think?"

"Darci, calm down now. Everything's okay. It's good you're telling me. We can get things straightened out now. Can you tell us where she is?"

Darci rambled for a few minutes, talking about the gun that wasn't real and taking Cindy in her car—although she only called her "the woman" and never Cindy. She was very upset, and Coppinger got her a drink of water and tried to calm her down. Finally, however, Darci told him that she could remember where the woman was, and she could tell him how to get there. "But don't make me go up there, all right? Will you promise I don't have to go up there?"

"Darci, you don't have to do anything you don't want to do."

"You're not going to tell anyone, are you? Please don't tell anyone what I told you."

Coppinger was stunned. She had just confessed a murder to a policeman. How could she expect him not to tell anyone? He kept talking to her, calmly, explaining what had to happen, and finally Darci agreed to ride in a car to show him where the body was. She didn't have to look at it, and he would keep her away from the actual site, but she needed to show him how to get there. She agreed to that.

Coppinger left the room and began to gather a

group of air force and Albuquerque police investigators to make the trip.

Elisabeth returned to Darci and sat down next to her. She put her arm around Darci's shoulders.

"Elisabeth, I killed her," Darci said. "My mother is going to hate me."

CHAPTER 8

It was nearing eleven o'clock in the morning when the little caravan of cars left for the Manzano mountains to find Cindy Ray. Throughout the night the officers had held out some hope that Cindy might be alive, but by this time, given the patchy information Darci had given Steve Coppinger, that hope was gone.

Tom Craig drove, and Darci sat up front with him. She had a washcloth to wipe her face with, and she was still upset, but she was under control, and she had no difficulty remembering the route they had to travel. In the backseat, behind Craig, was Steve Coppinger, and behind Darci was Elisabeth Koehler. She should have been off duty at seven that morning, but she had established a rapport with Darci, and the officers felt they needed her to go along.

Behind Craig's car were a couple of black-and-whites from the Albuquerque Police Department, an ambulance, and other cars from Air Force OSI. No one was exactly sure who would have jurisdiction. The crime had happened on national forest land, but the abduction had happened on the air force base. Local police, the FBI, or perhaps the military could possibly end up handling the case.

Each person in the car with Darci remembered slightly different details, but the general impression of each was the same: that Darci was remarkably in control most of the way to the scene. According to Elisabeth Koehler, as Tom Craig drove up I-40 toward the mountains—going *very* fast, without his safety belt on—Darci "just chatted."

Unquestionably, Darci was upset, but she was really quite composed. "She wasn't crying, as far as I remember," Elisabeth later explained. "We were talking about—it was the middle of the day. I was hot and thirsty. I wanted an iced tea. She talked about the intercom thing and how it was okay for Tom to go ahead and talk on it. She didn't mind; it was okay. And I asked her how—we were just talking about are we going to be able to see the body, is this the right way."

Elisabeth asked Darci whether Cindy had delivered the baby vaginally or whether Darci had done a C-section. Darci only said, "I took the baby." According to Elisabeth, Darci also said that she had used a model gun that looked real. "[Darci said that] it had the same serial number on it, shot blanks, that it was not a deadly weapon, and that that's what she used to get Cindy Ray to go with her."

Elisabeth also said that as they were turning onto Highway 14, Darci joked with her, saying, "Is this the point where I'm supposed to say I'm not going to say anything until I get my attorney? Is this the point where I'm supposed to be quiet?" But she wasn't serious: "She was joking. She continued to talk. She didn't stop talking after that."

The two men in the car did not remember Darci making these jokes, nor did they remember the mention of the gun. But if memories were different about a

LULLABY AND GOODNIGHT

few details, they were the same in one important matter. All three in the car remembered Darci recognizing the exit at Tijeras when she saw the name, and then saying that right at that point she could have turned left, under the freeway, and returned. And she thought about doing just that. But she decided to continue on to the right and into the Manzano mountains.

As the car drew ever closer to the turnoff and the site where Cindy's body would be found, Darci began to show more emotion. She became very upset, and finally she moaned, "Oh, God, don't let her be dead." But then she said, "She's dead. I know she's dead."

Highway 14 is a winding road, cut into a canyon full of junipers and piñon pine. At one point, near a sheer cliff, Darci said that was perhaps the point where her car had skidded off the road as she had been driving on the rain-soaked highway, returning to Albuquerque.

As Tom Craig spotted gravel roads, he kept asking Darci whether each one was the proper place to turn left again. But Darci would look and then tell him no, not yet. She had no trouble identifying Wantoms Road, the one she had taken the day before. But by the time she had reached this point, she was becoming increasingly agitated. She reached over the seat and grabbed Elisabeth's hand, and she repeated, "Oh, God, don't let her be dead!"

A little way up the road, Darci saw another left turn, and she suddenly became almost hysterical, screaming that she was afraid that the woman was dead and that she didn't want to go up there. But then she realized this was not the correct turn, and she calmed down and said to go a little farther. When she reached the correct turn, she went into hysterics all over again.

Coppinger hardly knew what to make of this: the extreme reaction, the delay, and then the same reaction.

In any case, Darci's reaction, as Craig turned up the little road and over the cattle guard, was to scream and cry. Up the road a very short distance was a clump of trees—a few fairly tall piñons, with some juniper and underbrush beneath. Darci pointed and screamed, "There she is. Oh, God, there she is. She's dead. I don't want to be here."

Elisabeth saw the body plainly, behind the trees but only a short distance from the road. Farther up the road, the body was harder to spot, because the trees obscured the direct line of sight.

Tom Craig drove on by and parked the car a little way past the actual site, and then he and other investigators got out and found the body. They quickly checked Cindy's vital signs, and then they instructed the other officers to secure the area and begin the initial steps of investigation.

Darci, meanwhile, was becoming frantic. Elisabeth was frightened by her wildness: "She was holding me and crying, hugging me, holding my hands, very upset to the point of almost screaming that she had done something terribly wrong, that she killed her, that she hoped she wasn't dead. She had mentioned that her Krugerrand was there. I asked her if she wanted me to ask the police to look for it and she didn't really respond to that but she said her Krugerrand was there and that she wanted to get out of there, and at one point she asked me to kill her. She said, 'Eli, kill me. Please kill me.'"

Darci had apparently heard some of the other nurses use Elisabeth's nickname, and she had picked up on it.

Darci kept pleading to be taken away from the

scene, but cars were packed in behind them on the narrow road. Elisabeth found herself frightened. Darci continued to scream and cry, and no one stayed near the car to help. But eventually the cars were backed out, and Steve Coppinger and Special Investigator Butch Flint came back to the car and honored Darci's request. Elisabeth, exhausted from the long ordeal, had to wait a little longer, but she too was eventually driven back to Albuquerque in another car.

Tom Craig stayed at the scene, and in fact, at one point drove to a little store on Highway 14 and called the FBI. Eventually, the APD (Albuquerque Police Department) would handle the case, under the direction of Tom Craig, himself, but Craig felt that the FBI had to be notified. Agent Gene Hughes, of the Albuquerque office of the FBI would end up working closely with the APD on the investigation, and they would later help to put together information about Darci's background in Oregon.

Coppinger and Flint drove Darci back to Albuquerque, took Darci to a secure office in the OSI headquarters, and received her formal confession. And it was on this return trip to town that Darci demonstrated one of those strange qualities that the defense would use to argue for her insanity, and the prosecution would interpret as part of her callousness.

As Coppinger drove away from the scene, he noticed that Darci changed immediately. "She calmed down completely, became very cool and collected." And she began, as on the trip up to the mountains, to chat with the men. "I'm still wearing the ring that I was then," Coppinger explained. "It's a Krugerrand gold ring. She noticed it and commented that she had a Krugerrand necklace and she began talking about her visit to South Africa."

Most of the way back to Kirtland Air Force Base,

Darci talked about her experiences in South Africa. When Coppinger and Flint took her inside the OSI offices, Darci accepted a soft drink that they offered her, and then she called her husband, with their permission. The conversation surprised Coppinger: "She called him up and asked for some clothing items, cosmetics and also kind of unusual, a book of photographs from South Africa. We had been carrying on a discussion about South Africa on the way down from the crime scene and she, I guess, wanted to show me the pictures she had taken while she was there."

Ray Pierce remembered much more emotion, however. He said that he had never known Darci to be so upset. She kept crying and telling him she was sorry. She told him that she didn't remember killing Cindy, but she knew that she had done it. She had taken the police to a place she never remembered seeing before, and yet, she had known how to get there. Ray was overwhelmed. He told Darci that her body might have committed the crime, but her mind hadn't. The woman he had married wasn't capable of doing such a thing.

Yet somewhere in the conversation Darci asked for the photos of South Africa. This was a woman who twenty minutes before had been in hysterics, screaming, "Please, kill me." But, she became so involved in her conversation about South Africa that she wanted to show a man—a man who was in the process of developing a murder case against her—her travel pictures. And she made the request in a phone conversation in which she was admitting to her husband that she *was* a murderer.

Madness or callousness? Or both? Or something too complex for most of us to comprehend?

* * *

LULLABY AND GOODNIGHT

Steve Coppinger and Butch Flint took Darci's statement about the crime—her true confession, as compared to the false confession story about the surrogate mother. Clearly, the investigators set out to put Darci at ease from the beginning. They had her sit down at a little table, and they turned on a tape recorder, but then both joked about the need for it only because they wrote so badly. They "got real official" and showed her their badges, but then they told her that any time she wanted to take a break for a Coke, or whatever, they would just stop.

Darci wanted to know how many times she would have to "go over it," and Coppinger assured her that they would only go through the story once. "Don't let anyone put anything in your mouth and that's it. We won't ask you again."

Flint advised her of her rights, and he did advise her that she was a suspect of an "alleged offense of homicide," and then he told her of her right to various protections, under the law. Darci waived her right to counsel. But then she asked, very calmly, what the punishment for homicide was. Flint hedged. "Uh, see, the word we use is suspected." And Coppinger added, "Yeah, you are guilty of nothing."

They took turns assuring her a couple more times each, that she was only suspected. "You're guilty of drinking a Sprite, that's what you're guilty of," Coppinger joked. And Flint threw in, *"Holding* a Sprite in your hand, that's the only thing I know of."

But Darci could not be so easily sidetracked. "Okay," she asked, "what happens if in this tape recording if I tell my story and it looks like I'm guilty?"

Coppinger told her that they weren't in the Soviet Union. A "complicated system" would assure her that she was physically all right, "that emotionally, and everything else you're stable and then at that point, uh, you get attorneys, there's a lot of discovery and things like that and, uh, you know, things you shouldn't even worry about at this point."

Interestingly enough, Coppinger, in bringing up the issue of emotional stability, was perhaps revealing his own sense of what might be Darci's defense. Maybe he suspected, himself, that Darci was unstable, or maybe he knew that would be the only argument in Darci's situation. Either way, it might have served as Darci's first suggestion as to how she would have to approach her case. What she saw in her life, however, was pressure and stress rather than instability.

As she began the interview Darci seemed very relaxed. When Coppinger asked her who lived in her house, Darci said that it was just she and her husband and two cocker spaniels. When he asked whether anyone else, relatives or whatever, lived there, Darci said, "Two black widows."

Coppinger laughed and Flint said, "Do you tolerate black widows?"

Darci joked, "No, we burn them."

As Coppinger asked about Darci's early background, going back to her medical problems in Portland, Darci gave some inaccurate answers, but perhaps ones she believed. She said that she had "lost a baby," and described other medical problems, such as endometriosis, that Dr. Sargent later denied. She claimed that she never told her husband about the problem because "he's never really shared in any of those women-type things that happen." But she added, ". . . if I were a man, I certainly wouldn't want anything to do with woman stuff either."

Darci told about getting hooked for a while on a

painkiller the doctor gave her, and she built something of a case that she had been through a lot of stress and multiple physical problems.

Coppinger continued to show a good deal of empathy for Darci's problems, probably to encourage her to open up. Darci told him how desperate she was to have a baby, how much it meant to her. She also revealed her prime motivation for all the lying she had done: ". . . the reason Ray married me in December is because he thought I was carrying his baby."

In court, Ray would deny that. He would say that he loved her and planned to marry her, and the timing had nothing to do with the pregnancy. Whether that is true or not, what is important is what Darci believed.

Simple statements also gave a hint of Darci's complicated motivations: ". . . I started letting everybody know that I was pregnant, I guess I wanted to be so badly." And then the pressure kept building. Finally she hinted of some mental difficulties: "I think I was losing touch. I was getting really desperate trying to figure out what I was gonna do, how I was gonna find someone to give me their baby now."

Coppinger, however, had her back up a little, and once again, in showing empathy, he perhaps planted some ideas for Darci's defense. He asked about the pressure on Darci from Ray and from her family. Darci talked about her family, told about leaving home because she wanted to be "her own person," about not being invited to her cousin's wedding.

Coppinger followed with, ". . . do you feel like inside there was kind of an internal thing that you actually really wanted to have a strong family and you weren't getting it?"

Darci's answer revealed her own sense of self in relation to her family: "Yeah, I did and . . . and for a long time I think I walked around with a chip on my shoulder because of the fact that I'm adopted, but I sit down and I've thought about it a lot and I don't think I can take all the blame myself for the way I feel about being adopted, because my oldest brother, whenever we had fights or anything, he would always say to me, he would say to me, '. . . I don't have to take that from you because you're not my real sister.'

"Uhm, my whole family has always treated me very special. I've always had everything I've wanted because I'm the youngest, I'm a girl, I'm adopted, I'm the only girl, but it's like I had all the cards in my hand as far as getting everything I wanted, but I don't . . . I don't know if I should have gotten everything that I wanted all the time, because it made me feel even that much more of an outsider and it put a lot of distance between my brothers and myself, and my youngest brother in particular. He's nine years older than I am and he felt this real, 'Well, gosh, Mom and Dad give you everything, and we didn't get anything when we were young.'"

At times, Darci said things that were startlingly straightforward. During her trial, the defense would later argue that one part of Darci's mind always believed she was pregnant, that she lived in a double kind of reality. But Darci told Coppinger and Flint, ". . . I had fabricated the pregnancy to the point where people were getting to the point, well she's getting supposedly overdue, you know, why aren't the doctors doing something?"

What built the pressure, more than anything, was her mother's phone calls, wondering when the baby would be coming, and it was that pressure that led to the story of the induction, and then the delay for a second date. And then added pressure led to the simple, logical conclusion: "I had to figure out some-

LULLABY AND GOODNIGHT

thing to do before five o'clock, didn't I, when we [were] supposed to go to the hospital."

Darci's story was that as she set out that day, she first filled her car with gas because she was going to leave. She was just going to disappear and let everyone wonder what happened to her. Coppinger asked whether she felt that her family didn't really care about her. "I think they care about me," Darci said, "but I think they wanted the baby more than . . . wanting to talk about what my situation actually was."

There is a circular kind of logic in this. She was the one who wanted the baby so desperately, and she was the one who had convinced them that a baby was coming. Yet from her perception, the pressure to have the baby was coming not from herself, but from her family. Instead of saying, "I didn't want to admit I had been lying all that time, so I went out to find a baby," her logic is that her family wanted the baby so much that she didn't dare let them down.

Another crucial question was why Darci took the gun with her. If she had only planned to drive away and disappear, and she hadn't taken so much as a toothbrush with her, why would she need a weapon? Why—unless she had a plan when she left the house? Darci's answer was that she kept the gun in the car for her own protection. It would not shoot, but it might scare someone off. After the crime, however, Ray looked for the gun at home and found it missing. He said it was normally in their house or in the garage.

Darci described her long wait outside the clinic and the conversation with Cindy in which she asked to talk to her about her own pregnancy and promised "not to hurt her." This, in and of itself, was an interesting statement. If the conversation was friendly, supposedly to invite Cindy over for iced tea and a chat, why would Darci tell her that she wasn't going to hurt her? She denied using the gun at that point, but she admitted that Cindy looked frightened. Wouldn't it seem more likely that Cindy's reactions and Darci's promise not to hurt her would only occur if she had been holding the gun in her hand?

Darci said her memory was patchy from that point on. She remembered little about her conversation with Cindy, and even though she could track the trip to the mountains the following day, she had lapses in what she recalled about the drive there with Cindy. But she did remember that she and Cindy were about the same height and that Cindy had dark hair, as did Darci. She also said that Cindy was "very, very pregnant." Cindy certainly had the qualifications Darci would have needed: someone ready to give birth, and someone who looked sufficiently like herself to be carrying a baby who would look reasonably like her child.

According to Darci's account, when she and Cindy reached the murder site, she only wanted to get out and talk. She portrayed this time as pleasant and friendly. While Darci emphasized her own stress, she expressed no empathy for a young woman who must have been terrified. Over and over she said that Cindy was relaxed and calm. And while she could describe Cindy and her clothing, even remember some details about their conversation, she had no idea what "the woman's" name was.

Evidence at the scene did show one clear footprint of Cindy's shoe. And the print had to have been made with Cindy standing, with her weight on her feet. So it is likely that Cindy and Darci did walk and talk. But when Darci was examined, she did not show the scratches that she should have received had a fight

LULLABY AND GOODNIGHT

occurred. There may have been some struggle, but it can not have been extensive.

Evidence also showed that Cindy was struck in the back of the head with a blunt instrument, perhaps the butt of the gun. Cindy was awkward, being so large in front, but she was strong and athletic. If Darci had come at her, with any warning, she certainly would have put up a very good fight. But if she were struck hard and stunned, she may not have been able to defend herself.

Darci claimed not to remember much of anything until she was heading down the canyon in the car, going very fast. But as she reached the valley, she certainly admitted to her own calculating mental process: "And then I started thinking, I can't just show up someplace with this baby in my arms around here and not have some kind of story."

This was Darci's fourth explanation for how she had obtained the baby. The first three stories—that the baby was her own, that it was a black market baby, that she had hired a surrogate mother to deliver the baby for her—were all told with equal sincerity. Certainly this last story was the closest to the truth, since objective evidence backed up much of it, and since it was clearly incriminating at that point. But Darci earned her right to be doubted by telling so many lies before. Surely no one will ever know whether Darci built a cover story of stress, amnesia, and a kind of mental break, or whether she finally told all.

What did seem clear to the psychologists and psychiatrists who later spent many hours with her—those hired by the prosecution as well as those on the defense side—was that the amnesia probably was real, and that the account, however self-serving, probably was close to, if not exactly, what she remembered. What was left wide open was the question of her capability of controlling her actions.

As to the lies she concocted before she told the truth, Darci's account was once again very strange. On the one hand, she admitted to calculations: She couldn't just show up with a baby unless she had "a story." Yet she told Coppinger and Flint that she actually believed the story about the surrogate mother: "Yeah, it . . . it . . . it's what I believed, it really is and then they brought the baby into me, I wanted to see her and they brought the baby in and they let me hold her and I had been holding her and all of a sudden I got the feeling that I had done something so bad like there was . . . there was something terrible there that I wasn't remembering and then the story I was remembering, it wasn't a story, it actually was [Darci starts to cry] and . . . and . . . one nurse and one doctor were sitting in there with me and things started flooding back, terrible, terrible things about driving in the woods and about a baby and about another person being there and that you had told me, the group had told me about a woman who was pregnant and she was missing and I started thinking about who was this person that I was getting while I was seeing in these . . . these images that I was getting while I was holding the baby and then I . . . I had started realizing that, my God, maybe it was the same person and maybe I had done something really terrible, and so then I asked for you to come in because of all the investigators that had been there you seemed to be the one that wasn't getting excited. The other guy that was with you, he has blue eyes, they're really bloodshot and he was like, he was being really excited and he was shaking over this whole thing and he was . . . he was playing this game with me of 'Come on you can tell me, I'm on your side,' but yet the tone of his voice and the actions were, 'Come on, wench, spill it, tell us the story and just get it over with, we want to get out of here,' and I had the feeling that . . . that if I said one thing, if I even said, my God, you know, I'm having these feelings, that they were just gonna slap on the cuffs and haul me off and so I asked for you because I figured I could sit down and . . . and tell you that these things were coming to me and I didn't know where they were coming from or why and this terrible feeling of something I had done and then when you and I were talking and all of it started coming back as we were talking more and more. And we went out there [Darci cries again] and we found her.

"I don't remember doing any of this though, really. I mean, it's . . . it's like a nightmare that you have at night and you wake up from and the bogeyman's not coming through your window, and there's not burglars walking around in your house.

"And I'm expecting to wake up any minute here, you know. It's like somebody slap me, or something, because it's still . . . it's still not there. I didn't, I mean, I can sit here and say that this is what's happened, but I didn't do this. I mean, I didn't. You know."

That, of course, became the great question. Was Darci out of control? Did she commit the crime, or did she act in some mental state that cleansed her of responsibility?

Before the interview ended, Steve Coppinger went back through the story, and he pushed Darci for more details. She did remember some. She remembered that she and Cindy, in their struggle, had fallen out of the car and onto the gravel road. In one of those curious moments that characterize Darci's conversations, when Coppinger asked her whether it was big gravel or small gravel, Darci laughed and said, "Sore gravel."

After the tape was turned off, Darci strolled around the outer office and looked at the pictures and plaques on the wall. She was still sipping at her soft drink. It was difficult for Coppinger to imagine that this was a woman who had committed a brutal murder less than twenty-four hours earlier. She seemed calm and controlled, and hardly aware of her peril.

Ironically, it had only been a few hours since Sam Ray had come to the same office. He had been nervous and worried, and very upset. Darci was placid by comparison.

When Tom Craig showed up to take her to the Albuquerque police station, she was friendly and cooperative. This was the blue-eyed man with the bloodshot eyes—the one Darci had disliked during the interrogation at the hospital. But she was perfectly friendly with him now. She got into the car with Craig and FBI Agent Hughes. The radio was on, and soon a news broadcast began. Hughes winced and Craig reached to turn the radio off. They didn't want her to hear a report of her own crime. But Darci told them it was all right, to leave the news on. As it turned out, the news did not include a report of the murder.

At the police station, Darci was examined for scratches or bruises, and she was photographed and fingerprinted. Throughout all these procedures, Craig said that Darci was pleasant, calm, and relaxed. She was obviously intelligent and much more articulate than most of the criminals he was accustomed to dealing with.

On Monday, July 27, Darci was formally charged with murder and kidnapping. Judge James O'Toole ordered that she be held under $500,000 bond in the

LULLABY AND GOODNIGHT

Bernalillo County Detention Center in Albuquerque. A preliminary hearing was set for August 6. Ray was still stunned by all that had happened, but he vowed allegiance to Darci.

Earlier, Tom Craig and his team of investigators had combed the murder site for clues, and they had found something clear-cut. When Cindy's body was removed, under her was Darci's Krugerrand necklace, the broken chain fitting the remainder of the chain that had been around Darci's neck when she arrived at the hospital.

This gave the prosecution conclusive physical evidence that Darci had been at the crime scene. Confessions can end up thrown out on technicalities or, for some reason, mistrusted, so corroborating physical evidence is crucial. Mr. Hartshorn, who had driven up the road and had gotten permission to shut the Volkswagen door, came forward and provided another key element: an eyewitness who had seen Darci at the crime scene, and had seen Cindy on the ground beneath the trees.

All the other evidence—the car key with human tissue in its grooves, the pathologist's report on the blows to Cindy's head, the witnesses who had seen Darci waiting in the clinic parking lot, the fact that Darci had not given birth—everything corroborated the essential story that Darci told and filled in some of the blanks in her memory. The case would not hinge on *whether* Darci had taken Cindy's life; it would depend entirely on Darci's psychological state.

Darci was confined in the Bernalillo County Jail, downtown in Albuquerque, and for a time she seemed to disappear. Everyone wanted to know who she was and what had motivated her. At the jail, the evaluation process began as mental health specialists were called in. Those who met Darci all had the same reaction: She was sweet, polite, and charming. She was depressed and fearful, and yet, she could converse with them as though she were the girl next door chatting over the fence. Reports circulated that other prisoners were harsh, even threatening, because they found her crime so disgusting, but jail officials denied that she was being mistreated.

Tom Jameson, a public defender who became one of Darci's lawyers, would later claim that Darci received brutal treatment upon entering the jail. He said that she was put in a small cell and all her clothes were taken away. Not even bed sheets or blankets were allowed on her bunk, nor could she have a toothbrush. While this was supposed to be for her own good, to keep all devices away from her that she could use to commit suicide, a guard was also looking in on her almost constantly. Few situations could be more intimidating and dehumanizing than to be left naked in a room and then watched all the time. Darci was terrified and constantly wondering what was to become of her.

Or at least that's what Darci told Jameson. Jail officials denied that such treatment ever took place. Darlene Carr, one of her jailers, reported that Darci was under constant watch, for her own protection. She said that Darci was very jumpy in the beginning, like a nervous "scared rabbit." She couldn't sleep much and wanted nothing to eat. But after a time, she adjusted. She began to read and write and exercise, and she became more talkative. But throughout her stay, until the following spring, she was kept in a nine-foot by seven-foot room for twenty-three hours of every day. She came out for two half-hour exercise periods only. It was a lonely existence, at best.

Shortly after Darci was jailed, John Bogren was

LULLABY AND GOODNIGHT

assigned to serve as her public defender, and Tom Jameson was added to the team a few days later. John Bogren was the man who handled all capital cases that came into the public defender's office. Since it appeared possible that the district attorney would go for the death penalty, Bogren received the assignment.

Bogren had a touch of the Colombo in him. Normal dress for him around the office was a pair of jeans, a T-shirt, and an unbuttoned flannel shirt. He was an intense man who hated the death penalty and saw it as his job to "keep people alive." His graying hair and mustache were a little wild, his manner sort of blue-collar. He was a transplant from Chicago, but he seemed to thrive in the casual atmosphere of New Mexico. He had a way of shuffling his feet, waving his arms, speaking in bursts, swearing, and above all, saying exactly what was on his mind.

Tom Jameson was quite the opposite. He was a natty looking young man with dark hair and glasses, button-down collar shirts, and a neat mustache. His voice rang with sincerity and poise. He came across as a very nice person who cared a great deal about Darci. But in one regard he was much like John Bogren: He spoke his mind, openly and sometimes even passionately.

When these two men met Darci, both of them were shocked. Public defenders become accustomed to the hard characters they often have to deal with. They are sometimes forced to defend people they can hardly stomach. But Darci was from another world: neat, clean, well-spoken, innocent. She behaved like a frightened little animal, and both of them responded with a desire to protect her. They knew what she had done, but they couldn't believe for a minute that she was dangerous. Surely, she was a victim herself.

As the case developed, it began to take on a very

high profile. Bogren and Jameson knew that this would put pressure on the DA's office to play hardball. They soon found out that the "boys across the street" were not willing to plea-bargain in any way that looked reasonable to them. Bogren decided to ask Jackie Robins to join the team. She was New Mexico's chief public defender, and that gave her the power to sink money into the case. Mental health experts didn't come cheap, but from all appearances, the DA's office was going to spend big to bring in expert witnesses.

Jackie Robins seemed rather mild-mannered on the surface, but she could be a bulldog. A small, dark-haired woman with glasses, she was usually polite, but she shifted into another gear at times, becoming aggressive. She was not the leader of the team, but she brought clout to the threesome.

Robins also brought the commitment to pursue a defense of mental illness. Bogren hated psychological mumbo jumbo, but he knew that Darci had committed the crime. The only possible defense was a psychological one. Even more, he had met with her and seen the contradiction: She did not seem capable of cold-blooded murder. He thought that a jury might agree. Surely, the initial reaction of everyone hearing the story was the same: No normal person could do such a thing. And that was on the defense team's side. But he and Jameson and Robins knew something else. New Mexico laws made a mental illness defense almost impossible.

Still, it was the only chance, and they felt that if ever a case could make it on those grounds, this was the one. Above all, the defense team came to believe absolutely that Darci deserved their commitment. Their passions were united in that regard. They were certain that Darci needed help, not punishment, and they were going to do everything in their power to give her the representation she deserved.

A grand jury was called for August 6. Darci was charged with first-degree murder during a kidnapping, which meant that the prosecution could, if it chose, seek the death penalty. An additional charge of child abuse was brought against Darci, since the procedure she had used put Millie's life in such serious danger. At this point, Greta Thomas was handling the case for the prosecution. She presented the basic evidence and received a ruling that granted a trial.

Soon after the hearing Harry Zimmerman, born in New York and educated in Ohio, was assigned to the case. He was a young man, in his thirties, but he already had plenty of trial experience with the DA's office. He had learned to love cowboy boots since moving to Albuquerque, maybe partly because he was very short, but he made no attempt to look the part of the local southwesterners. His curly hair always seemed rather disheveled, and his beard gave him a certain professorial appearance. As an undergraduate he had majored in journalism, minored in dramatic arts, and his secret dream was still to become an actor.

Zimmerman's partner, Michael Cox, added soon after, was as experienced as Harry and an effective cross-examiner. He was also a bearded man, but a relatively quiet person, not as demonstrative as Zimmerman. His manner was controlled and considerate.

If the defense had the advantage that most people assumed Darci must be "crazy," the prosecution had perhaps even more advantages. Darci had disturbed a taboo. Killing an expectant mother was something inhuman and repulsive. The crime was so disgusting that not many people were comfortable with the idea that Darci might end up back in society. The person-on-the-street impulse, in other words, was to dismiss Darci as mentally ill, but not to feel a great deal of compassion for her either. She was, in their minds, a kind of aberration and should be shunted off somewhere, never to be seen, never to be a threat to normal people again.

Both teams of attorneys had the same problem. Both had to make Darci human. The defense wanted to prove that she was an abused child, a pitiable little girl who had suffered and finally cracked, but someone who could be restored and someone worth restoring.

The prosecution had to show that Darci's motivations were actually understandable and even rather common. They had to prove that she was a greedy young woman who wanted something, planned a way to get it, and then carried out the plan—much the way any other thief would operate.

The defense team had another huge disadvantage. Virtually no one in New Mexico had been successful with an insanity defense since a change in the law in 1982. The defense would have to prove not only that Darci had psychological problems, but that she was out of control and unable to understand the difference between right and wrong. New Mexico allowed no temporary insanity plea, and so the mental disease had to be proved as a long-standing problem.

Even more difficult, the state allowed three verdicts: not guilty, guilty, or guilty but mentally ill. On the surface, "guilty but mentally ill" would seem a compromise verdict. Most people who hear the term assume that it means that the guilty person would be treated differently from a person convicted of being "guilty." It implies, for instance, that the person would receive care, would perhaps be placed in a mental hospital rather than in a prison. But that is not the case. In fact, "guilty but mentally ill" is really only another guilty verdict. Every criminal entering a prison in New Mexico is evaluated and given mental care according to the needs perceived by prison officials (some would say that all prisoners receive the same absence of care). Or in other words, "guilty but mentally ill" would be a victory for the prosecution.

If that wasn't difficult enough, the law does not allow juries to receive instruction on what verdicts mean. Jurors probably assume that "guilty but mentally ill" means something quite different from "guilty," at least in terms of treatment, and so they would tend to see such a verdict as a compromise.

This situation left the defense with a tough battle ahead of them. But they remained committed to the diagnosis they were receiving from the psychiatrists they had hired to evaluate Darci. They believed she was seriously mentally ill.

On the other hand, the prosecution had a challenge to achieve a verdict of first-degree murder. Women are rarely put to death in the United States, and certainly a pretty, innocent-looking nineteen-year-old with mental difficulties of some sort—whether "insane" or not—would win the sympathy of a jury. The same people who might feel that she must be taken out of society might hesitate to put her to death.

And could the prosecution prove premeditation, which was necessary for a first-degree murder charge? Darci claimed that stress had led her to an irrational, impulsive decision. Zimmerman and Cox would have to show planning and considered decision making. Once again, a jury might see enough premeditation to convict for a life sentence, but they might be more likely to buy the defense's notion of an impulsive act under stress if they thought the ultimate result would be the young woman's death.

Still, Zimmerman and Cox would go for the death penalty in Darci's case if they thought it was justified. What they hoped, instead, was that the case could be plea-bargained. That's also what the defense wanted. But both sides soon realized that they were very far apart on what Darci's sentence should be.

CHAPTER 9

When Sam came home from the hospital after seeing his little daughter for the first time, his Mormon "brothers and sisters" were there. Carolyn Yoss, the president of the women's organization known as the Relief Society, had so many calls from people who wanted to help that she couldn't give everyone things to do. Brother Greer, the president of the Elders' Quorum, stayed at the trailer, answered the phone, helped Sam review his insurance papers, and helped him think through the things he would need to do. Bishop Prettyman began arrangements to have Cindy's body shipped home to Utah, and he rarely left Sam's side.

Msgt. Ed Dickson helped Sam look at his options with the air force. He set up a memorial fund in the community that would eventually bring in thousands of dollars, intended especially for the baby and for Luke. He also spent many hours with Sam, just talking. Ed was a religious Christian, and he and Sam had often talked about religion in the past. Now they shared their perspectives and tried to get a grip on what death meant in the context of Sam's trust in a future life.

The children were Sam's major concern. He never

left Luke for a minute. When arrangements had to be made at a funeral home or on base, Sam took Luke so that his son wouldn't have to face any additional insecurity. Sam's father had flown in on the first available flight, and he went with Sam almost everywhere. He entertained Luke while Sam filled out papers or met with police and air force investigators, but the three stayed together.

Over and over Luke kept asking the same question: "Daddy, where's my mommy?" At two-and-a-half, he was a blond-haired boy, with large, bright blue eyes, and he was remarkably articulate. He had always been active and happy, but he had turned quiet now. He could be distracted at times, and he would seem to return more or less to normal. But then he would run back to Sam, and when he did, he would ask the same question again.

Each time Sam tried to explain. Mommy was in heaven with Heavenly Father. If Sam and Luke were good boys, they would see her again someday. In time, Luke could give the answer as easily as he could ask the question, but he still kept asking. Sam held him and hugged him and tried to comfort him, but Luke was preoccupied with his question. He started to wet his pants again, even though he had been toilet trained for a time.

Sam had some decisions to make. He had no trouble with most of them. The baby's name would be Amelia Monik, and she would be called Millie. Cindy had chosen the name Amelia as one of her favorites when she was only fifteen—back when she had first met Sam. Sam's mother's name was also Millie, and she and her husband loved Cindy very much.

Sam knew that Cindy should be buried in Payson, close to her family and friends. He also decided almost as quickly that he wanted to go home too. He

LULLABY AND GOODNIGHT

had decided earlier that he would leave the air force at the end of his six-year hitch so he could return to college full-time. The only question now was whether he would try to get out sooner. The air force, under the circumstances, was very cooperative about allowing him to resign before his commitment was up. An air force benefit also took care of transporting Cindy's body home, and insurance would give him some money to go on for a while, so he could go back to school. An additional insurance benefit paid off his trailer, so he had a home he could take back to Payson.

Things began to fall into place, and within a few days Sam was thinking he would probably leave the air force if he could work out all the details. One thing about these arrangements did worry him. He wanted to care for Millie himself, but he wondered what he could do with her while he went to school. He talked things over with his mother and sisters, two of whom were in high school and still home. He was not sure his mother could handle a little baby again, but she wanted to. She told Sam to bring the baby home to her, and she would take care of her during these early months, and her daughters would help.

Sam decided that would be best, but he also decided he wanted Luke with him. If he parked his mobile home in Payson, he could let Luke spend the days with Grandma and then be with him during evenings and nights. Sam could also spend time with Millie every day.

With that the plan took shape. But it all happened in a daze. Each day was busy, with arrangements to be made, questions to answer. But the nights were horrible and long. It was then that Sam had time to think about Cindy, to feel the emptiness. Sam almost never cried around people, and some of them worried that he was holding his emotions too well, that he would be better to let himself mourn. But at nights, alone, he lay in bed and cried, feeling more alone than he ever had in his life.

He would go home, go to college, raise his children, go on with life. But what did it all mean without Cindy? His trust in God and in his eternal commitment told him that he would see her again. But right now the wait seemed more than he could live with.

He searched inside for compensations. And he did find some. He felt that God had warned him, prepared him, with the dream. That didn't take the sting away, but it somehow meant that God was there, trying to get him through it, softening things a little. He concentrated on the temple vows, tried to think of time as a grand continuum and these intervening years as a very small part of the whole. At least his faith was secure and he was sure that he would see Cindy again, remain sealed to her forever—with the children. Above all, he did have Luke and Millie. Millie could have died so easily, but she hadn't, and something in her lovely newness helped Sam believe that life was meant to go on.

Somehow, Sam had to make something good come from all this. Cindy quickly enlarged in his own mind as a sort of symbol of what truly good people were capable of being. He didn't want the image of Darci's destructive act to linger in everyone's mind. He knew that Darci's dark actions would long be remembered by all who knew the story, but he didn't want Cindy's simple kindness and love to be lost. Somehow, he had to represent her in his life, and he had to make sure that her story survived. Mormons, throughout their history, have found ways to make something good out of tragedy and pain, and something of that tradition

LULLABY AND GOODNIGHT

spoke to him now, and told him that he could use this experience in positive ways.

Each day Sam went to the hospital. He held little Millie in his arms, talked to her, looked into those already bright eyes that reminded him so much of Cindy's. The nurses surrounded him and tried to teach him how to care for her. But Sam thought he knew enough about that. What he needed right now was simply to hold her.

The time with Millie was the best part of each day. The hospital offered to keep her longer than usual—free of charge—even though she was doing very well. That way, Sam could take care of all the details of leaving Albuquerque and the funeral arrangements, and then pick her up as he drove to the airport when he left for Utah.

The story of Cindy's murder shocked everyone who heard it. Most everyone was angered and disgusted, but Sam was the most important person who had to decide what to think of Darci. His attitude would affect his life so deeply.

During that awful night when Cindy had been missing, Sam had imagined a rapist or some sick attacker—a man. When he had learned that the baby was alive and Cindy still missing, he pictured black marketers, men willing to kill for the profit of selling his child. He was enraged as he imagined such utter callousness. What he hadn't thought of was a woman. And when he did learn that a woman was involved, he immediately asked, "Who worked with her? Who else was involved?" He assumed that profiteers were behind the scheme and that Darci had only been used to draw Cindy in.

But gradually the story came out that only Darci was involved. And early reports stressed the idea that

Darci was infertile and therefore desperate for a baby. Sam and Cindy had known a couple in Germany who had been unable to have children. Sam remembered the compassion Cindy had felt for them; he had felt great empathy for them himself. He could see how that kind of pain could lead to some sort of psychological obsession. And so he pictured a woman in pain, psychologically unstable, desperate—someone he could forgive.

He saw no value in focusing on the criminal, anyway. Some victims filled the rest of their lives with hate, and something in Sam said that he would harm his future relationship with Cindy by allowing that sort of distortion to creep into his own thinking. Cindy would have forgiven Darci; he could do so too. Dismissing the hatred and anger didn't exactly relieve him of the pain, but at least it didn't add any.

The press also wanted to know about Cindy and about Sam. His trailer was shown on local television, and his address was printed in the paper. People started showing up, mostly well-wishers and supporters, but also reporters from outside the area. Sam's friends tried to protect him from all that, but on some occasions Sam chose to speak to the reporters. He wanted them to know who Cindy was; he was tired of seeing her as nothing more than a face on TV, merely the "murdered woman."

Sam talked to one reporter from the *Atlanta Journal,* who wrote a long feature story for his paper. In this and future articles and interviews, a surprising voice began to take shape. Sam's manner was always quiet, subdued, but never angry. And he was always more than generous with Darci. The crime was startling, bizarre, but somehow in the middle of it all, emerged a sense that someone—the very person most deeply damaged—had refused to lose his head and his heart.

Not long after the crime, Sam issued a press release:

> The family of Cindy Ray would like to make the following announcement. A very unfortunate chain of events has left two little children motherless and a husband longing for his wife. This catastrophe will affect their lives for many years. Even though the situation has long-lasting effects, we wish to express our feelings to other parties involved. We wish to say that we feel sympathy for women who can not have children of their own. Let it be known that no hard feelings are harbored toward other parties involved. We are sure Cindy feels the same way. We also wish to express our deepest gratitude to any persons, even remotely involved in any way, for helping our family through this difficult time.
>
> Sam, Luke, and Amelia (Millie) Ray

In subsequent interviews Sam expressed similar feelings. Some wondered if he wasn't actually holding back his anger and grief. Maybe he would explode one day. But that would not happen. In fact, he spent much of his time trying to help his friends and family handle their anger the same way.

Larry Giles had a harder time. He was irate when he got the news of his daughter's death. On the phone, when Sam broke the news to him, he raged about wanting to get even with the person who had done this to his little girl. But Sam calmed him, and Larry soon found perspective.

On Sunday, Sam spoke to his Mormon ward, even though the bishop had told him to stay home and not subject himself to more pain. But Sam wanted to talk. He knew how people were struggling, and he felt he had to help them. As Sam stood at the podium, the chapel was silent. No one had suspected that he could manage this so soon after the tragedy. But there were things he felt he needed to say. He reminded his fellow believers that something glorious had happened. Cindy had accomplished her goal in "mortal life." She had lived a short time, but she had lived as she should. Most people never achieved so much.

He thanked the ward members for their great outpouring of love. He had never seen people care so much and give so much in a time of need. He bore testimony of his faith, and he asked the members not to be bitter about what had happened. He told them —without mentioning the dream—that he had been prepared for what had come, and that things were actually happening as "they were supposed to," however tragic it all seemed on the surface.

Finally, he told the congregation not to be scared, not to pull in and hide away from the world. He had seen much in his police work, and he knew what awful things happened in the world. But no one need fear that God had withdrawn support and protection. Cindy's time had come, and it was not wrong for her to go. Life was too full of joy for people to withdraw from all that was good.

Throughout the ward, Sam's attitude spread. Much of the anger and frustration was replaced with a desire to follow Sam's example. For many, this was one of the most moving and important religious experiences of their lives, as they saw the teachings of their religion actually manifested in a young man who had every excuse to give vent to desires for revenge.

Sam had hoped to have the funeral quickly, but Cindy's body was not released for a few days. An autopsy was required by law. And so Sam wasn't able

LULLABY AND GOODNIGHT

to leave Albuquerque until Monday afternoon. The funeral was scheduled for Wednesday in Payson.

The community of Albuquerque and the air force opened its heart to Sam—with money, with letters of support, with help in all the arrangements he had to make. Delta Airlines did the same. Officials from the airline made special arrangements for Sam to board the airplane privately, without having to walk through the terminal. They placed Sam and his father, with Luke and Millie, in the first-class section, and the crew gave them special attention and help.

Sam's dad held Millie most of the time, while Sam looked after Luke, who was still quiet, for the most part, and still very confused. He was interested to see his sister, but he was not his usual lively self. He was still asking his question: "Where's my mommy?"

As the airplane ascended out of Albuquerque and then arched around to the north, Sam looked out the window and saw billowy thunderheads scattered over the valley and against the mountains. It was all very beautiful and dramatic, and as the airplane climbed over the mountains among those thunderheads, Sam looked down and saw the mountains where Cindy had died and the canyon where Darci Pierce had driven back to Albuquerque with Millie.

He was struck by a thought that had not crossed his mind until now. He wondered what it was like to die, for the soul to leave the body. Did Cindy rise up like this airplane? Did she see down into this canyon as Sam was seeing now? Did she know what was happening? Had she known that Darci Pierce had her baby and was driving down that canyon with her?

He had wondered before what she must have thought as Darci had first taken her from the clinic parking lot at gunpoint and driven her up the canyon.

D. T. Hughes

She must have been most concerned for the baby; she must have wondered what Darci wanted and what she would do. And then an idea struck Sam so clearly that he had no doubt it was true: Cindy would have put the safety of the baby ahead of her own. She had actually died not just *because* of the baby—which limited her ability to fight Darci off—but *for* the baby. At her best, she could have run, could have fought, but she would hesitate to do that when losing her own life would also destroy the baby. She couldn't have known exactly what Darci had had in mind, but she must have done everything possible to placate Darci, to gamble her own life for the sake of the baby inside her.

And she must have prayed. It would be like Cindy to pray constantly in such a situation. She trusted so absolutely in prayer.

But what about the end of the struggle, as she left her body in the grass under those junipers below? Had she been able to look down and understand what was happening? Surely, if she had known what Darci was doing, then she would have prayed again. More than anything, she must have asked that her baby would survive and be taken back to Sam.

The doctor who had looked after Millie had said that she was in perfect health; he had called it a miracle. The police said that solving the crime within hours was rare and very fortunate. Sam knew this from his own police work. Cindy must have known that she was not likely to survive. But she must have prayed for her baby. After her death it seemed likely to Sam that she had prayed for the baby to be taken safely to her husband.

It seemed right. It was a kind of miracle, but Cindy had created miracles before with her prayers.

And Sam wondered. What was Cindy thinking now? Did she know what he was doing? Did she

LULLABY AND GOODNIGHT

approve? He remembered their conversation that Monday night, just three days before her death, when he asked her how she could handle what was coming. "I don't know. But I will," she had told him. Sam hoped that she was satisfied with him. He hoped he could always handle things in ways that she would feel good about. He wished he could consult with her from time to time, to get her help, but since he couldn't, he was glad they had talked that night, and she had given him some idea of the direction he should go.

Delta Airlines had made special arrangements at the Salt Lake airport. Sam and his father, with the children, were taken off the airplane first, and ushered not through the walkway, but through a side door and down some stairs and then into a private room where the family was waiting. Cindy's parents were there, and so were Tonie and Mark. Sam's mother was also waiting, along with a friend who was assistant chief of police in Payson. He had driven Mrs. Ray to the airport.

Kipper had received the word of Cindy's death in North Carolina, where he was now assigned as a missionary. After some hard soul-searching, he had decided to complete his mission and not come home. He knew that Cindy had wanted him to be a missionary more than anything, and he could best honor her by staying.

Sam greeted everyone and tried to get some sense of how they were handling things. He tried to comfort everyone. Cindy's father had overcome his early fury, but he was nervous. Sam found out that he was trying not to drink, not even to smoke, because he knew how much that would mean to Cindy. Cindy's mother seemed very quiet and controlled, but Sam sensed in her a good deal of anger about what Darci had done to her daughter. Tonie held up well, and Sam knew she was trying to help him. He also saw the pain in her eyes, behind the outward show of optimism.

Airline officials gave the family time, and then they moved them around the terminal in vehicles, so that no one needed to walk through the building. Sam and his family were delivered directly to the car that the family friend had driven. So he and his parents and children, along with the friend, drove the sixty miles home. Millie was so tiny that she could hardly be strapped into the car seat, and Luke was shy and quiet amid all these new experiences. He had spent little time in his life around his grandparents. He would soon get to know them much better.

In Payson, final funeral and burial arrangements had to be made. Sam kept himself busy. One of the things he wanted was some special flowers for Cindy. To get them he went back to the little flower shop where he had bought corsages for high school dances. The woman there, a neighbor, had assisted him many times. On his first visit, long ago, he had told her that he needed a lot of help, since he didn't know about such things. Over the years, she had always advised him, teased him, and helped him pick out just the right thing. This time she remembered him with affection, and she tried to help him again, even though her store had been closed for a time and was not yet entirely reopened. Sam chose a dozen red roses for Cindy, and he picked out a bouquet for his children to give their mother. On the ribbon were printed the words OUR MOMMY.

The funeral was rather typical of Mormon services. It was poignant but not overly sad. The theme was upbeat and optimistic about Sam and Cindy's future together. Marjean Wilson, mother of one of Tonie and Cindy's closest friends, talked about Cindy's growing-up years in the neighborhood, her tomboy antics, her

LULLABY AND GOODNIGHT

love of life, her ability to organize and apply herself—and above all, her love for people, and her willingness to forgive.

Bishop Harward, Cindy's former bishop, wept for quite some time. But when he finally got control of his voice, he gave another fine eulogy, describing Cindy's good qualities. Most touching was a little tribute that Larry Giles had written for his daughter.

Sam spoke again, saying many of the same things he had told his friends in his ward in Albuquerque. He was tall and straight and handsome in his dress blue uniform, his military haircut and mustache. He was in control, never cried. There was sadness, loneliness in his voice, but at the same time, resolution. "I'll take my little kids," he told them, "and I'll raise them as their mommy wanted them raised. And one day we'll be together again—as a family."

Throughout the service no one mentioned the exact circumstances of the death. The emphasis stayed upon Cindy and her triumph in living such a good life. Outside, in the foyer, reporters took notes, but sometimes they stopped writing and merely shook their heads, amazed at these people—and especially Sam—who knew how to keep on going.

The family took videos of the funeral and the burial. One touching scene shows Sam standing at the head of the grave after his father had said the dedicatory prayer. He has on his Security Police beret, along with his uniform, and he is holding little Luke, who has fallen asleep on his shoulder. He is rocking Luke, slowly back and forth in a steady rhythm, as he looks down at the blue casket, draped in flowers. For a half minute or so, no one approaches him, and he simply stands there with his little boy, alone, with people all around him.

In the crowd is Tonie, her hair permed the way

Cindy had once had hers, and looking much like Cindy. She is greeting people with a smile; she is not destroyed; she seems set upon surviving. She is smiling and wishing people well, the way Cindy would have done.

Larry is caught for a moment in the video, chewing gum rather rapidly. He speaks to people, but he seems distant, as though he isn't exactly there.

A few people are standing back, wiping their eyes, looking at the casket, shaking their heads, talking in hushed tones. Some of the men have on western style shirts, and no one looks very slick or polished. But the voices, picked up only in bits and pieces, sound rather normal. Laughter is heard from time to time, and one senses that these people are not devastated. They know how to deal with death. They simply refuse to see it as tragedy.

After the burial, Sam returned with others to the church where the funeral had been held. There, a dinner, prepared by the Relief Society, was served for the family. People had done their crying for the day; the mood now was mostly cheerful.

Sam returned to his home after the funeral, but it was a hot July day, with a long evening ahead, and he really wanted to get away to have some time for himself. He and Mark took Luke and they drove up into Payson Canyon. They stopped at the grotto, an area where a waterfall forms a pool beneath a cavelike formation. It was one of Cindy's favorite spots in the canyon, and she and Sam had been there together a number of times. Back when she had wrestled with her high school worries and problems, she had come here to think.

Luke played and Mark and Sam talked. They tried to avoid the painful topics, but both of them knew that they shared something. They had been married to

LULLABY AND GOODNIGHT

sisters who were very close and very much alike. Perhaps no one could understand Sam's loss quite as well as Mark.

After a time Mark walked with Luke back to the car, and he left Sam alone. Sam leaned against a little tree and cried for a time, and then he prayed, trying to think what lay ahead for him. He knew he had to hold himself together. In front of people, he could be strong, even give them strength, but alone, he felt as though he might sink down and give up. He knew all the things he believed, but he also knew what it was going to mean to get up each morning and go about life with half of himself missing.

But he couldn't do this. He couldn't wallow in the pain. He looked down at the ring on his hand, blurred by his tears. To the world, he was no longer married, and the ring said that he was. So he slipped it off and dropped it in his pocket. He hoped Cindy would understand. He wasn't ending anything. He was deciding to move ahead with the life that fate had handed him.

The day after the funeral Sam drove to Provo to spend some time in the temple. After attending the endowment session, where he once again repeated the vows he had made with God—and with Cindy—he sat alone in the Celestial Room, a place set aside for contemplation at the end of the ceremony. As he sat there, a man approached him. He asked Sam whether he had time to come to the sealing rooms to take part as a proxy for some marriages being performed for the dead. Mormons believe that certain holy ordinances, such as baptism and marriage, must be performed on earth, and therefore they trace the names of their ancestors who never had the opportunity to receive these on earth and they do proxy ceremonies for them.

Sam agreed to help. He followed the man to a sealing room—one of the small, elegant rooms, with the chandelier in the center and the mirrors on both sides. First he watched as other couples knelt at the altar and took the vows, and then he knelt at the altar himself. He shut his eyes and imagined Cindy across from him. But he listened closely, recalled the words, and vowed within himself again that his marriage would last forever.

A few days after the funeral, Sam and Larry Giles, along with little Luke, drove back to Albuquerque. Sam had final arrangements to make in order to be released from the air force, and he had to pack his trailer and get it ready to be transported by the air force to Utah.

When Sam had paperwork to fill out, Grandpa would take Luke riding on an elevator or out for walks—just as Sam's father had done the week before. Larry enjoyed being with Luke; it seemed to help him deal with the loss of his daughter.

After Sam and Larry returned from Albuquerque and set up the trailer, Sam took Luke and went to Castle Dale, Utah, to spend some time with Tonie and Mark. Luke found more comfort in being with Tonie than with anyone. Tonie looked and sounded much like Cindy, and when she held him, he seemed to find something familiar. He nestled close to her more than to anyone else other than Sam.

Sam enjoyed Mark and Tonie, and the three of them took their kids and drove into the mountains, took picnics, and simply tried to make the best of a very hard time. Mark and Sam went bow hunting, and they tried to fill their time with activities that took Sam's mind off the past. Sam had made arrangements to start at BYU, but he had a couple of weeks to get through, and Tonie and Mark helped him make it.

LULLABY AND GOODNIGHT

When fall semester began Sam quickly settled into a routine. He would take Luke to his parents' house in the morning and drive to Provo. Sam's parents had loved Cindy very much, and now they poured out their love on Millie and Luke. And so they were secure and well taken care of and that was something Sam could feel good about.

After classes he would return and spend an hour or two with Millie and Luke and his family, and then he would go back to the trailer with Luke. He wanted to cook dinner most nights and have Luke with him, so that Luke would know that he still had a home.

Luke was gradually becoming more secure now that he had his grandmother with him every day and Sam with him every evening. But he continued to ask about his mother, and he seemed younger, less confident than he had when Cindy had been with him. He was a handsome little boy, and his little sister looked much like him. She had very little hair, but what she had was fine and light, very different from her mother's—and Darci's. She was tiny like her mother, however, and Sam saw Cindy's eyes, Cindy's smile. She was unusually alert and aware of things for her age. Sam saw intelligence in those lively eyes. When he held her, small as she was, it was the one time each day that he felt some direct attachment to Cindy.

Evenings, once Luke went to bed, were long. Sam had plenty of studies to do, and in that sense was busy, but life seemed hollow and lonely. In his classes he felt different, older than most, and separated. One day when a freshman girl began to flirt with him, cute as she was, he had the urge to say to her, "Say, do you ever do any baby-sitting?"

But what usually did happen was that he would start to get to know people, and then his story would come out, and from that time on they would treat him differently from before. Sam could live with that. He understood that people were shocked by the bizarre crime that had changed his life so much. What he struggled to live with was the absence. He and Cindy had shared everything, and now, suddenly, he had no one to talk to—at least no one to share his deepest feelings. He was not one to spill out his emotions, and he felt a certain need not to worry his family and friends. As a result he told people he was doing fine, and in many ways he was, but the loneliness was sometimes almost more than he thought he could stand. He was surrounded by nearly thirty thousand students at BYU, but he felt disconnected, separated from his past and from his companion. At the same time he was disconnected from his present, from the people around him, by the events of the past.

Sam decided that he would not despair; he would fight the grief. He would make something good come of his life. Luke and Millie represented for him a reason to make the best of things.

But one day that fall, at lunchtime, the loneliness seemed more than Sam could handle and he walked to the temple, just a few blocks from campus. He went around the east side to the bench where he and Cindy had sat on the cold January day—in the rain—and he had asked her to marry him. The day was pretty this time and the fall colors were ablaze on the mountains just above the temple. And yet that day in the cold January rain had seemed infinitely warmer.

As Sam sat on the bench and looked up at the temple he thought of the scene all over again—almost five years before. He had sat in exactly the same spot, and he had held Cindy on his lap and said, "Will you marry me . . . *in the temple, forever?*" She had been so happy, and so had he. He thought about the ring and how much she had loved it. He remembered how they

LULLABY AND GOODNIGHT

had laughed and talked about their future. It had all seemed like a fairy tale, and now this . . . the present . . . seemed such a distortion of what they had thought was theirs.

He got up and walked back to campus, not really consoled. People were streaming around him again, and he didn't feel a part of them or of anything.

That night he drove back to Payson and he held Luke and Millie in his arms. They represented the one hold he seemed to have on this world anymore. They symbolized both what he had and what he didn't have.

CHAPTER 10

During the fall and winter the two teams of lawyers prepared their cases. Both sides tried to learn all they could about Darci's past, and both listened to the mental health experts they had hired. Darci was complex, confusing—an enigma—but the defense held to its position that she was insane, and their experts felt they could make a strong case for that position. The prosecution was just as certain that Darci knew exactly what she was up to and carried out a premeditated crime. She had some mental problems, from their point of view, but she was certainly in control and responsible for her actions.

Zimmerman and Cox claimed that they had nothing against Darci. If their experts had told them that she had disabling mental problems, they would have been willing to plea-bargain and then seek help for her. But in fact, they came to believe, as they listened to their forensic experts, that Darci was basically a self-serving thief.

As the trial approached, New Mexico's chief district attorney dropped the death charge, probably because of the unlikelihood that a jury would send a teenager to her death. Both sides continued to work for a plea bargain, but the lawyers on the two teams tell differing versions of what happened in their negotiations.

Zimmerman, by his account, offered a deal in federal court. In the federal system Darci could receive better therapy. But the defense turned this offer down because they didn't like to give a federal judge the right to set the sentence. They feared that Darci would receive a very lengthy sentence, and they didn't like putting control over Darci's release in the hands of the judge.

Defense lawyer John Bogren, however, denies that this approach was viable for Darci. He wanted to see her sent to a hospital, not a prison, and he saw little advantage in the federal system over a state penitentiary. By his account, he and his partners bargained for a sentence of twenty-seven years, with opportunity for therapy. That way Darci could possibly be paroled in half the twenty-seven years, and with good therapy be able to go on with her life. They believed that she was no danger to society once she worked out some of her problems. To this day the defense lawyers are bitter that the prosecutors refused to grant Darci that much of a chance.

But Zimmerman and Cox felt that anyone who could commit such a brutal crime *was* a danger. If she were not so ill as the defense claimed, why should she walk free in as few as thirteen-and-half years when people were spending more time in jail for lesser crimes?

So the two sides never came close, and that meant that the trial would go on. Meanwhile, Darci became deeply depressed. At one point she went into a kind of catatonic state. For a whole day—twelve hours—she didn't move, but lay on her bunk and stared straight ahead, hardly even blinking. She seemed in another world.

During the trial Darci's apparent catatonia would be debated and denied by the prosecution. And she apparently did respond at times. But Darlene Carr, who observed Darci continuously that day for three hours, said that Darci never so much as blinked the entire time. Tears rolled out of her eyes, but her eyes did not move, and she lay completely still.

As spring came, Sam knew he would have to testify. In March, as the trial was about to get under way, he and Mark and Larry Giles drove to Albuquerque. Sam was feeling a little more like himself now, and the three of them laughed and avoided the subjects that only brought on pain.

Sam learned from Harry Zimmerman that he would be the first witness. He, along with Larry and Mark, sat in Zimmerman's little office and talked about the case. Larry was especially interested to know who this woman was who had killed his daughter.

"Well, I'll tell you something," Zimmerman said. "If I had known what I just found out a couple of days ago, I might've gone for capital homicide."

"What do you mean?" Larry asked.

"We heard from a librarian over on base. She said she saw Darci and Cindy in her library, both of them there at the same time, about two weeks before the crime. She didn't realize it until she saw both their pictures in the paper."

"Were they talking to each other?" Larry asked.

"She didn't see that. But they could have, very easily. The way I figure it, Darci picked her out. All she would have had to do was start a conversation with Cindy. 'Oh, say, you're expecting too; when's your baby due'—that sort of thing. Then she maybe says, 'So do you go to the clinic on base? What day do

LULLABY AND GOODNIGHT

you have your appointments?' Cindy says Thursdays at such and such time, and Darci decides to wait for her after her appointment. Remember, she was going to do this whole thing a week earlier, and then she put it off and had that woman lie to her husband and everything, and then she could have—"

"Wait," Larry said. "What's this about doing it a week earlier?"

"Well, yeah. I guess you don't know about that."

And on the conversation went. But Sam wasn't listening. The hair on the back on his neck was standing up. Chills were running through him. He had instantly put it all together: The day that Cindy had gone to the library, two weeks before the murder; that was the day he had had the dream. At the same instant that Darci may have targeted Cindy, Sam was home in bed, and he had had that incredibly intense, incredibly real dream.

The wheels had started in motion that day, if the librarian was right, and Zimmerman's theory was right. And on that day Sam had received the warning. The delay, for some reason—Zimmerman said it was because Sam went with Cindy for the appointment that week—had given them time for the temple trip, time to have the talk about Cindy's possible death. It all made sense.

Maybe. It was just a guess. Zimmerman didn't know for sure that it had happened that way. But it all seemed to fit together.

For now, however, Zimmerman needed to talk with Sam about his testimony. They reviewed the questions that Harry had for him. "It's not so much what you say," he told Sam, "but I want to get you up there before that jury. I want them to see that a nice young man has lost his wife and that he's trying to raise his kids by himself. I want them to get some idea about how much in love you two kids were. The defense is going to try to make Darci the victim, but we can't let the jury forget that you're the one whose life got ripped apart."

Zimmerman leaned forward at his desk. "Sam, look, I don't want you to fake anything. That won't work. But I'm going to push you a little up there on the stand. And if you can show me a little emotion, that would help a lot."

But Sam was not good at that. He never showed much emotion in public, and he certainly didn't know how to play the actor.

The courtroom in the downtown Albuquerque courthouse was often filled, not only with local spectators but with news reporters from around the country. It was a little early in the year for the air-conditioning to turn on, but all the body heat usually made the room uncomfortable by mid-afternoon. All the same, Judge Richard B. Traub, an experienced, sometimes crusty administrator, kept the trial going for long hours each day. A gray-haired man with wire-rim glasses, he would peer down at the attorneys with impatience at times, and he brought to the complex case a no-nonsense kind of practicality.

The first week of the trial was spent in *"voir dire,"* the selection of the jury. Most of the questioning was done with the entire group together, but individuals were asked questions as well. After the case ended, this process would be called into question, since one of the jurors would reveal that he hadn't told the entire truth about himself. But no one knew that at the time.

The jury was rather young, fairly well educated, and a fair cross section of American culture. Harry Zim-

LULLABY AND GOODNIGHT

merman felt pretty good about the group. John Bogren was not sure. He wondered whether they wouldn't be too skeptical about his complicated psychological defense. He hoped for one—at least one—who could find enough empathy to agree with him that Darci was seriously ill.

For four weeks these jurors sat in the neatly paneled courtroom and considered all the information. In the end they had no luxury to announce that the whole matter was too complex to decide. They were expected to come to unanimous agreement. Everyone outside the courtroom read the papers, formed their opinions, and the most common opinion in the street was that Darci should be "put away for good."

But talk is easy for those who don't have to make the decision. The jurors had to look at the pretty young woman who sat before them each day. She dressed simply and neatly, and she sat, most often, with her head down. She never showed any reaction to what was happening. Often it seemed that she was hardly there. Maybe that was so. Darci had always moved into her own fantasy world when pressure was on her.

On one occasion, as Darci was led from the courtroom during a recess, her mother was the witness on the stand. Her mother had broken down as she described Darci's hatred of her, and again as she talked about the pain of learning what Darci had done. As Darci walked by her mother, she reached out and patted her mother's arm. It was a simple gesture, and it didn't seem calculated to impress the jury. It appeared to be Darci's way to say, very simply, that she was sorry—for everything. Some would argue that Darci only knew how to pretend sorrow, that she really only cared about herself. That may well be the case. But it was a touching moment, and one which caused those in the room to hope that all this ugliness could somehow, someday be made right again. But the very thought was a reminder that Cindy could not be brought back.

The trial began with opening statements by the lawyers. Both sides established the main theses of their cases. Michael Cox led off for the prosecution, and he introduced the essential picture of Darci that he wanted the jury to remember. He said Darci was a con artist, a great actress, and a liar. He warned the jury that the defense would make a case that Darci was insane, but one of the problems with that, he claimed, was that the defense mental health specialists had listened to Darci too trustfully, and they had accepted her version of things rather than the reality of what had really happened. The liar, in other words, had built her own defense—by lying.

Cox also stressed a key concept for the prosecution. Everyone was saying that Darci's crime was bizarre, but in fact, her motivations were fairly simple, very clear, and based on greed and inconsideration of others, rather than on some complicated psychological problem.

Finally, he emphasized that Darci did not act on impulse. She planned ahead, knew exactly what she wanted, and went about the crime in a cold, heartless manner.

Cox also made the case that the murder was carried out with time to deliberate. In Darci's own confession, she admitted that she almost turned back on at least two occasions. Or in other words, even if Darci didn't plan the crime days ahead of time, she could be shown to be deliberating and premeditating throughout the hours she waited for Cindy, and during the time that she drove with her in the car and then talked to her at the crime scene.

The crime, Cox contended, was carried out with great precision and control. Darci performed a perfect operation under primitive conditions. Her expertise implied that she had prepared herself with the knowledge of how a proper C-section should be carried out. She was even interrupted at the moment she was about to begin, took care of the intruder in a controlled way, and went back to her ugly work. She then protected herself from detection. Even though she would be portrayed as in a hysterical state, she thoroughly washed her hands somehow—probably in the little stream nearby. She left the blood where it might help her establish her story, but cleaned it from her hands and arms, and then she used her own dress to wrap the baby, not Cindy's—which would have been incriminating. Every step, it would be said, was carefully carried out with an eye to pulling off a crime. Where is the madness in all of this?

Crucially, when Darci finally admitted to her crime, one of the first things she said was, "I killed her." If her memory of the murder was gone, how did she know this?

Cox argued that Darci, the consummate liar and actress, failed to pull off her crime, so she was forced to act out another falsehood to save herself from prison. If she couldn't fake a pregnancy and then steal herself a baby, then she could fake insanity and not have to pay for her crime. But Darci, according to Cox, was not insane, and his experts would prove it. Darci was "intelligent, careful, ruthless, almost totally self-centered, and extremely deceitful."

He concluded: ". . . the kidnapping, mutilation, murder of the woman, and taking of the child was not the product of a diseased mind, but the product of a diseased, hardened soul, and that is the very essence of criminal responsibility, and will lead you to find her guilty of the crimes charged."

Michael Cox sat down and Tom Jameson stood up for the defense. Cox had painted a ghastly picture, and Jameson would have to say, in effect, "Look over there. Look at Darci. Can you really buy the story you've just heard? No one could be that calculating. Only someone crazy could do something like this." It was what most people tended to believe, and it was what Jameson had to get the jury back to.

The first words Jameson spoke were, "May it please the Court, prosecution, ladies and gentlemen of the jury, this case is about insanity. It's about the insane acts of an insane mind." He then told his version of what had happened. The facts were much the same, but the stress was on the bizarre nature of things. He said that when Darci showed up at the hospital, she had a "wild story" to tell, and he repeated this phrase several times. People were "puzzled" by the story; it was "unbelievable" and "strange."

He brought out the contradictory, surprising elements of Darci's behavior. Cox had made the pregnancy seem nothing more than a calculated lie, but Jameson stressed the symptoms Darci experienced that would seem to indicate that she did go through a pseudo pregnancy. The surrogate mother story had been an example of Darci's dishonesty to Cox, but to Jameson it was another wild story, told with conviction. "It was rather eerie because she appeared to believe it completely." And he stressed how much she loved the little child she claimed to have delivered.

Jameson also emphasized the idea that Darci's moods were shifting rapidly throughout the long night of her interrogation. On the way to the crime scene she had talked in "normal tones" and seemed "very pleasant," and then had become hysterical at the site. Cox had quoted one of Darci's statements to Elisabeth Koehler: "I killed her." Jameson quoted another: "Oh my God, I hope she's not dead."

Jameson also denied Cox's claim that Darci had planned the crime. How could she if she didn't even take an instrument with her to perform the cesarean?

True, Darci had confessed to the crime, and the defense would not argue those essential events, but Jameson called on the jury to listen to her confession and notice how choppy and fragmented the account would be, full of gaps and illogical jumps. And didn't it all begin with an idea that only an insane person would consider reasonable? Didn't Darci want to talk to Cindy and ask her whether she wouldn't give Darci her baby?

Jameson, at that point, introduced the key to their defense. Darci was suffering from a dissociative disorder, which he described for the jurors: "The doctors will explain that for most of us, identity, memory, and reality mesh together nicely. They work in tandem. They work in conjunction. . . . Doctors will explain that within Darci's brain there's a disease that short-circuits memory, identity, and reality, and that in various episodes these components no longer mesh. They miss. They fly around wildly, and that in certain episodes they can decompose very rapidly, and why this is important is that they will explain to you that lies are evidence of this disorder. They will explain to you that lies are Darci's way of filling in the blanks because there are blanks at various points in her life. . . ."

The prosecution had already called Darci ruthless, but Jameson promised that her life would not show that. The nineteen years of her life would show that she could be compassionate, loving, a good friend, someone who had never hurt anyone before. She was, in fact, a bright, caring person, but she was also characterized by strange, unexplainable elements in her behavior. She had had trouble adjusting to the idea that she was adopted. She had trouble at times adjusting to school situations. Above all, she had told wild, bizarre lies all her life. They weren't told to take advantage of anyone, or to gain anything; often, they were merely her fantasies, which she seemed to believe were real. Out of these fantasies grew an obsession: She would marry the perfect young man and create a perfect life. Part of that fantasy of perfection was a baby, and she really did fear that she could not give birth.

Jameson rehearsed the story of Darci's growing obsession in some detail. He detailed the medical problems and then the genuine symptoms that convinced everyone that Darci was pregnant. He described the nursery that Darci had prepared, her every action indicating that she actually believed she was expecting. The obsession produced a kind of "momentum that was bubbling inside of her brain." As she waited outside the clinic in the hot sun, still planning only to talk to Cindy and ask for her baby, the momentum pushed her deeper into madness. ". . . as she sat there or as she paced there her brain bubbled and churned until Cindy Ray came into the car to talk, to maybe share a cool drink." The defense view, in other words, was not that Darci kidnapped Cindy, but that Cindy agreed to sit in the car and talk.

Jameson concluded by saying, "At the beginning of this case you took an oath as jurors, and in that oath you said that you would listen to the facts of this case and judge them as truly and as honestly as you could. We promise you that in the defense of Darci Pierce we

LULLABY AND GOODNIGHT

will present it as honestly and as truthfully as we know how."

The prosecution called their witnesses first. What Zimmerman and Cox set out to do was present the simple facts of the case—with the slant toward the lying and conning. Eventually, the real battle would be over Darci's mental state, but the prosecution would not call its own mental health specialists until the defense introduced their insanity argument.

Sam was the first witness. When he took the stand, Harry asked him to recount his and Cindy's lives a little: How they had met, their years of marriage. He asked the court to admit as evidence a picture of Sam and Cindy, with Luke and Millie superimposed. He tried, in other words, to humanize Sam and Cindy as a nice young couple, very much in love, starting a family, undeserving of such malignant treatment at Darci's hands.

For the most part Sam answered Zimmerman's questions in his policeman's style. He was direct, detailed, careful. But at one point, when Zimmerman asked him about the night he had spent alone, wondering about Cindy, and then learning of her death, Sam's eyes glistened and his voice tightened. He did not break down, but the jury saw the restrained emotion and surely must have empathized.

Zimmerman also had an important point to make. The defense wanted the jury to feel that Cindy might have gotten in the car with Cindy out of friendship and shared experience, both advanced in their pregnancies—or both seeming to be. Darci had said that she had merely invited Cindy to talk to her, to share some iced tea.

But none of that made sense to Sam. Cindy was in a big hurry to pick up Luke from the baby-sitter. She had already had Sister Rosemary call Sam because she was concerned about that. In addition, in Cindy's purse the police had found the special temple undergarments that Cindy and other endowed Mormons wear. Sam explained that she normally took them off and wore normal undergarments when she went to her appointments, merely to avoid questions about something that was sacred to her. But she always hurried to put them back on. The only reason she would have left the clinic without putting them on was that she was in a hurry to pick up Luke. But if she had planned, from the beginning, to wait to put them on until she returned home, she would not have taken them with her. Clearly, she was feeling pressed for time when she left the clinic.

Zimmerman also had Sam explain his philosophy about dealing with an assailant. He told the jury: "She was supposed to go along, try to gain confidence in an attempt to get an advantage until she found a time where she could get away. She was supposed to head toward people if possible and if she had any control over the situation at all, she was supposed to try to put the other person—gain their confidence enough that she would put down their guard and she would have a chance to get away from them."

That philosophy would explain why Cindy didn't put up a fight in the beginning when Darci had the advantage—with a gun—and why she might chat with Darci as they drove along. If she remembered what Sam had told her, she would be trying to get Darci to relax so that she could find a chance to escape.

Zimmerman finished the account with details of Sam's long wait and suffering on the night Cindy was missing. He wanted the jury to remember what agony

LULLABY AND GOODNIGHT

Sam had gone through and what a loss he had experienced.

In cross-examination Jackie Robins tried to get Sam to say that Cindy was no longer shy, now that she had been selling Tupperware and getting out in the world. Sam bristled: "This sounds a little too black-and-white. It was more of a process. Cindy was not afraid to talk to people that she knew. She wasn't afraid to go meet people in an environment where she felt comfortable, but when she went into public situations, when she went into a group of people . . . she just kept to herself, and even though she was developing more of an ability to go talk to people she never met before, I didn't know her to go and introduce herself to people she never knew for no reason. Does that answer the question, I hope?"

Jackie Robins changed the subject.

CHAPTER 11

Ray Pierce was the next witness. Zimmerman asked him to tell about his life with Darci and to describe the way Darci had made him believe she was pregnant. The story was astounding, but Ray came across as a nice young man—very young—clean-cut, straightforward. There was simply no question that he had believed, as everyone else had, in Darci's deceptions. But he also came across as loyal to Darci. He refused to characterize their marriage as troubled. In his version, all was well at home, and the two had been very much in love. He also said that he had married Darci because he loved her and not because she had told him she was pregnant.

After Ray's testimony, the witnesses who followed continued to bring out Darci's building need to have a baby and her manipulations to pull off her deceit. The progression was not always in chronological order, but the whole story gradually took shape. The witnesses included Darci's obstetrician, Dr. Sargent; Jerry Fisher and Robert Mohr, employees at Montano Acura; nurses and doctors from both the base Ob/Gyn clinic and the UNM Medical Center; patients at the clinic who had seen Darci waiting in the parking lot on the

LULLABY AND GOODNIGHT

day of the crime; Theron Hartshorn, who had come along the road as Darci was preparing to take the baby; the pathologist who performed the autopsy on Cindy; and the air force and Albuquerque policemen and investigators who dealt with the case.

The defense approach in cross-examination was not only to admit to the facts of the case but to emphasize them. Jacky Robins did most of the questioning, and she usually did little more than have the witness recount his or her testimony. In effect, the defense was saying, "We agree. All this happened." The slant, of course, was sometimes a little different. The prosecution worked on its theme: that Darci was a calculating liar and actress. The defense would occasionally get the chance to bring out some element of the bizarre in Darci's behavior. But for the most part, the stories meshed: Darci had killed Cindy and taken the baby. The only question was whether she was responsible for her behavior.

The state rested on the morning of the third day. They had presented their case succinctly and clearly. They had created the picture of Darci they wanted. The defense had to change that, and so the approach was to use Darci's life as her defense. The first witnesses were Darci's parents, and then her brother and sister-in-law and her aunt. Ray's parents followed and eventually came Darci's cousin, Kurt Davenport; her sixth-grade teacher, Sharon Gray; friends from her childhood; colleagues where she had worked; and close friends. The thesis in all these testimonies was a delicately balanced image of Darci. On the one hand she was kind and loving, sweet with children, concerned for friends in need. On the other hand, everyone had also noticed certain bizarre elements in Darci's behavior.

The prosecution would constantly challenge the idea that Darci was insane. Again and again, Cox and Zimmerman would ask witnesses whether Darci hadn't seemed a normally functioning human being. And the witnesses would admit that Darci operated very well except for a few little quirks. The defense had to grant that, and in fact, it was part of the total picture, as they perceived it. Darci did manage all right, considering the trauma of her childhood and the growing difficulty she was having in keeping her complicated psychological problems under control. In that regard, she was remarkable. She managed to be a decent person, a good friend, etc., in spite of all her challenges. Nonetheless, everyone who knew Darci knew how strange she could be. And so the witnesses were asked to tell the wild stories, the bizarre elements of Darci's life: her obsession about being adopted; her sexual activity with her cousin at age six; her outlandish imagination; her moments of "lost time"; her sudden, wild outbursts and her "adjustment problems" in school; her sexual promiscuity; her obsession with having a baby; the lies she told but seemed to believe; and her complicated medical history.

Two images of Darci evolved throughout the trial, and yet, the two were based on the same information. Was Darci a deceiving liar or an insane woman who believed her own fantasies? Since the two sides argued little about the facts of the crime, the decision of the jury had to come down to the expert witnesses, the psychologists and psychiatrists who would attempt to sort out Darci's actual motivations. Four mental health experts appeared as witnesses for the defense, and two for the prosecution. Their testimonies were long, often tedious and complicated. The jurors must have felt overwhelmed at times as they tried to sort out all the conflicting opinions, the psychological

LULLABY AND GOODNIGHT

terminology, and the legal definition of insanity. But in the end, it would be the testimony of these experts that the jurors would have to use as the grounds for their decision.

During the long night after Darci had arrived at the hospital with the baby she called Amanda Michelle, many people observed her. Most would later say that Darci seemed controlled, chatty, wide-awake, and normal. But one person saw her that night who had quite a different impression. That person was Dr. Teresita McCarty, and it would be her impression and subsequent diagnosis that the defense case would be founded upon.

When Dr. McCarty took the stand, called by the defense, she was led by John Bogren to give the account of her first observation of Darci. Dr. McCarty had come into the small conference room on the morning of July 24, and she had found Darci with Elisabeth Koehler and Dr. Graham. The first, long interrogation had ended and the investigators had taken a break. Koehler was questioning Darci at this point, and trying to use her closeness to Darci to convince her that she must, for the sake of the mother of the baby, reveal what had really happened. Dr. McCarty saw Darci sitting in a wheelchair with an IV in her arm. She was holding the baby, and she was delicately stroking its hair with one finger. She looked "very pretty."

Dr. McCarty also heard the "pleasant conversation," the "chatty, sort of friendly voice," but she noticed that Darci's answers were "very vague." Nurse Koehler was asking questions and Darci, when pressed for details, would say, "I don't remember," or "I don't know."

Dr. McCarty's immediate impression, even before she asked Darci any questions, was that she "was in the midst of a dissociation." She illustrated, for the court, what she meant by dissociation. She told the story of a little girl who might, for instance, eat some chocolate cake after her mother had told her not to. If the jurors were to think of the little girl as someone who dissociates, she might have a part A and part B to her psyche. Part A might hear the mother's warning but part B would not. So when the mother comes back and finds a piece of the cake eaten, she asks the little girl whether she took a piece. Part A doesn't know that part B ate the cake, and so part A answers No. The mother sees chocolate around her daughter's mouth and has to conclude that the little girl is lying. But the little girl has no idea that she has done anything wrong.

Dr. McCarty eventually concluded her illustration by saying: "And being in that room with Darci on the day after this crime happened was like being with that little girl with the chocolate around her mouth.... Because she was telling a story that all of us knew was not true or very likely was not true because we knew she hadn't had this baby. And yet she was telling us a story that was obvious to me, she believed, about going to Santa Fe and getting the baby from a surrogate mother.... so her belief in the story led me first to think that she was dissociating.

"The next thing was that the story that she was telling us was so vague, it was like a fairy story. Well, 'How did you get to Santa Fe and how did you get back?' And, you know, it was like, to her, it was like, well, you follow the yellow brick road, you know. It's like it didn't matter. You just get there. It's like if you ask a kid how does Santa Claus get down the chimney. Well, he just does. So then when they would press her on streets and things. It's like, well, she said [she] didn't know, but in a way that showed it doesn't bother her either, I mean, it didn't matter. And that is as close as I can give you as a sense of what it was like to be in the room with her and it was a dissociating sense."

Having reached this conclusion quickly, Dr. McCarty, after listening for a time, asked Darci whether she had "ever forgotten anything before." Darci's answer was that she had forgotten something in the sixth grade: ". . . she told me a story about how she had been in the room grading papers, when two students came outside the door and were taunting her through the glass door and next thing that she remembered was that the glass was broken. She had no memory of how that happened." All this she told in a natural, "friendly, chattylike, perfectly ordinary" tone of voice.

It was only one example, but Dr. McCarty was reasonably sure that Darci had a dissociative disorder. After spending twenty-one further hours with Darci, she concluded that, indeed, Darci was seriously mentally ill, that her early diagnosis of a dissociative disorder was correct. She also, after the further interviews, diagnosed Darci as having suffered a pseudo pregnancy and a "factitious disorder." She documented some history of substance abuse, and she discovered features or borderline and narcissistic personality disorders.

Under Mr. Bogren's guidance, Dr. McCarty set out to define each of these mental problems. She said that a dissociative disorder was "when there are more than one personality states present in a person, usually two or more. And it's when the person has inconsistency or changes in their memory, behavior, and patterns of perceiving the world."

This definition, as well as the diagnosis, would be much debated before the trial was over, but Darci's "lost time" experiences were the issue. Did she check out of reality at times and do things that she would later not remember? Did differing "ego states" exist within Darci that bordered on being separate personalities cohabitating one mind?

For the first time, Dr. McCarty introduced the theory that Darci was probably abused as a child, even though objective evidence for abuse as a small child was not available. An incident of an uncle and a neighbor making advances toward Darci would eventually come out, but these were hard to establish as traumas that could affect her so powerfully. The fact of Darci's very early sexual activity, along with her dissociating, was evidence to Dr. McCarty that sexual or mental abuse had occurred. Commonly, abused children repress the memory of their abuse, and this very protective technique can become the genesis of a dissociative disorder. Dr. McCarty thought it therefore reasonable to assume that some sort of abuse had occurred. The reaction to her adoption and her dysfunctional family could also have affected Darci and played a role in the development of a dissociative disorder.

Darci also reported to Dr. McCarty that she had heard voices inside her head, although Dr. McCarty gave no report about what they said or how they affected her behavior. But it was a common symptom, Dr. McCarty argued, of people who suffer from dissociative disorder.

Dr. McCarty spent much of her testimony trying to explain the various ways that dissociative disorders could manifest themselves, and what she generally described was a state in which various parts of a person's mind may operate separately from each other, taking over that person's actions at different times, and showing up as very different styles of behavior. Sometimes these parts are not even aware of each other. What Dr. McCarty did not claim was that Darci had a fully developed multiple personality. She could not claim that separate personalities with different names and voices and styles—and with no knowledge of each other—operated in Darci's head. What she saw were divisions that were more subtle than that, mere parts or ego states to a somewhat more combined personality. What people of this sort experience, she said, are gaps in memory when they escape the present and do something that they later do not remember. They tend to cover themselves by learning to fill the gaps with guesses at what might have happened.

If a child, for instance, begins to experience these gaps, as Darci said she did in the sixth grade, rather than to admit to the gap, they will often make something up to hide what to them is an embarrassing situation. This habit of covering is easily perceived as lying, when in fact, it may only be an attempt to account for what the young person doesn't know how to explain. Often such children are placed under great pressure to explain their actions and they feel they have to come up with something.

Eventually Dr. McCarty speculated about (she said she "sort of came up with") the parts to Darci's personality, "six consistent states that I could see operated at the time when I first saw her . . . around the time of the crime that I could also see evidence existed before that time." She knew that it would take further work with Darci to pin down these states, but for the purposes of the trial, she could at least try to give some sense of what was happening in Darci's head when she committed the crime.

The first state was the one that thought she was pregnant. Dr. McCarty was certain that this state "really, truly believed that she was pregnant . . . and expecting to deliver soon." That part "had the weight gain and had the breast enlargement and had missed periods and had all the physical changes consistent with pregnancies.

"Then I think there was another part, part two, that was simulating pregnancy; that's the part that I gave the diagnosis of factitious disorder to. This part knew she wasn't pregnant, but probably had [known] about part A, so knew that there was also a part that really believed she was pregnant and this part helped part A out. This is the part that in one of the testimonies or one of the statements Mrs. Pierce said she learned to move her abdomen muscles so that it would seem like the baby was moving and so this part simulated pregnancies but knew it wasn't . . . really pregnant."

The third part Dr. McCarty identified was "really hard to say. I think that was a surrogate mother. This part was so dissociated that Mrs. Pierce viewed her as a totally other person. There was no chance—she had no clue that this part was part of herself." This part she had given the name Sherry Martin and she used both with the admissions clerk at the hospital, when she convinced her to lie about the delayed induction, and again at the hospital when she tried to explain the source of her baby. This was the fairy tale she was telling when Dr. McCarty first saw her and reached the conclusion that Darci was dissociating.

The fourth part, or state, felt that "she was sterile and had endometriosis." This part of her mind was hopeless, convinced that she would never have a baby. It reasoned that the only way she would ever get a baby was to talk another mother into giving her hers. "And I think, maybe, that's the part that was able to at least piece together enough information to figure out that this baby had not come from her surrogate or even from herself. . . ."

Parts five and six were angry parts, according to Dr. McCarty. The fifth one was the one that killed Cindy and the one that had no memory of breaking the window in the sixth grade. Part six was always angry at her mother. Darci reported to Dr. McCarty that she had, on at least one occasion, hidden behind a door with a gun and thought about killing her mother. This angry part—that did not act but did remember—could be considered separate from part five, the one that did not remember.

Dr. McCarty was sure, with further treatment, she could understand the parts better, have a more exact sense of how many existed, and could treat Darci. What was needed was a kind of "family reunion," in which all the parts would come to understand each other and function as one person. Darci would have to face the probable traumas of her childhood and deal with them, so that she could integrate these parts of her mind. But her disorder was "not at all unusual," and could be treated.

When Dr. McCarty tried to speculate about what happened to Darci on the day that she killed Cindy, she presented a scenario of Darci going to the base only because she was aimlessly wandering. She ended up at the hospital "because that's where a pregnant person might end up." She trusted Darci's own statement that she waited outside the clinic to ask Cindy whether she could have her baby. For Darci, that would not be irrational, given the way the parts of her mind could dissociate and reason in contradictory segments. It would be the surrogate mother part of her mind that would find that request logical. Since she had no instrument with her, Dr. McCarty reasoned that she probably had no plan to take the baby by C-section.

When Darci drove home but then turned around when she saw her husband home, Dr. McCarty concluded that this decision was made by the part of her that knew she was not pregnant. When she chatted with Cindy, learned a few things about her, the part that did believe she was pregnant was perhaps operating. She was just one pregnant woman talking to another. At the crime scene, when Mr. Hartshorn showed up, she remembered his presence later because it triggered another self, the one that protects Darci, the one that knew she wasn't pregnant. That part may have known what she had just done, but Dr. McCarty thought it probably didn't know.

A key to Dr. McCarty's testimony was that something must have triggered the angry part in her to set off the more violent action of strangling Cindy. Later, in summation, Mr. Bogren would add his own speculation about what might have caused that angry reaction. But Dr. McCarty saw a calmer part taking over to perform the actual surgery. The strangulation was "a violent, impulsive, uncontrolled thing," but the cesarean required "careful consideration." And then, once Darci had the baby in her arms, the state that thought she was pregnant returned.

Dr. McCarty's theory about Darci's driving to the Acura dealer was that she merely knew people there who had been friendly to her, and she didn't know where to go. When she arrived at the hospital, she still thought she had given birth to a baby, but when the doctors asked to examine her, the second part took over and wouldn't allow it. This part "didn't want to bust the pregnant part's bubble. . . ."

Mr. Bogren led Dr. McCarty through further speculation about why Darci would remember some periods of her experience and not others, but McCarty had to admit that all this was very difficult to say for sure. Still, when it came to the crucial question, she felt she could answer unequivocally. Bogren asked, "In your opinion, Doctor, to a reasonable degree of medical certainty, could Darci Pierce control her actions on July twenty-third, 1987, during these switches and changes in her personalities?" And Dr. McCarty replied, "No, I don't think so. She could not control her actions." And was she insane, according to a legal definition of insanity? "Yes, she was."

Mr. Bogren passed the witness to the prosecution. Harry Zimmerman stood up and walked toward the witness stand. "Good afternoon, Dr. McCarty," he said in a friendly voice, but he was about to attack.

The first step was to establish that Dr. McCarty and Dr. Jean Goodwin, the two prime psychiatric witnesses, were really peas from the same pod. Dr. McCarty answered yes, that she had received her resident training from Dr. Goodwin, and that yes, the two of them had authored a number of articles on child abuse together. Obviously Zimmerman wanted the impression that he was not dealing with a matter of two independent researchers arriving at the same conclusion. Rather, he wanted the jurors to believe what he believed: That two people who tended toward the same types of diagnoses, who were especially interested in child abuse and dissociative disorders, had formulated—together—a theory about Darci's behavior.

The next step was to show just how theoretical it all was. He asked Dr. McCarty how much time she spent with Darci on that first occasion. McCarty said it was fifteen to thirty minutes. Had she interviewed Darci?

No. "And your testimony today is that as a result and, in fact, your impression before you asked any questions was that she was in the midst of a dissociation?"

Dr. McCarty answered simply and firmly, "Yes."

"That was within a few minutes after your arrival?" Zimmerman emphasized.

"Uhm-hum," Dr. McCarty answered.

After a few more questions, Zimmerman came back to the collusion he suspected between the two psychiatrists: "And you later communicated that fact [the dissociations theory] as part of your consultation with Dr. Goodwin, didn't you?"

"Yes, I did."

When Dr. McCarty restated her convinction that Darci believed her own story about the surrogate mother, Zimmerman asked whether people facing criminal charges didn't tend to lie to protect themselves. Dr. McCarty said that they often did.

Zimmerman then zeroed in on the crucial definition that Dr. McCarty had given to dissociation: the presence of two or more personality states. She admitted that there were other definitions and that her definition was similar to that of a multiple personality disorder, which she did not claim Darci to have.

Zimmerman attacked other elements of the testimony. He challenged the idea that any proof existed for a severe trauma in Darci's life and that she was ever sexually abused. Dr. McCarty was firm in her opinion, but the jury was reminded that these were theories rather than established facts.

Thereafter, for some time, Zimmerman shadowboxed with Dr. McCarty over whether Darci in fact suffered from a dissociative disorder or perhaps a character or personality disorder. Throughout the trial the definitions of disorders and illnesses, as defined by the Diagnostic and Statistical Manual of

LULLABY AND GOODNIGHT

the American Psychological Association, Third Edition, Revised *(DSM-III-R)*, the handbook used by mental health specialists to diagnose mental disorders, would often come up for debate. Zimmerman argued that borderline and narcissistic personality features, child abuse, sexual aggression, and emotional trauma were not listed as criteria for diagnosing dissociative disorder. Dr. McCarty admitted that, but she said they were listed as associated factors.

What Zimmerman tried to get Dr. McCarty to say was that certain actions—lying, shifting moods, fighting, acting aggressively or violently, running away from home, and abusing substance—were all items in the list of diagnosing factors of a personality disorder. But Dr. McCarty held to her guns. True, they could be evidence of personality or character disorder, but they could also be associated factors of a dissociative disorder.

This matter was very important because personality or character disorders are typical of criminals. Such disorders are not part of a legal definition of insanity. Dissociative disorders have also usually not been granted as insanity defenses, but the multiple personality disorder was the disease that might come closest to convincing the jury that Darci was debilitated and unable to control herself.

Zimmerman did get McCarty to admit that Darci had reported certain abnormal mental traits only after having been interviewed by mental health specialists. She, for instance, had never reported hearing voices when she had been asked by a counselor at Catholic Social Services, or on the in-take form at the jail. But after talking with psychiatrists for a time, she started to claim to hear voices, have memory gaps, hallucinate, etc.

Finally Harry Zimmerman took Dr. McCarty back

through her account of Darci's switching "selves" on the day of the murder. What he obviously hoped to do was show the jury just how theoretical and tentative all this guessing was, and at the same time, make the theory sound confusing, maybe even silly.

Dr. McCarty had said that Darci was aimlessly wandering when she ended up at the base hospital. But Darci claimed she had gassed up the car and was going to leave. When Zimmerman asked about that, Dr. McCarty said, "That was one of the things, one of the parts." This was typical of her attempts to try to keep her theory together. She really did seem to be grasping at straws at times. She had said, for instance, that the surrogate mother part of Darci had waited for Cindy. Zimmerman questioned, "Was it the surrogate mother part that used the gun to take Cindy off base?" Dr. McCarty answered: "I would think that was the same part that got angry, part two, as I've defined it, that used to point guns at her mother behind a door so that her mother wouldn't see. I think that part probably felt that Mrs. Ray couldn't see the gun, whether or not she did, and I don't think we know whether she did. . . . I think at that point she may have had Mrs. Ray a little bit confused with both herself and her mother, and I think that part could have assumed that Mrs. Ray did not see the gun and certainly that it didn't involve her, because that part of the mother never knew about the gun before."

The jury surely must have found such statements confusing and farfetched. And once Dr. McCarty was starting to sound rather scattered and thin on evidence, Zimmerman pointed to what he saw as the great weakness of Dr. McCarty's case: "Now you've talked a lot about 'possibly' and you have talked a lot about—understanding it's really speculation on

LULLABY AND GOODNIGHT

your part—what was operating at any particular time...."

Dr. McCarty held on to her position, but she must have sounded a little desperate. "Excuse me, I think there is a dissociative disorder and there are different parts operating at different times. I've done the best map that I can do without [Darci's] assistance. You know, she is either not able or is not quite able to tell us at this point, all the details."

Yet the jury must have remembered Darci's confession, which they heard on tape. She sounded much more coherent and systematic than Dr. McCarty. Maybe that was because one of her states was talking, and that state could tell the story from that one point of view. But a jury of lay people must have found themselves wondering about this six-part Darci. For them, perhaps *that* was the fairy tale being told by a person who clearly believed her own story.

CHAPTER 12

The trial of Darci Pierce became a battle of "shrinks." Dr. McCarty's theory was only the beginning. One of the mental health experts the defense introduced was Dr. Susan Brayfield-Cave, a clinical psychologist from the University of New Mexico. Dr. Cave had done some of the initial workup on Darci, administering a host of tests. She introduced the terms that continually reappeared throughout the trial. Virtually every mental health expert, including Dr. Cave, diagnosed Darci as having narcissistic and borderline personality disorders. Narcissism is an extreme self-absorption or self-centeredness. Borderline personalities live on the edge between fantasy and reality and sometimes believe their own fantasies, even though they do not become outright psychotic; they have great trouble with relationships and therefore tend to cling and become dependent on those they do create; they are impulsive and given to dramatic mood shifts.

Dr. Cave also saw a tendency in Darci to dissociate, as did all the others. But the question would persist: Did Darci merely use dissociation as a defense mechanism, or did she slip into separate personalities?

Other questions persisted: Did Darci actually experience a pseudo pregnancy or did she fake those symptoms entirely? Did she have a factitious disorder, which is a fixation on certain physical ailments and a pattern of faking or simulating those ailments? Another related disorder that some would mention was somatic disorder, which is the tendency to have multiple physical problems or diseases. Did she have enough physical problems to indicate such a disorder? Was Darci actually more accurately defined as having an antisocial personality, which is a character disorder, not legal insanity?

Every authority talked about the *DSM-III-R,* with all its complicated definitions, schematic axes, "contributing symptoms," numerical symptom requirements, and heavy jargon. Surely the jurors must have wanted to scream, "But is she *crazy?* That's what I need to know."

The defense lawyers all said she was. Dr. Cave began with her array of tests, and concluded that Darci was very complicated and very ill. Dr. Goodwin certainly agreed, but she had a "grab bag" way of talking, jumping around, naming off diseases and disorders, and pulling up details of information from various sources, from various times in Darci's life. She would mention Darci's claim to have been raped—which had never been mentioned in court—and then admit that it wasn't really ever proved a rape but only a baby-sitter becoming flirtatious with her. Or she would imply that Darci had experienced "lost time" on many occasions but then be hard-pressed to give more than one or two examples. At one point, Dr. Goodwin tried to explain Darci's personality with its divisions and parts: ". . . I feel that what kept Darci functioning so well for so many years in between her behavior problems in grade school and the crime was that she had pretty good cooperation going between this side of her that thought she was pregnant—this side that's kind of young and very feminine and very interested in babies and pregnancy—and this side that's kind of older and more masculine, very survival oriented. So I think for a long time they cooperated pretty well and kept out some of the sides of her that are more out of control. . . .

"As I see it, the side of her that's very survival oriented knows a lot about the side of her that's naive and kind of cheerleaderlike and friendly. That side of her knows very little about the side of her that's more survival oriented, manipulative, does the lying, keeps things going, so there was a lot of cooperation, I think among the personality states and that's usual. People have, I think, a misconception a lot, because of fiction, which is the way that most people get introduced to this disorder, that I know. The side of the personality will be like black-and-white, and, you know, the black side will know nothing about the white side and the white side will know nothing about the black side. It's actually more complicated than that."

This is actually one of Dr. Goodwin's more lucid moments. At least it contains a kind of explanation of what she thought was going on inside Darci. Perhaps the more sophisticated jurors were able to picture this split person, with dark and light sides, and maybe they could imagine some sort of breakdown, in which a kind of madness would take over.

But Dr. Goodwin talked a long time and said a great many things, and all of it together must have seemed a veritable maze to the jurors. Yet this was a Harvard medical school graduate, and underneath it all was an absolute conviction that Darci was unable to control herself on the day of the crime. The jurors had probably come to the trial ready to believe that. The defense team may have made a mistake by putting Dr. McCarty on the stand. What sounded complex but possible in Dr. Goodwin's words often sounded bizarre and even fabricated when Dr. McCarty spoke. The six personalities jumping in and out on the day of the crime, some of them vaguely defined, the "maybes" and "mights" and "possiblys" strewn throughout the language, and all the conclusions that sounded more like science fiction than science—all that must have been very difficult to swallow.

Even at that, if the prosecution had brought in equally confusing witnesses—only with different conclusions—the impression of craziness might have combined with the common person's impulses, and said, in effect, "Okay, just as I suspected; this woman is nuts." But the prosecution brought in only two mental health witnesses, one a psychologist and one a psychiatrist, and they were both remarkable for their orderly, clear explanations, their systematic approaches, and above all, their appeal to common sense.

Dr. Julieann Lockwood met many hours with Darci and she reviewed videotapes of Dr. Goodwin's interviews along with all the tests that others had administered. She also did some testing of her own. As the head of the New Mexico Department of Psychiatry Forensic Service, she had done hundreds of forensic evaluations.

Dr. Lockwood was a neat, attractive, graying woman, whose style inspired confidence. Her approach was to review the tests and interviews that the defense's mental health experts had used, but to do so systematically and carefully, and essentially to contend that in many cases the defense experts had jumped to rather extreme conclusions on the basis of very little information. What had sounded so theoretical and invented by the defense, in other words, was, according to Dr. Lockwood, just what it sounded. Typical of Dr. Lockwood's analysis was her statement about Darci's dissociations: "... she is basically an intelligent young woman who is focused essentially on herself, her own needs, her own desires, who is very much involved with her own wishes, who uses as basic coping strategies, ways of dealing with stress, withdrawal, disengaging."

She went on to explain that most people have contradictory elements to their personalities. Most of us are thoughtful at times and impulsive in other moods. "These kind of contradictions are not unusual, particularly in young adults and adolescents. . . ."

Doctors Cave, Goodwin, and McCarty had created a wild picture, with multiple personalities bouncing about in Darci's skin, a *kaleidoscope*, to use Dr. Goodwin's word. But Dr. Lockwood stopped the spinning pieces and presented a coherent design. She used a quotation from Darci to describe what was going on inside her: "I grew up in a . . . fantasy world. I created a utopia for myself. I never faced reality or problems." To this, Dr. Lockwood added, ". . . I think that really describes her coping strategy, that she copes primarily by disengaging herself from the problems at hand by focusing on her wishes and . . . letting her heart, if you will, rule her head in terms of what behavior she then engages in and I think this has been a lifelong pattern."

What had been, in other words, a form of madness—a shattered psyche—for the defense, became, in Dr. Lockwood's explanation, a "coping strategy." The important distinction Dr. Lockwood made was between dissociation as a defense mechanism and an actual dissociation disorder. We all find our ways of dealing with stress, and according to Dr. Lockwood, Darci's way was to disengage from reality, to make up fantasies, to go into a little dreamworld. But it was a conscious coping method that had become a habit. Dr. Lockwood simply found insufficient backing for the idea that Darci was splitting off into separate personalities. As she reviewed records, tests, reports of Darci's friends, she found very few documented incidents of Darci doing anything extraordinary. There was the well-discussed event in sixth grade when Darci had apparently broken a window and had not remembered doing it. But the memory loss was Darci's own report, and even if it was taken as a clear-cut example of a lost-time experience, where were all the others to back up the concept of shifting ego states?

Dr. Lockwood described people she had treated with dissociative disorders. They were dysfunctional people, unable to hold jobs, confused and stressed and frightened by their lost-time experiences. By contrast, Darci was known as a charming, fully-functioning person. Her husband, family, and friends reported no awareness of any shifts between personality states. They did report that she exaggerated, even lied, and that she could be manipulative and self-centered.

If Darci had mental problems, according to Dr. Lockwood, they were not terribly mysterious. She disengaged from reality when she came under stress. Or she used the childish method of fantasizing. In conversations, she used verbal methods of avoiding subjects that caused her stress, and this explained some of her inappropriate or unpredictable shifts when she was being interviewed by policemen. Why would she talk so much about South Africa with Steve Coppinger on the way back from viewing the woman she had murdered? Because that was her consistent method, immature as it was, of running from things she didn't want to deal with. Why would she make jokes in the middle of conversations about the murder? Once again, as a coping method, a defense mechanism that had become an ingrained habit.

What Dr. Lockwood saw in Darci were many elements of an antisocial personality: "There was no indication in her behavior of . . . empathy . . . for the dead woman. . . . She never called her a woman, she never called her Cindy, Mrs. Ray. . . . She always called her 'the victim' . . . until I finally pushed very hard and insisted that she use another word and then she finally did. But her choice of words was constantly 'victim' as if, again, to disengage herself, to keep that distance from herself and this human being that she had come to know, however briefly."

Dr. Lockwood refused to buy into the defense's concept of shifting personalities on the day of the crime. What Dr. Lockwood saw was an obsession to have a baby, and two choices: to give up the lie and level with her husband, which she considered doing, or to "get" a baby. "In Mrs. Pierce we see no marked impairment of functioning. We see no obvious eccentricities. We see no hallucinations or delusions which in any way relate to the crimes with which she is charged."

Finally Dr. Lockwood reminded the jury of all the deliberating Darci did during the process of the crime. She considered leaving, just disappearing, but she didn't do that. She went to the hospital and the Ob/Gyn clinic on base—the most obvious place to find a pregnant woman. She waited for Cindy for two hours, during which time she had plenty of time to think about what she was doing there. She abducted Cindy, whether with the gun or not, and drove home, where she saw her husband's car and made the

LULLABY AND GOODNIGHT

decision to go to a secluded place. She drove for quite some time, during which she considered turning back at least twice. She claimed to have chatted with Cindy before finally striking her. Through all this, she had time to consider her actions, and she even admitted to thinking she should not continue. Rather than a series of personality shifts, what Dr. Lockwood saw was a persistent, self-centered, goal-directed, carefully accomplished theft.

Dr. Lockwood only hedged on one point. She could not say with assurance what was actually going through Darci's mind at the actual moment of the strangulation and cesarean. Needless to say, the defense was quick to jump on Dr. Lockwood's uncertainty on this one point, but perhaps John Bogren would have been better off to leave the issue alone. Once he forced Dr. Lockwood to take a position, her statement was more damaging to Darci than the admission she had made in the first place. She told Bogren: "I think that is the crucial moment at which I have some degree of uncertainty. In my opinion, my psychological opinion, Mrs. Ray was essentially irrelevant to Darci Pierce. Obtaining the baby was the relevant act. Whether at that moment she was so focused on obtaining the baby that she thought nothing beyond that, only the process that would go into—only the reasons for continuing to . . . hit [Mrs. Ray] on the head and drag her to an excluded spot— the question of whether she carefully weighed the negatives, I can't be certain of. But if she did not intend at that point to do her further harm, if it was not in her mind at that point to do her further harm, then hitting her on the side of the head and dragging her from the car to another excluded area is totally inexplicable."

Mr. Bogren must have swallowed hard, but then he

came back to the same question: "So if I understand you, you cannot say to a reasonable degree of medical certainty what her intent was when she struck Mrs. Ray on the side of the head; is that right?"

But Dr. Lockwood replied, "I can say with reasonable psychological certainty that her intent was to obtain the baby in any way she could."

Bogren shot back, "But you don't know what her mental state was when she did that?" And Dr. Lockwood granted that. Maybe Bogren should have stopped. Instead, he followed with, "If you don't know what her mental state was, how do you know what her intent was?"

Dr. Lockwood's answer was long and complete. She listed all the actions of Darci's entire afternoon that had led to that moment: the clear intent to get to the point where the baby could be taken. Bogren was left with an image he didn't want. Supposing a robber marched into a bank with a gun, held it on the teller and demanded money. And supposing, at the last moment, this thief had second thoughts or doubts—or some other psychological confusion. Supposing he even regretted the act. The thief still planned and carried out the crime. The state of mind as he picks up the money is not really the issue. Could he argue that he wasn't guilty because, at the last moment, he didn't remember what had happened, or he "lost control"?

The other mental health expert hired by the prosecution was a real pro. Dr. Resnick was a professor from Case Western Reserve University medical school, a psychiatrist, and expert in law as it pertained to psychiatry. He had taught in the law school as well as the medical school, and had even given classes in effective court presentations for forensic mental health experts. He had been contacted by Dr. Lockwood to do an evaluation on Darci. He was asked to decide whether she had been capable of forming intent in the crime and whether she was legally insane under the laws of New Mexico. He collected sixty-five documents that he reviewed, including tests and transcripts of other experts' interviews, and then he spent nine-and-a-half hours with Darci.

More than any other witness, he presented a systematic, orderly catalog of findings, with specific conclusion based on specific evidence. More than anyone, even Dr. Lockwood, he appealed to the common sense of the jury. A balding man, wearing reading glasses and a neat blue suit, he looked authoritative, and his style was orderly and confident. His conclusion was that Darci exhibited symptoms that could classify her as an antisocial personality. She hated her mother and expressed teenage fantasies of killing her. She had run away from home once, and viewed her trip to South Africa as another occasion of running away, even though she had a scholarship. She was openly defiant to her parents. She had committed vandalism, abused drugs, and she had gotten in repeated fights. She lied constantly. She had been promiscuous to the point of reporting, as a younger teenager, to sex with four to seven "strange men" in a week. She had once talked with others of having someone run over her sister-in-law, whom she hated, so that she could take her brother's baby as her own.

All this, Dr. Resnick saw as consistent with many of the criminals he had dealt with before: people without remorse (and he saw none in Darci) and people who could not sustain relationships. He agreed that Darci was narcissistic and showed borderline tendencies in her fantasizing, but he did not believe that she was legally insane. He saw almost no evidence of dissociative disorder, and certainly not of multiple personality disorder.

One of the things Dr. Resnick did was to listen to Darci's own opinion about herself. Dr. Goodwin and Dr. McCarty had trusted Darci's accounts of lost time or voices in her head, but they rarely trusted Darci's self-analysis. They had looked for interpretations for all her actions. But Darci often explained herself rather simply and surprisingly. She told Dr. Resnick how she faked her pregnancy, for instance, by wearing baggy clothes, putting on weight, letting her abdomen hang out, walking awkwardly, and rippling her muscles to give the impression the baby was moving. When he asked her how she could pull this off, she said she was a skilled actress. When Dr. Resnick asked how good she was, Darci replied, "Give me a script," which he took to mean that she thought she could play any role that was required of her.

She admitted to Dr. Resnick that she considered stealing a baby from a newborn nursery as one alternative (showing no concern for the parents whose child would be lost). When he asked why she didn't admit to her husband that she was not pregnant, she explained her motivation: "Well, I just didn't want him to catch me in a lie. I was afraid I would lose him."

Darci had claimed in her confession that the gun she set in her lap "didn't involve" Cindy Ray. But she told Dr. Resnick that she got the gun out because she "didn't want Mrs. Ray to leave." She did tell Dr. Resnick that she had heard voices in her head since she was eleven or twelve. They were men's voices, speaking gibberish, but she could get rid of them by changing positions, and they never told her to do anything, nor did they bother her much.

Dr. Resnick was not impressed by Dr. McCarty's analysis and diagnosis. He said that young medical students had a tendency to learn about all sorts of diseases and then start diagnosing all of these rare diseases in their patients. But experienced physicians learned that "when you hear hoofbeats, assume it's a horse and not a zebra." In his view, Darci's actions—the hoofbeats—pointed to antisocial behavior, which was a "common horse." But Dr. Goodwin's diagnosis of atypical dissociative disease with strong elements of multiple personality disorder was an attempt to put stripes on the horse, to identify a zebra where very little evidence existed. ". . . Dr. Goodwin happens to have a particular interest in multiple personality disorder. It is a special area of interest. She's published in it. So in my view, rather than see a horse as a horse, she was looking for a zebra."

And it was Resnick's common-sense style that was especially convincing: ". . . Another example where I feel Dr. Goodwin just simply overcalled normal phenomena . . . [was when] she asked Mrs. Pierce the question, 'Have you ever had the feeling that your actions were controlled by others?' and the defendant, Mrs. Pierce, answered yes. And in Dr. Goodwin's original report, this is listed as one of the evidences of the atypical dissociative phenomenon which is really the aspect of multiple personality. But on the videotape when Dr. Goodwin later clarified what did it mean that she felt that others controlled her actions, Mrs. Pierce answered, 'Well, as a child my mother controlled my actions. When I worked, my boss controlled my actions,' a perfectly rational, understandable phenomenon that all of us could answer. But this, to Dr. Goodwin, was evidence of multiple personality states."

Harry Zimmerman had believed from the beginning that the one thing he would have to convince the jury of was that Darci was not very different from any other criminal, and in Dr. Resnick he had found the expert to make exactly that case. Bogren had to hope that Dr. Resnick had gone too far. His manner was confident and systematic, but maybe the case all seemed too "wild" to be summarized in such simple terms.

As John Bogren took the witness, he tried to break apart the diagnosis of antisocial personality. He pushed and Dr. Resnick held when he thought he could, and let go when he knew his case was weak. Bogren finally got Dr. Resnick to admit that the diagnosis might not hold up. One of the elements in a complete diagnosis of such a personality disorder was that the person could not hold a monogamous relationship for a year. Bogren contended that Darci had been promiscuous when younger, but had stuck with Ray for about two years (before the interlude with Kathy Landrum).

Dr. Resnick didn't fight. He said that if this was true, his diagnosis would have to be adjusted. But it didn't matter, he claimed. Whether Darci could be diagnosed as antisocial or only as having many antisocial traits—which everyone had already described—was not the real issue. The question was whether she was insane.

That was true. But Bogren had made a little crack in the wall and some of Dr. Resnick's veracity was now called to question.

But Bogren was unable to break Resnick's considered, reasonable demeanor, nor get him to back off his basic position. Bogren seemed to become frustrated with the coolness of the man. Later in the cross-examination, Bogren returned to the issue of whether Darci really acted the way an antisocial person would. Hadn't her manner when she told the lie in the hospital been bizarre, so cool and calm? Resnick, however, answered that this was exactly how antisocial people acted; they were effective liars. Bogren sounded frustrated when he responded, "Usually though . . . they tend to get a little defensive, don't they?"

"Well," Dr. Resnick said, in his own calm style, "the more skillful the antisocial personality, the more they keep their cool, look you in the eye and lie."

"And she's a skillful, cunning, antisocial person?"

The tone of the question was sarcastic and unbelieving. But Resnick didn't respond to the sarcasm. He simply stated, "She's a very skillful liar."

"Well, her lies weren't being believed; how skillful could she have been?" Bogren shot back.

Calmly, again, Resnick replied, "Well . . . the tale was unraveling but she did her best and she came up with some very plausible stories to explain the mud, the blood. She did a very good job for someone whose story was unraveling."

The cross-examination eventually ended with Bogren having attacked Resnick's theory in every way he could, and Resnick unshaken. When Harry Zimmerman took over for redirect he simply had Dr. Resnick restate the crucial point that whether Darci was a clear-cut antisocial personality, or whether she only had strong features of antisocial behavior, was not really important. The only real question was whether she was mentally ill, by legal standards. In Dr. Resnick's opinion, she was not. He had interviewed her for nine-and-a-half hours, and he had not seen a single indication that she suffered from dissociative disorder or multiple personality disorder.

The prosecution had rested its case earlier, but they had brought mental health experts as rebuttal to the experts the defense had used. Now Zimmerman announced that the state was finished. Immediately, however, Mr. Bogren announced that the defense had one more witness. An argument at the bench ensued. The prosecution saw no reason why the defense wanted to bring in one more psychologist—the fourth mental health expert they would use. Everything had been said on the issue, hadn't it? But Bogren argued that the defense now needed to answer some of the questions raised by the prosecution experts. Judge Traub allowed Dr. Norman Katz to take the stand.

Katz was a clinical psychologist, not a psychiatrist, and a confident, scientific-sounding witness. Clearly, the defense knew by now that Dr. Goodwin, and especially Dr. McCarty, had not come off well against the more systematic Dr. Lockwood and Dr. Resnick. Someone needed to make the diagnosis of "dissociative disorder, atypical type" seem reasonable and scientific.

Dr. Katz described dissociative disorder as much more common than anyone had believed before the last ten years of research, and he explained the usual connection of the disorder to child abuse. He countered Dr. Lockwood's description of such people as being dysfunctional and stressed. Many of them, he claimed, "would seem very healthy. They might seem like they know what they're doing." They can even be in the midst of dissociation, be asked a question, answer it normally, and return to the unreal environment inside their heads. This, of course, was a possible explanation for Darci's being able to deal with Mr. Hartshorn in the middle of what may have been a dissociative experience.

Darci's sexual activity at age six, he believed, made the likelihood of sexual abuse very high. He was certain that Darci was out of control at the time she committed the crime: "Although Darci had had episodes of having violent fantasies in the past and had episodes of getting into minor trouble, she had never before done anything close to this kind of violent act. My clinical impression in reviewing materials and talking with Darci is that the entire circumstances of her life, her dissociative disorder, and the pressures of discovering that she was not pregnant when she had convinced herself she was, at one level led her to do something over which she had no control."

It was one more statement by one more expert, and maybe by then most of the jurors had decided which theory they could believe. But the tone was clinical and reasoned. Perhaps many of the jurors still found themselves wondering whether a sane person could have done what Darci had done. In that sense, the use of Dr. Katz was an attempt by the defense to get in a final lick, to make their theory stick.

But Michael Cox did the cross-examination, and he was able to make Dr. Katz look rather foolish at times. Katz admitted that telling lies calmly could be an indication of dissociation, but it could also be an indication of antisocial behavior. And yes, dissociation could be a conscious coping style and Darci had admitted to using that technique of dealing with stress.

Perhaps most important, Dr. Katz, under cross-examination, came off sounding as though he didn't know the case nearly as well as other experts had, especially Dr. Resnick. He had spent five hours with Darci and claimed to have reviewed all the documents. But he was confused at times and demonstrated some rather large gaps of knowledge. He was not clear about the crime scene and exactly what steps Darci took to conceal the body. Was he aware that no blood prints were in or on the car, indicating that Darci had washed thoroughly before she returned with the baby? No, he had not been aware of that. Was he aware that Darci had picked up the clip from the gun, with mud from the scene on it, and put it back in the car, obviously another attempt to conceal her involvement in the crime? No, he had not been aware of that.

Finally, Cox ended with, "But it is true, isn't it, Doctor, that the defendant considered other options besides killing a woman and taking her child by force?"

"Yes, she did."

"In the past she had fantasized about killing a woman to get her child, had she not?"

"Yes, there was one episode in that fantasy."

"She arranged for someone else to run over the woman so she would not be linked to that crime, did she not?"

Dr. Katz might have come back with a number of responses. He might have said that this was a mere fantasy, and she had never moved to carry it out. He might have said that in a dissociative state, people often fantasize, and this was a precursor to the dissociative state in which she committed the crime. He might have admitted, one more time, that he hadn't known about that, since the impression one got was that, indeed, he was not aware of all this.

But instead, his answer was a weak, "Uh-huh," and Michael Cox had no further questions.

Bogren was tired. When the judge sent the jury out and then asked the counsel for both sides whether they wanted to work on instructions to the jury "for a while," Harry Zimmerman said, "We're pretty well covered—have ours together."

But Bogren told the judge, "My brain is fried."

He had a legal argument he wanted to make, and he just didn't feel that he could be coherent at the moment. The judge decided to excuse the jury for the weekend. After three weeks of testimony, most of it

LULLABY AND GOODNIGHT

technical and complex, everyone was tired. At 10:30, Monday morning, the jury would return and the attorneys would make their final arguments.

Over the weekend, according to Judge Traub's instructions, the jurors were not to discuss the case with anyone—not family or friends or anyone else. They were to keep an open mind. With that the jury left, and the lawyers began preparation for their last efforts to move the jury to their sides.

CHAPTER 13

On Monday the court reconvened and received final legal instructions. The lunch recess had come and gone before the time finally arrived for each side to make its summation. Harry Zimmerman would go first.

He stood before the jury, leaned on the podium, and spoke in a thoughtful, organized style. At times there was passion and indignation in his voice. He had to walk a narrow line. He had to make a plea for justice, for a proper response to a vicious crime, but he couldn't seem to beat up on this delicate-looking young woman still seated before him. She had never spoken, never been called to the stand to witness, but something in her sad, submissive posture must have appealed to the jury.

Zimmerman started with his major theme—the same one Cox had introduced in opening statements. "Ladies and gentlemen, what this case has presented to you was the consummate actress trying to pull off the ultimate con job. Darci Pierce certainly was expecting a baby. The evidence is indisputable that Darci Pierce was expecting a baby." The clever choice of the word *expecting* was not an accident.

"While there's no doubt that Darci Pierce was expecting a baby, Darci Pierce was not expecting the baby to come from her own womb. Darci Pierce was expecting to get a baby in any way possible to keep with her scenario." He then described all the lies that had led to the day when she had to have the baby. She had received confirmation from doctors that she was not pregnant, but she continued to lie, "and the lie continued to snowball, month after month, and eventually she killed for her goal, and she lied to cover it up."

Zimmerman restated the claim of the prosecution that Darci acted with premeditation and control. He saw in her formal confession all sorts of admissions of weighing right and wrong, deliberating. He pointed to the single most damaging statement, in his opinion—the one thing the jury should not forget. When Darci described convincing Kelly Lyden, the hospital receptionist, to lie for her, she said, "So that bought me more time to try to figure out what I was going to do, or get up my nerve to say something [to her husband]." Zimmerman told the jury to notice the "weighing process" that was going on. Darci contemplated her actions, and she chose a course.

The real question, according to Zimmerman, was whether Darci had any long-standing disease that directly affected the crime. If Darci only responded to temporary pressures, as Dr. Katz claimed, that would not be an argument for insanity under New Mexico law. Then, Zimmerman put in sarcastically, "But I don't know whether you want to rely on Dr. Katz. He didn't really know a lot about the case."

He argued that no real evidence existed for the defense claim for shifting personality states. He then attacked the defense in its most vulnerable area. Dr.

McCarty had made up her mind about Darci before she even asked a question. "That's a pretty quick diagnosis, folks." Why did this happen? Because this was Dr. McCarty's special area of interest. And wasn't she tied directly to Dr. Goodwin through studying with her, and writing articles with her? Wouldn't she pass on her diagnosis to Dr. Goodwin? "They were looking for a conclusion that they eventually found." This, he concluded was "very unscientific." He reminded the jury how often these two doctors said they were only speculating and conjecturing, and yet, according to instructions, juries should discount conjecture and stick with solid evidence.

The first test for insanity was whether Darci knew what she was doing and understood the consequences of her action. But no evidence existed that she was frenzied, distorted in perception, or disorganized in her thinking. She knew the gun would keep Cindy in the car. She accomplished her goal, delivering the baby and passing it off as her own for a time. She knew exactly how to deliver the baby, and she did it very skillfully.

Afterward, she knew she had killed Cindy, and admitted it was wrong. Understanding that what she did was wrong completes the second test for sanity. Why else would she do so much to avoid detection, if she hadn't known what she had done was wrong?

Test three: Could she have prevented herself from committing the crime? Nothing showed that she was in some wild state, hearing voices or responding to a delusion. She understood the option of telling her family the truth, but she decided against that approach.

Also, Darci didn't have to use the gun to get Cindy in the car in order to be guilty of kidnapping. If she used the gun for that purpose at any point along the way, the crime was the same. Cindy was held against her will. And certainly, Darci had put the baby in serious danger of losing its life, and that was child abuse.

Zimmerman began to sense that he had gone a little longer than he wanted, and so he moved, quickly, to his final point, a repetition of the theme which he wanted the jury to hold in mind as they began their deliberations: "Some people yearn for money and power. But I submit to you, ladies and gentlemen, that what is the difference between this defendant here and someone who goes to a convenience store or anybody on the street, shoots them in the head, and takes the contents of their pocket? She knew what she wanted; she went after it; and she got it. And didn't have the moral fiber *not* to take what she wanted."

He walked toward the jury, and his voice took on more force, more intensity, but he was still very controlled. "Yeah, it's a bizarre act, but you can see it was done for a rational reason and in a very cold, calculating, and mechanical way. The state maintains that when you get back and review the evidence and the jury instructions you've been provided, you'll find this defendant guilty of first-degree murder, willful and deliberate murder, and felony murder as the result of the kidnapping. But you'll find her guilty of kidnapping. You'll find her guilty of child abuse. And that this defendant has been proven sane beyond a reasonable doubt. There is no common sense doubt about the sanity of this defendant. Thank you."

Judge Traub then gave the jury a fifteen-minute recess and cautioned them, once again, not to discuss the case until all the arguments had been made.

It was three in the afternoon when Mr. Bogren began his summation. He knew that he had his work cut out for him. People liked to believe that common sense can rule, and Harry Zimmerman had argued that the jury should let their common sense tell them that Darci was not insane. Dr. Lockwood, Dr. Resnick, and now Harry Zimmerman, had attempted to dispel the idea that something bizarre and crazy had happened, and the jury had had plenty of time to get used to the strangeness of the crime. It must have been rather satisfying to think that maybe the world hadn't turned upside down after all, that this crime could be explained the way most crimes could: an act of greed and self-centeredness, by an essentially "bad apple." Everyone in the jury—everyone in the world—had known kids who fight and lie and cheat, and finally do something that gets them into big trouble. If Darci could be explained that way, everyone could go home feeling rather comforted that such a person had been "taken off the street."

The other possibility, that there are people who are so immensely complicated that they can walk around among us seeming perfectly normal, even charming, but who can suddenly strike down even someone like Cindy—or anyone else for that matter—that possibility is not something anyone likes to believe. Could the jury really buy into this defense?

The defense had to rebuild the idea of the bizarre, crazy world in Darci's head, but they had to deal with the difficulty of understanding this kind of craziness. What Bogren obviously decided was that the time for further explaining, further psychological claptrap, was gone. He had to appeal to the emotions, the instincts of his jurors, and convince them to remember what they probably believed in the beginning: that something was wrong in this case—that normal people just didn't do things like this. His approach was to be a little scattered, a little wild, perhaps to create a sense of the madness that he wanted them to feel.

LULLABY AND GOODNIGHT

Bogren, with his shuffling manner and disheveled appearance, was perhaps better prepared to create a sense of that craziness than was the rather sedate Ms. Robins, or the natty Tom Jameson. Bogren looked out of place in a suit; he kept his tie a little loose; his mustache drooped over his upper lip; his speaking style was the opposite of Zimmerman's. He whined at times, waved his arms, pleaded, and his organization was anybody's guess. But what he pounded on, repeated dozens of times, was one theme: "Something is wrong here."

His first point was that the prosecution had distorted the truth. He began a long, scattered laundry list of claims that he believed were never proven. But he chose rather trivial examples. Even if the prosecution really had made the claims—which no one could remember at that point—they were minor matters in a case with plenty of crucial questions. Obviously, Bogren wanted to impugn the veracity of the prosecution, to imply that if some little things were wrong, perhaps all sorts of things were wrong.

Bogren then jumped to another claim that was not easy to understand: "They put on an expert to tell you to ignore your instincts, to ignore your intuition, to ignore the evidence, to ignore the law, to put your common sense aside and find her guilty. But use your common sense. Ask yourself where your instincts have gotten you so far in life. They tell you that Darci Pierce is guilty of first-degree murder. This case is about as far away from first-degree murder as we are from the north pole."

But the jury must have wondered who was this expert he was referring to? Hadn't the defense experts stretched the imagination as much as anyone had? Bogren didn't tie it down. If the case was so far from first-degree murder as he claimed, why not explain why he thought so. His summation would continue this way throughout—jumping about, making emotional stabs that often remained unexplained.

"They tell you that it was a willful murder," Bogren argued, "that she carefully weighed the consequences of her actions, for and against, when neither of their experts could conclude, and yet we and you are to conclude, that that is true beyond a reasonable doubt." The jurors must have stopped to ask themselves what he meant by that. In fact, both Lockwood and Resnick had been firm and clear in their diagnoses that Darci was not mentally ill. They had only admitted that they were not certain exactly what was going through her mind at the moment of the crime. But Bogren didn't want to be logical and reasonable. He was getting mad, appealing to emotion—what he called common sense—and he was trying to bring the jury with him into the emotion of his argument.

Not only had Dr. Resnick listed his proofs that Darci had weighed her actions and deliberated on her choices, Harry Zimmerman had reviewed them. What the jury had heard was a clear argument for that position. That didn't make it true, but it is hard to believe that a response that was equivalent to "Oh, yeah!" would persuade them to think differently.

The jurors were given no chance to consider. Bogren kept jumping, kept gesticulating, kept getting angrier. Whether any of the jurors were moved by the technique is difficult to say, but the impression may have been that the man was desperate and frustrated, rather than considered and accurate.

Bogren did, however, make some crucial points for his position. He told the jury that to convict Darci of felony murder, they had to conclude that Darci had formed a specific intent to commit murder at the time that she abducted Cindy. "The key to intent is the key to the case. Even Dr. Lockwood, in her report, says that she can't say what the intent was when she struck the victim." To Bogren it was clear that if the prosecution couldn't prove this intent, they had no case. The action could have been caused by an "irresistible impulse," which would be proof that the defendant was legally out of control. The jury did not have to believe that Darci Pierce suffered from a mental disease. The real question was whether she ever, "on any sane and rational level" formulated the intent to take the baby. That intent was necessary to convict Darci of first-degree murder.

Bogren again tried to get the jury to forget everything they had heard during the three weeks of court and go back to their first impulses: "No one in their right mind could contemplate successfully creating the cesarean operation with a car key."

Then he moved to the appeal that he would make time and again. "Putting the insanity issue aside, the state has failed to prove beyond a reasonable doubt the crime of first-degree murder or the crime of kidnapping. You know that. They can stand here and speak in statements about what shows premeditation. The evidence does not show it. The key to this case is that the cesarean was performed with a car key. That is the key to the intent."

But Bogren did not take on the list of evidences that the defense had presented. He merely went back to that impulse that might speak to a juror and say, "How could she have planned if she had no knife?" Time and again he repeated his refrain: "You know that." He wanted them to feel something at gut level and forget about all the expert testimony.

Dr. Resnick had made the crime seem rather logical, but now Bogren listed questions that he felt the prosecution couldn't answer. He pointed out all

Darci's illogical actions—going to Kirtland Air Force Base to commit the crime, taking the baby to the hospital and telling such a wild story, not concealing the body, not taking a knife, etc. And then again, "They tell you to ignore your instincts, but your instincts tell you that what she did made no sense. Even Tom Craig, who dealt with liars all the time, admitted that Darci's calm lies raised the hair on the back of his neck."

Bogren then read off quotations of people who perceived her actions as bizarre, and hit the refrain again: "I tell you not to ignore your instincts, your intuition, your common sense. . . . When the answer is not simple, and the simple answer is not logical, then the answer simply is not simple."

Bogren knew he had to dispel the idea that his own expert witnesses were loose and given to conjecture, and that the state's experts were more scientific and systematic. He claimed that the state had brought in "slick, professional" witnesses, whereas the defense had used the workaday mental health specialists who commonly work with such people as Darci. "Maybe their answers seemed somewhat bizarre, but so were Darci's actions. . . . Maybe Jean Goodwin wasn't the slick witness the state put on for professional testifying, but you knew that lady knew what she was talking about." She had perhaps given a graduate course in dissociative disease when the jury might have wished for a basic course, but it was clear the woman knew her material. And she knew that Darci was almost surely a victim of child abuse.

By contrast Dr. Resnick had claimed that when a child is having sex at six that's a precursor to an antisocial personality disorder. "I say to you when you're having sex at six, you know something happened. It's learned behavior. When you have a girl who sleeps . . . with a knife under her pillow and a gun underneath her bed, you know something happened."

All this was proof to Bogren that Darci had a long-standing disease. He took the many proofs that Resnick had used to prove antisocial behavior and tried to show that all of these were actual precursors to a multiple personality–type disease. He mentioned the white light Darci claimed she saw when she got angry, her withdrawal from people, her fantasies about killing her mother or her sister-in-law. In fact, he argued, Darci lost control, was literally out of her mind at the time of the crime. He named other examples of how bizarre her behavior was: her conviction that she was pregnant, her catatonic state in jail, her ability to believe her own lies.

And again, "You know she has a multipersonality-type disorder. You know that."

"I will give you a rational explanation for the crime," Bogren stated. "Or maybe it will be an irrational explanation for an irrational crime." What he presented was roughly the explanation that his experts had given, but simplified, without all the shifts of personalities. He portrayed basically a two-part Darci, under pressure, and finally driven beyond control. But he asserted "facts" with little regard to past testimony. For instance, he said Darci didn't know whether she was pregnant or not, "but it's finally hitting her that she isn't." That, of course, is directly contradictory to Darci's own account.

But the key to Bogren's "rational explanation" was that once out in the mountains, Cindy must have gone for the gun. That could have triggered Darci's violence just when she was about to get back in the car and drive Cindy back. He admitted that he didn't know that was true, but he offered it as one explanation for what pushed Darci over the line.

In any case, Darci, at the moment of the crime, was out of control. "Darci Pierce went to sleep and woke to discover that she killed someone. And that simply is the truth. I know what you're thinking. You're thinking, 'So what? So what if she was insane? Look what she did.' She sits there and she scares you. Because she could be the girl next door. The woman who baby-sat for your child. And it's scary to think that someone who appears to be so normal can be so crazy. But that's it. She was a nice, loving, caring person or all these people wouldn't come to court to tell you that. . . . You don't go from that caring person who shares, who loves, who loves children, who loves dogs, to the type of murderer that could complete that kind of crime. There's something in between here. The 'so what' is that you're sworn to follow the law. The law is that if you're out of control and cannot prevent yourself from doing it, you're not guilty. It's the law that we all live by, and we are a nation of law and not of men. So I'm going to ask you today to do what the law says you have to do."

He then moved to his powerful emotional pitch: "This whole case is a contradiction. Everything you heard is a paradox. There's a lot of things that I haven't said. But you could feel it. You know that something is wrong here. You could feel the devil in this courtroom. You know that's true. On July twenty-third, 1987, Cindy Ray was brutally murdered. She was brutally killed by an insane person. On July twenty-third, 1987, a miracle happened. Amelia Ray was born. She was delivered by the same insane person—a person who was a loving, caring person, who took that baby to the hospital. That total disregard for her own safety or being caught . . . and that is the extreme paradox in this case. It is a bizarre crime. It deserves a bizarre explanation. On behalf of all the people who have come to speak on Darci's behalf, who still love and care about her, we thank you for your consideration in this matter."

Bogren had to hope that much of the technical information that had been presented over the last three weeks would make less of an impression than the gut-level appeal that only a crazy person could do what Darci had done. He would later say that he hadn't meant devil when he said the "devil was in the room"; he had meant demons. But his point was merely that something felt wrong, not that any satanic force was involved.

The prosecution would have one last chance for rebuttal. Michael Cox would now have his word. He got up, approached the jury, knowing they were tired and had already heard two long speeches. He promised them he would be brief. His style was softer than Zimmerman's, but reasoned and precise—a complete contrast to Bogren.

Bogren had argued that the car key was the "key to Darci's intent." Since she didn't have a weapon, she didn't have intent to kill anyone or perform a cesarean. Cox countered that the intent didn't have to be formed before she left home. She could have made the decision at the parking lot, and then she may have realized that she had to make do with whatever she had. She did go home, and she may have gone there to get a knife. Why did she go to the mountains if she didn't have intent to conceal what she was going to do?

She had shown she could control her impulses in the past. But on this day, she chose to act, sacrificing Cindy.

Cox did not believe that Darci thought up the dissociative disorder defense on her own. But she was an excellent actress. She had told Dr. Resnick that she could prove her acting ability. Once Dr. Goodwin began to suggest the kind of experiences that could be used to create an insanity defense, Darci came up with plenty of them.

Cox scoffed at John Bogren's theory about Cindy "going for the gun." The jury had received instruction about speculation. This was clearly speculation without evidence, and a grasp at a theory that exonerates Darci from responsibility. But where was the struggle? Where were the scratches on either woman's hands or face or arms? This theory should not even be considered, since there was no evidence for it.

Finally Cox focused on one moment: when Mr. Hartshorn drove up, and Darci knew exactly what she was doing, and knew how to get rid of him. She understood that she had to conceal what she was doing, and she was under control. Where is this impulsive, irresistible urge the defense described? How, right in the middle of the act, could she stop and take care of business and then go back to her madness?

The jury did not start its deliberation until late in the day. They had time to choose their foreman, but little else. The next morning they convened again, and at one point asked for individual copies of the jury instructions, but received the answer from the judge that such copies were inappropriate. They recessed for lunch, and then at about three in the afternoon, they requested information about whether there was a difference between felony murder and first-degree murder. Judge Traub sent back the answer that there was no difference.

LULLABY AND GOODNIGHT

Shortly thereafter, after only a few hours of actual deliberation, the jury returned. The members filed into their seats and sat down. One woman was crying. The foreman handed over the slips of paper, and the judge read the three verdicts: "We find the defendant guilty but mentally ill of murder in the first degree as charged in count one."

The foreman was asked whether the decision was unanimous, and he said that it was.

"We find the defendant guilty but mentally ill of kidnapping as charged in count two."

The judge asked the foreman whether the decision was unanimous, and he said that it was.

"We find the defendant guilty but mentally ill of child abuse as charged in count three."

Again, the decision was unanimous.

Darci did not move. She was dressed in a dark blue jumpsuit issued at the jail. She sat, seemingly in some other world, still looking down at the table. But not far away, her mother, dressed in her expansive blue flowered dress, cried openly, the tears running down her cheeks.

"Guilty but mentally ill." It was the prosecution that celebrated. Darci was going to prison.

But what did the decision really mean? If the jury had said "guilty," the decision would have been clear. That would have meant that the jurors had accepted the opinions of Dr. Lockwood and Dr. Resnick that Darci was not very different from most criminals. She was fully responsible for her crime. Or if the jurors had acquitted Darci, again the decision would have made sense. The jurors would have demonstrated that they trusted in Dr. McCarty's and Dr. Goodwin's theory that Darci suffered a dissociative disorder so severe that she had not really acted on her own will when she committed the crime.

But what did "guilty but mentally ill" mean? What did the jury believe? They obviously had come to a compromise decision. After all the wrangling over Darci's mental state, the jurors had not been able to conclude that she was normal. Yet at the same time, they weren't willing to exonerate her. She was not a psychotic, powerless to control herself.

Finally, then, what the jury apparently wanted was, first, to keep Darci off the street. They did see her as too sick, and perhaps too dangerous, to walk free. Yet they also didn't feel that she was a common criminal. What they wanted—and this has been corroborated by the statements of some of the jurors—was to see Darci receive counseling. They expected her to be sent to a mental institution, not to a prison for hardened criminals.

So who won? In a certain sense, the defense actually made its point with the jury. The jurors couldn't convict Darci without the qualification that she was mentally ill, which to them apparently meant that she should receive help more than punishment.

One is left to wonder what the decision would have been had the choice for the jury been strictly between guilty and not guilty. No one will ever know what the jury might have done in that case, but apparently their decision was for a compromise position.

When Judge Traub later pronounced the sentence, he actually gave Darci the minimum sentence he might have given. He sentenced her to life in prison without parole, but he allowed the other sentences—for kidnapping and child abuse—to run concurrently. In New Mexico "life in prison" means that the prisoner will be eligible for parole after thirty years. This means that Darci could get out of prison at age forty-nine. In a recent case, a prisoner serving a life sentence in New Mexico appealed that he should have the right to reduction of his sentence for good behavior, the same as anyone else. But he lost his case. As things now stand, "life" still means a minimum of thirty years. Darci will probably get out of prison someday, but not until at least the year 2017.

The defense lawyers, to this day, bitterly contend that Darci won her case with the jurors but lost it with the state of New Mexico. "Guilty but mentally ill," they contend, means nothing. Darci was sent to the same prison in Grants, New Mexico, under the same conditions she would have been kept under, had she received a guilty verdict. When she entered the prison, she was given a psychological evaluation, but so does every other inmate. The prison does have a resident psychologist and a visiting psychiatrist, but according to Bill Chambreau, Darci's social worker, Darci has received little help. When Darci was sentenced, the defense team presented a plan for Darci's psychological care. It included extensive therapy by someone who understood dissociative disorders. Darci needed, in the view of the public defenders, to go through the thorough process of identifying her divided personality states and coming to understand her own confusion about her identity. Then she needed to integrate the parts of her shattered self. No one at the prison is trained to do that, however, nor is anyone attempting such a treatment. Darci's sole treatment, according to Chambreau, who has kept in touch with her, was to give her a drug that was meant to control seizures—something Darci had never really suffered from. The drug made her sick, and so she stopped taking it. The newspapers portrayed that as her refusal to receive help. But Chambreau is convinced that Darci is only being punished; she is receiving no help for her mental problems.

Bill Chambreau works out of the public defenders'

office. He has worked with thousands of criminals during his career. He shares some of the style of his friend John Bogren. He is taller and a little neater, but equally informal and equally outspoken. He is absolutely convinced that Darci's life is being wasted when, in fact, she is capable of living a productive life.

Don Moriarty, assistant warden at the prison, denies Chambreau's charges. He says that Darci is receiving care. He does admit, however, that her case is handled the same as any other. The fact that she received a "guilty but mentally ill" verdict has no effect on the approach the prison takes.

New Mexico, in effect, has created a verdict for a jury to choose, but it has not created a commensurate sentence. Since jurors are not instructed on what the different verdicts mean, what has really been created is an illusion. The jurors are allowed to think that they can reach a compromise position when in reality the law creates a basic imbalance: two "guilty" verdicts, one "not guilty."

Or at least that's how the defense lawyers see it. They remain deeply committed to their belief that Darci is mentally ill and should not be housed in a prison with ordinary criminals.

Early in 1990, the public defender's office lost an appeal to the state supreme court on Darci's behalf, but they lost it on a narrow three-to-two vote. The appeal was primarily based on another strange twist in the Darci story. Shortly after the trial ended, one juror, Tom Griego, began to make statements to the press that he had made up his mind very early in the case. He had known all along that Darci was not insane because he had experienced mental problems of his own, and he had been in a mental hospital with people who were much crazier than Darci. During *voir dire,* prospective jurors had been asked about past mental problems and Griego had not admitted to any such problems. Darci's lawyers contended that she deserved a new trial, given the biases and falsehoods Griego was admitting to, but the state supreme court ruled that the one juror's actions did not cancel the work of the entire jury.

So Darci remained in jail. Perhaps that's exactly where she deserves to be. Perhaps she was everything Harry Zimmerman said she was, and perhaps she continues to try to manipulate the system to her own advantage. But a few questions do remain: Did Darci receive the kind of treatment the jury intended for her? Can anyone ever be acquitted for mental illness in the state of New Mexico? Does Darci deserve more help than she is getting?

But then, others might ask whether she deserved the death penalty. If Dr. Resnick's assessment is correct, and Darci's real problem is a character disorder, some would say that she got off very lightly. She was allowed to live.

Epilogue

I have talked with most of the people who were directly affected by the murder case of Darci Pierce, and I discovered lots of victims. It is one of those cases that doesn't go away. It gnaws. It has powerful effects on people.

The defense team, for instance, all spoke of strange dreams, strange emotions not just during the trial but since. The case seems to haunt them. John Bogren remains angry to this day. He still feels that the DA's office could have done the greatest justice by offering a reasonable plea bargain that would have given Darci a shorter sentence and some genuine care.

Bogren believes that he had an impossible task. He had a defendant who appeared sane. He didn't dare put her on the witness stand because she would have sounded too ordinary, too much under control. He had a witness who happened onto the crime and heard Darci say, in a controlled voice, that she would have to be left alone with her friend. He can explain that as one of her personality states in operation, but how could he convince a jury of that?

Yet what gnaws at him, and at Tom Jameson, Jackie Robins, and Bill Chambreau, is that in their own minds they won the case. They convinced the jury that Darci was mentally ill, and what did they get for it? Nothing. Darci went to prison, the same as she would have had she been given a straight guilty verdict.

All the defense lawyers speak of Darci in similar language: She is one of the loveliest persons they have ever known. They would trust her to baby-sit their children. You cannot be around her, they say, without seeing that something is wrong, that something doesn't add up. Only some deep psychological problem could explain her actions, given who she normally is. Bogren is accustomed to dealing with people with long criminal records and hardened attitudes. But Darci is not a threat to anyone. He understands the impulse to put her away, and maybe she should have been kept out of society for a time—at least until some of her problems were worked out. But he sees no purpose in her being locked up for thirty years.

Bill Chambreau continues to stay in contact with Darci, and he shares Bogren's resentment over what the system has done to Darci. Tom Jameson, who has now left the public defender's office and has a private practice, is just as certain now as he ever was that Darci was legally insane when she committed her crime. He feels that if Darci couldn't be acquitted on an insanity plea, no one in New Mexico ever will until the law is made more reasonable.

But in San Diego I heard quite a different opinion. Harry Zimmerman has left Albuquerque. He now teaches at the University of San Diego law school. He warned me from the beginning: "As you get into this thing, don't get sucked in by Darci. She's a born manipulator. She knows how to use people to her advantage, and she can come across as the sweetest woman who ever lived."

Zimmerman argues that if an objective listener goes

back to Darci's confession before she had talked to any mental health people, she presented a much more accurate picture of who she was and how she operated. Every step of the way was calculated. It was she who said, "I had to have a story." It was she who taught herself to ripple her muscles to fake the movement of the baby. It was she who lied to her husband, her family, and everyone she knew, and who went to every length to make those lies stick.

Zimmerman spoke to many people who knew Darci well, and every one of them spoke of her charm. But he couldn't believe it until he met her, by accident, when she was brought to the DA's office before the trial. He found her stunningly pretty, simple, and lovely. Yet as he traced her history, he discovered no end of examples of her ability to look into a person's eyes and tell whatever lies were helpful to her at the moment. He believes very strongly that Darci realized quickly that her only defense would be insanity, and that she began to present experiences from her past according to the leads she got from the psychiatrists who tried to build a case for her defense. She is a chameleon, in his view, and if insanity was needed, she sensed immediately how to make herself appear insane. And McCarty and Goodwin were taken in because they wanted to be—they saw what they looked for.

No, Harry Zimmerman told me, this is not the girl next door. This is not the sweet kid. This is an actress. This is as cold a killer as you will ever meet. He feels that justice was done insofar that it *can* be done in this case. The only real justice would be to have Cindy back.

But if Zimmerman accused McCarty and Goodwin of seeing what they wanted to see, Bogren is just as adamant that Resnick was a hired gun, or to use his term, a "prosecution whore." Bogren would claim that Resnick was paid a great deal of money to come to Albuquerque and say what the prosecution wanted him to say. He nicknamed the man "Dr. Death," and felt that his slick performance on the witness stand was calculated to put Darci in prison, not to deal honestly with her mental problems.

Of course, Zimmerman denies the accusation entirely. He claims to have set out to find solid forensic experts who could come in with no preconceived notions about Darci and make an accurate assessment of who she was and what made her act.

So the deep but opposing convictions about Darci persist. Those who loved her admit that they are confused by what she did. Those who must suffer from her crimes have no idea what could have caused her to act so brutally. But almost everyone continues to feel powerful emotions, whether it be pain, anger, resentment, or indignation.

In Payson, Utah, what remains is much pain but little bitterness. Cindy Ray's parents are each with other partners now, but they remain friends, and they look back with some regrets about Cindy's life at home. They wish things might have been better in some ways, but they also remember wonderful times together, when everyone was home. Vickie cannot talk long about Cindy without crying. Her memories hurt too much. Larry married again after his divorce, only to have his second wife die. And so his life has continued in pain. But he has not lost his resolve. He has kept his vow. He gave up both drinking and smoking, and he began to attend church again, as Cindy always wanted him to do. It is his way of honoring her wish, and he believes, as other Mormons do, that Cindy knows that he has changed his ways. He has now married a third time, and his life is better than it has been in some time. Still, the pain hangs on. He has tried to push all the anger away, and has done pretty well. But Cindy was someone he loved so very much, and he never goes a day without thinking about the loss of her. Kipper and Tonie feel the same way.

But if there is a loss in Payson, Utah, there is also a loss in Portland, Oregon. What mother expects to see her daughter commit murder? I spoke with Sandra Ricker only briefly, but I could tell immediately that her pain is as great as that of Larry and Vickie Giles. Mrs. Ricker has a dignity about her, an honest acceptance of her daughter's actions, but she is also upset and disappointed with a system that imprisons her daughter but fails to treat her. She honors Darci's wish not to give out personal information, but she says, "There's another side to this whole story. Darci isn't like what you heard about in the papers or what you heard in the trial. And in a way, I'd like to tell all about it. But Darci doesn't want me to, and I'm going to honor her wish on that."

I remembered the big woman in the flowered dress sitting on the witness stand, sobbing as she told the jury that Darci had hated her because she was so fat. But now she told me, "Darci loves me very much. And I love her. I always will, no matter what she did. I know she's mentally ill, and that's why she did it. I just wish someone could help her."

Once the trial was over, Ray Pierce wanted to slip out of the limelight. He was not eager to talk to anyone about the case, and especially not the press. He was portrayed as the ultimate innocent—or perhaps the unwitting accomplice—by the press. But the truth seems to be that he was taken in by Darci's skill in manipulating information, and by his own tendency to distance himself from the female issues of Darci's life. Above all, he seems very young, and

LULLABY AND GOODNIGHT

certainly stunned by all that happened to him. He waited for a time before he sorted out what he wanted to do, but he has now divorced Darci and has remarried. He wants nothing else to be known about him.

And what is Darci's life like? She, too, is vigorous about defending her own privacy. She doesn't answer mail, and she has filed a letter that requests of prison officials that no information about her be released. She wants to talk to no one except for a very few friends and family who continue to be loyal to her.

I was only able to learn that she rises at 6:00 A.M. with all the other women in the correctional facility. During the day, all prisoners either work or receive skill training. The evening is given to counseling or to group sessions, or perhaps arts and crafts and other activities. Psychological help is available if prisoners choose to receive it, and Darci can be educated in such fields as computer science, business, and hotel management.

That's what the prison officials say. Bill Chambreau laughs. But he, too, honors Darci's wish to reveal nothing about her life in prison. What he does say is that she's managing pretty well. She's accepted her lot in life and is making the best of it. She is certainly not happy with what has happened to her, but she knows she must go on with life as best she can. He says that she does feel genuine remorse for what happened. He feels that the press has never given her credit for that, but that people who know Darci know how deeply she loved the little baby she thought was hers for those few hours, and her regret is to know that she caused the baby such harm by taking her mother away. Darci, the little girl who was given away, understands better than anyone what damage she has done to this other little girl, who will never know her mother.

Harry Zimmerman doesn't see Darci, but he

doesn't buy this picture at all. He has heard that Darci does very well at the prison. She is a manipulator, and she's in a perfect position to control the many weaker personalities around her.

Which picture is true? I don't know. I have tried very hard to decide how I feel about Darci. But like so many others who have known her, I remain confused. I certainly feel sorry for her, but I wonder whether she is capable of feeling remorse. I honestly don't know.

What I do know is that among the many victims, one person seems above the anger, if not the pain. I have never met anyone quite like Sam. My first response was that he was too good to be true. I sometimes doubt that his motivations can be quite so lofty as they seem, and yet, I have never seen him do anything or say anything that is inconsistent with his basic view of the whole experience. He does not hate Darci. Those who were with him from the first moment he learned what had happened to Cindy say that he did not once express any anger toward her from the beginning. I have watched other cases and so often have heard family members cry out for the death penalty after they have seen a loved one murdered. Sam never did that. His impulse from the beginning was to try to understand, to forgive, and to place his emphasis on going on with life. Luke and Millie were his focus from the very beginning.

Every night Americans watch the news and seem to learn of some new horror: children killing their parents, drive-by shootings, children killing children, parents beating their babies to death. Sometimes we feel as if there is no limit to the heart of darkness, to the depths to which humans can plunge. As the horror creeps into our homes, we pull back, ever more frightened by the possibilities outside. Somewhere we look for some sign that humans can rise to the heights

LULLABY AND GOODNIGHT

we have always expected of our heroes. Yet every day the press seems to drag another hero down, as well. Somewhere in all this, I think we want badly to believe that good impulses can survive, that goodness can walk around on two legs.

I don't offer Sam as a great hero. He's just a young man trying to make his way in the world. In most ways, he's like all the rest of us. But something in him is very right, and you feel it when you're near him. In most ways, he may be no better or worse than the next guy, but in one regard, in one instance in his life, he did something finer than one usually sees on this planet. He paid the ultimate price, lost the dearest soul in his world—and he harbored no hatred. I talked to him a few days ago, and I told him about my conversations with the defense lawyers. I told him how concerned they were that Darci was getting no treatment. I half expected a little chink in his armor, some evidence of clay feet. I really thought he might tell me that he had nothing against her, but she did after all, get what she deserved. But what he said was, "Well, that's one thing about your writing the book. Maybe it will put a little pressure on someone to give Darci some help."

When Sam read the first draft of this epilogue, he told me that I had missed the point. "It's not my natural inclination to be so forgiving. I used to be a real hothead. But Cindy taught me how to forgive. Since all this happened, I've just been trying to behave the way she would have wanted me to."

So maybe Cindy's the hero of our story.

Sam got married about two years after Cindy's death. It was what Cindy told him he should do. His wife is a petite woman, even smaller than Cindy. And she's blond, not dark. In fact, Luke and Millie, who both have very light hair, look quite natural with their new "mommy." Sometimes in grocery stores, people comment on how much Millie looks like her mother.

Sam graduated from Brigham Young University in 1990, and he took a teaching job outside the state of Utah. He wants to start over. Luke has struggled at times. He has not forgotten what happened, even though he was only two-and-a-half when his mother was killed. In the summer of 1990, Sam and his new wife had a little boy, named Bradyn (called Brady). Luke was happy to have a little brother, but during the last months of the pregnancy, he began to express his fear that the "lady who wants our babies" would come and kill his new mother. Sam and his wife took Luke for counseling. He's a bright, active, much-loved little boy, five-years-old at the time his new brother was born, but he will need much love and support to ensure that he does not end up damaged by what he experienced at such an early age.

But in all these sad stories, there is one bit of loveliness. I have fallen hopelessly in love with little Millie. She seems to me, somehow, a wondrous child. Her short blond hair and her round cheeks make her seem a pixy, and her blue eyes dart about, full of life and humor. Her long eyelashes give her a soft, beautiful quality. She is a little chatterbox, with a face so animated that I can't listen to her without laughing. She talks precociously, with a remarkable vocabulary, and she notices everything—and *asks* about all she sees. I feel a constant sense of her intensity and vitality when I am around her. It's as though she's kept her mother's life and added her own.

Or maybe that's only the metaphor I choose for her. Maybe I see more in her than really exists. Maybe I want so badly to believe that something good can come of all this ugliness that I overreact to this little light, which, to me, shines ferociously. I never met Cindy, but I've come to care about her immensely, and I suppose I want to look deep into Millie's blue eyes and find Cindy there.

I'll admit it; I too believe, with Sam, that Cindy knows what is happening to her children, and to Sam. And I believe that she has accepted what has happened, and approves.

The truth is, Millie has a tough life ahead. Sooner or later she has to be told. And then, we don't know how she will handle it. Sam thinks that maybe this book will help, because she will have a chance to hear the whole story, to learn more about her mother, and maybe see that the best course is to forgive Darci and go on with life. And that's what we all hope. We hope that when evil strikes, that it won't always be met with revenge—more evil. With so much evil in the world, we have to hope that it can sometimes be conquered with plain old goodness. And that's what I hope for little Millie. I want her to survive. And I want Cindy to survive with her. And I want Darci to survive, too, along with Sam Ray and Ray Pierce, the Rickers and the Gileses.

I keep thinking that the world can survive if we can just follow Sam's example. I'm not dumb enough to believe that this book can end with a "happily ever after," but I want to believe that darkness isn't spreading over the face of the earth.

No. It's more than that.

I believe with Sam that darkness can't win, and won't.

Author's Note

Lullaby and Goodnight is not a fictionalization. It is a true account, based on interviews, police documents and trial records. To protect the privacy of a few individuals whose connections to the case were sensitive, I assigned arbitrary pseudonyms. Most of the names in the book, however, are unchanged.

I am indebted to all those who took their time in sometimes lengthy interviews, to provide me with information. Above all, I appreciate the help of Sam Ray, who, at great emotional expense, revealed to me the details of his experience.

D. T. Hughes